Nobody writes mysteries better than
the Queen of Suspense!

After thrilling readers for forty years,
#1 *New York*

MARY

is still "

(*The Washi*

Praise for *I'VE GOT YOU UNDER MY SKIN*

"For 40 years—and about as many books—Mary Higgins Clark has been entertaining the masses with clever and affecting suspense stories. And she does so again in *I've Got You Under My Skin*, a classic whodunit with multiple twists. . . . With her trademark quick but not rushed pace, Clark ratchets the suspense to nearly unbearable levels before unveiling the truth in a conclusion that stuns in more than one way. Score another winner for the woman who has been nicknamed—with good cause—the queen of suspense."
—*Richmond Times-Dispatch*

"For those readers who have been fans of Clark's stories over the years, this is just another perfect addition to their collection. For new readers, this will be an introduction to one of the most successful mystery writers of recent times. Clark doesn't pile on the gore but rather . . . the suspense. She makes reading her books an enjoyable experience."
—*Huffington Post*

"Clark's books keep getting better. The suspense she manages to generate will keep readers up all night. Her writing style is always approachable, her characters are finely limned, and her plots are believable. *I've Got You Under My Skin* is a shining example of all these strengths."
—*Bookreporter*

I'LL WALK ALONE

MARY HIGGINS CLARK

I've Got You Under My Skin

POCKET BOOKS

New York   London   Sydney   Toronto   New Delhi

Pocket Books
An Imprint of Simon & Schuster, Inc.
1230 Avenue of the Americas
New York, NY 10020

This book is a work of fiction. Any references to historical events, real people, or real places are used fictitiously. Other names, characters, places, and events are products of the author's imagination, and any resemblance to actual events or places or persons, living or dead, is entirely coincidental.

First Pocket Books paperback edition April 2015

POCKET and colophon are registered trademarks of Simon & Schuster, Inc.

For information about special discounts for bulk purchases, please contact Simon & Schuster Special Sales at 1-866-506-1949 or business@simonandschuster.com.

The Simon & Schuster Speakers Bureau can bring authors to your live event. For more information or to book an event, contact the Simon & Schuster Speakers Bureau at 1-866-248-3049 or visit our website at www.simonspeakers.com.

Interior design by Jill Putorti

Manufactured in the United States of America

10 9 8 7 6 5 4 3 2 1

ISBN 978-1-4767-4908-2
ISBN 978-1-4767-4910-5 (ebook)

For John
And our Clark and Conheeney children
and grandchildren with love

Acknowledgments

AND SO ONCE AGAIN, THE TALE HAS BEEN TOLD. Last night, I wrote the last words and then slept for twelve hours.

This morning I woke up with the joyous understanding that all the dates with friends that I have cancelled can be reinstated.

But it is so satisfying to tell another tale, to share another journey with characters I have created and come to care deeply about—or not.

As always, for the last forty years, Michael V. Korda, my editor, has been the captain of my ship. I send him twenty or twenty-five pages at a time. His phone call "The pages are fine," is music to my ears. Let me repeat even more fervently, Michael, it's been grand working with you.

Marysue Rucci, the new editor in chief at Simon & Schuster, has been a marvelous friend and mentor. It is a joy working with her.

The home team starts with my right hand, Nadine Petry, my daughter Patty and my son Dave, Agnes Newton and Irene Clark. And of course, John Conheeney, spouse extraordinaire, and all of my family.

Abiding thanks to copy editor, Gypsy da Silva and to art director, Jackie Seow. Her covers make me look so good. Thanks as well to Elizabeth Breeden.

It is time to start to think about what comes next. But I will put that off just a little while. After all, tomorrow is another day.

Prologue

Dr. Greg Moran was pushing three-year-old Timmy on the swing in the playground on East Fifteenth Street in Manhattan, not far from the apartment.

"Two-minute warning," he laughed as he gave another push, just strong enough to satisfy his daredevil son, but not strong enough to risk having the seat flip over the top of the swing. A long time ago he had witnessed that scene. No one was hurt, because it was a child safety seat. Even so, with the long arms that went with his six-foot-three frame, Greg was always super careful when Timmy was on these swings. As an emergency room doctor, he was all too familiar with freak accidents.

It was half past six, and the evening sun was sending long shadows across the playground. Now there was even a slight chill in the air, a reminder that Labor Day was next weekend. "One-minute warning,"

Greg called firmly. Before bringing Timmy to the playground, Greg had been on duty for twelve hours, and the always busy emergency room had been absolutely chaotic. Two cars filled with teenagers racing each other on First Avenue had collided and crashed. Incredibly, no one had been killed, but there were three kids with very serious injuries.

Greg took his hands off the swing. It was time to let it slow down and stop. The fact that Timmy didn't attempt a futile protest meant that he must be ready to go home, too. Anyhow, they were now the last ones in the playground.

"Doctor!"

Greg turned to face a powerfully built man of average height with a scarf covering his face. The gun he was holding was aimed at Greg's head. In an instinctive movement Greg took a long step to the side to get as far away from Timmy as possible. "Look, my wallet is in my pocket," he said quietly. "You're welcome to it."

"Daddy." Timmy's tone was frightened. He had twisted in the seat and was staring into the eyes of the gunman.

In his final moment on earth, Greg Moran, age thirty-four, distinguished physician, dearly loved husband and father, tried to throw himself on his attacker but had no chance to escape the fatal shot that hit with deadly accuracy the center of his forehead.

"DADDYYYYYYYY!" Timmy wailed.

The assailant ran to the street, then stopped and turned. "Timmy, tell your mother that she's next," he shouted. "Then it's your turn."

The gunshot and the shouted threat were heard by Margy Bless, an elderly woman on her way home from her part-time job in the local bakery. She stood for long seconds absorbing the nightmarish event: the fleeing figure turning the corner, the gun dangling from his hand, the screaming child on the swing, the crumpled figure on the ground.

Her fingers trembled so badly it took three tries before she was able to punch in 911.

When the operator answered, Margy could only moan, "Hurry! Hurry! He may come back! He shot a man, then he threatened the child!"

Her voice trailed off as Timmy shrieked, "Blue Eyes shot my daddy . . . Blue Eyes shot my daddy!"

1

Laurie Moran looked out the window of her office on the twenty-fifth floor of 15 Rockefeller Center. Her view was of the skating rink in the middle of that famous Manhattan complex. It was a sunny but cold March day, and from her vantage point she could see beginners there, wobbling unsteadily on their skates, and in sharp contrast others who moved across the ice with the grace of ballet dancers.

Timmy, her eight-year-old son, loved ice hockey and planned to be good enough to play with the New York Rangers by the time he was twenty-one. Laurie smiled as her mind filled with the image of Timmy's face, his expressive brown eyes sparkling with delight as he imagined himself in the position of goalie in future Rangers games. He'll be the image of Greg by then, Laurie thought, but quickly gave herself a mental shake and turned her attention to the file on her desk.

Thirty-six years old, with shoulder-length hair the color of honey, hazel eyes more green than brown, a slim build, and classic features untouched by makeup, Laurie was the kind of woman people turned to take a second look at when she passed by. "Classy and good-looking" was a typical description of her.

An award-winning producer at Fisher Blake Studios, Laurie was about to launch a new cable series, one that she had had in mind even before Greg died. Then she had put it away—she felt people might think she had conceived it because of his unsolved murder.

The premise involved reenacting unsolved crimes, but instead of using actors, gathering the friends and relatives of the victims to hear from their lips *their* version of what had happened when the crime occurred. Whenever possible, the actual setting of the crime would be used. It was a risky venture—with great potential for success and also for chaos.

She had just come from a meeting with her boss, Brett Young, who had reminded her that she'd sworn she would never touch another reality show. "Your last two were expensive flops, Laurie," he said. "We can't afford another one." Then he pointedly added, "Neither can you."

Now as Laurie sipped the coffee she had carried in with her from the two o'clock meeting, she thought of the passionate argument she had used to persuade him. "Brett, before you remind me again how sick you are of reality series, I promise you this one will be different. We'll call it *Under Suspicion*. On page two of the folder I gave you is a long list of unsolved criminal cases and others *supposedly* solved where there is a real possibility the wrong person went to prison."

Laurie glanced around her office. The glance reinforced her determination not to lose it. It was large enough to have a couch under the windows and a long bookcase that showcased memorabilia, awards she had won, and family pictures, mostly of Timmy and her father. She had long ago decided that her pictures of Greg belonged at home in her bedroom, not here where they would inevitably bring to everyone's mind the fact that she was a widow, and her husband's murder had never been solved.

"The Lindbergh kidnapping is the first on your list. That happened about eighty years ago. You're not planning to reenact *that*, are you?" Brett had asked.

Laurie told him it was an example of a crime that people talked about for generations because of its horror, but also because there were still so many lingering questions about the case. Bruno Hauptmann, an immigrant from Germany who was executed for kidnapping the Lindbergh baby, was almost certainly the one who made the ladder that went to the baby's bedroom. But how did he know the nanny went to dinner every night and left the baby alone for forty-five minutes at exactly that time? How did Hauptmann know that—or who told him?

Then she told Brett about the unsolved murder of one of the identical twin daughters of Senator Charles H. Percy. It happened at the beginning of his first campaign for the Senate in 1966. He was elected, but the crime was never solved, and the questions remained: was the sister who was murdered the intended victim? And why didn't the dog bark if a stranger had entered the house?

Now Laurie leaned back in her chair. She had told Brett the point is that when you start to mention cases like this, everyone has a theory about it. "We'll do a reality show about crimes that are anywhere from twenty to thirty years old, where we can get the point of view of the people who were closest to the victim, and I have the perfect case for the first show: the Graduation Gala," she'd said.

That's when Brett really got interested, Laurie thought. Living in Westchester County, he knew all about it: Twenty years ago, four young women who grew up together in Salem Ridge graduated from four different colleges. The stepfather of one of them, Robert Nicholas Powell, gave what he called a "Graduation Gala" to honor all four girls. Three hundred guests, black tie, champagne and caviar, fireworks, you name it. After the party, his stepdaughter and the other three graduates stayed overnight. In the morning, Powell's wife, Betsy Bonner Powell, a popular, glamorous forty-two-year-old socialite, was found suffocated in her bed. The crime was never solved. Rob, as Powell was known, was now seventy-eight years old, in excellent physical and mental shape, and still living in the house.

Powell never remarried, Laurie thought. He had recently given an interview on *The O'Reilly Factor* in which he said he would do anything to clear up the mystery of his wife's death, and he knew that his stepdaughter and her friends all felt the same way. They all believed that until the truth came out, people would wonder if one of *them* was the murderer who took Betsy's life.

That's when I got the go-ahead from Brett to contact Powell and the four graduates to see if they would participate, Laurie thought exultantly.

It was time to share the good news with Grace and Jerry. She picked up her phone and told her two assistants to come in. A moment later the door of her office flew open.

Grace Garcia, her twenty-five-year-old administrative assistant, was wearing a short red wool dress over cotton leggings and high-button boots. Her waist-length black hair was twisted up and clamped with a comb. Tendrils that had escaped from the comb framed her heart-shaped face. Heavy but expertly applied mascara accentuated her lively dark eyes.

Jerry Klein was one step behind Grace. Long and lanky, he settled into one of the chairs at Laurie's desk. As usual, he was wearing a turtleneck and a cardigan sweater. It was his claim that he intended to make his one dark blue suit and his one tuxedo last for twenty years. Laurie had no doubt that he would succeed. Now twenty-six, he had joined the company as a summer intern three years earlier. He had turned out to be an indispensable production assistant.

"I won't keep you in suspense," Laurie announced. "Brett gave us the go-ahead."

"I knew he would!" Grace exclaimed.

"I knew he had from the expression on your face when you got off the elevator," Jerry insisted.

"No you didn't. I have a poker face," Laurie told him. "All right, the first order of business is for me to contact Robert Powell. If I get the go-ahead from him, from what I saw in that interview he gave, his stepdaughter and her three friends will very likely go along with us."

"Especially since they'll get paid very well to cooperate, and not one of them has any real money," Jerry said, his voice thoughtful as he recalled the background information he had gathered for the potential series. "Betsy's daughter, Claire Bonner, is a social worker in Chicago. She never married. Nina Craig is divorced, lives in Hollywood, makes a living as an extra in films. Alison Schaefer is a pharmacist in a small drugstore in Cleveland. Her husband is on crutches. He was the victim of a hit-and-run driver twenty years ago. Regina Callari moved to St. Augustine, Florida. She has a small real estate agency. Divorced, one child in college."

"The stakes are high," Laurie cautioned. "Brett has already reminded me that the last two series were flops."

"Did he mention that your first two are still running?" Grace asked, indignant.

"No, he didn't, and he won't. And I feel in my bones that we have a potential winner with this one. If Robert Powell goes along with us, I almost bet the others will as well," Laurie said, then added fervently, "At least I hope and pray that they will."

2

First Deputy Commissioner Leo Farley of the New York Police Department had been rumored to be appointed the next police commissioner when he unexpectedly put in his retirement papers the day after his son-in-law's funeral. Now, more than five years later, Leo had never looked back at that decision. At sixty-three, he was a cop to his fingertips. He'd always planned to be one until he hit mandatory retirement, but something more important had changed his plans.

The shocking, cold-blooded murder of Greg and the threat that the elderly witness had overheard— "Timmy, tell your mother that she's next, then it's your turn"—had been sufficient reason to decide to dedicate his life to protecting his daughter and grandson. Ramrod straight, average height, with a full head of iron-gray hair and a wiry, disciplined body, Leo Farley spent his waking hours on constant alert.

He knew that there was only so much he could do

for Laurie. She had a job she both needed and loved. She took public transportation, went for long jogs in Central Park, and in warm weather often ate lunch in one of the pocket parks near her office.

Timmy was another matter. In Leo's mind there was nothing to prevent Greg's killer from deciding to go after Timmy first, so he appointed himself as his guardian. It was Leo who walked Timmy to Saint David's School every morning, and it was Leo who was waiting for him at dismissal time. If Timmy had activities after school, Leo unobtrusively stood guard beside the skating rink or the playground.

To Leo, Greg Moran was the son he would have created for himself, if that had been possible. It was now ten years since they had met in the emergency room at Lenox Hill Hospital. He and Eileen had frantically rushed there after they received the call that their twenty-six-year-old daughter, Laurie, had been hit by a cab on Park Avenue and was unconscious.

Greg, tall and impressive even in his green hospital togs, had greeted them with the firm assurance, "She's come to, and she'll be fine. A broken ankle and a concussion. We will observe her, but she'll be fine."

At those words, Eileen, desperate with worry about her only child, had fainted, and Greg had another patient on his hands. He grabbed Eileen quickly before she fell. He never left our lives again, Leo thought. He and Laurie were engaged three months later. He was our rock when Eileen died, only a year after that.

How could anyone have shot him? The exhaustive investigation had left no stone unturned to find someone who might have had a grudge against Greg, unthinkable as that was to anyone who knew him. After they had quickly eliminated friends and classmates from consideration, the records had been scoured in the two hospitals where Greg had worked as a resident and staff director to see if any patient or a family member had ever accused him of a mistaken diagnosis or treatment that had resulted in a permanent injury or death. Nothing had come to light.

In the DA's office the case was known as the "Blue Eyes Murder." Sometimes an expression of alarm would come over Timmy's face if he happened to suddenly turn and look directly into Leo's face. Leo's eyes were a light china-blue shade. He was sure, and both Laurie and the psychologist agreed, that Greg's killer must have had large, intense blue eyes.

Laurie had discussed with him her concept for a new series, leading with the Graduation Gala murder. Leo kept his dismay to himself. The idea of his daughter gathering together a group of people, one of whom was probably a murderer, was alarming. Someone had hated Betsy Bonner Powell enough to hold a pillow over her head until the last breath had been squeezed from her body. That same person probably had a passion for self-preservation. Leo knew that twenty years ago all four young women, and Betsy's husband, had been interrogated by the best-of-the-best homicide detectives. Unless someone had managed to make his or her way into the house undetected, if the series was given the green light, the murderer and suspects would all be together again — a dangerous proposition.

All this was in Leo's mind as he and Timmy walked home from Saint David's on Eighty-ninth Street off Fifth Avenue to the apartment, eight blocks away on Lexington Avenue and Ninety-fourth Street. After Greg's death Laurie had moved immediately, unable to bear the sight of the playground where Greg had been shot.

A passing police cruiser slowed as it drove by. The officer in the passenger seat saluted Leo.

"I like it when they do that to you, Grandpa," Timmy announced. "It makes me feel safe," he added matter-of-factly.

Be careful, Leo warned himself. I've always told Timmy that if I wasn't around and he or his friends had a problem they should run to a police officer and ask for help. Unconsciously, he tightened his grip on Timmy's hand.

"Well, you haven't had any problems that I couldn't solve for you." Then he added carefully, "At least as far as I know."

They were walking north on Lexington Avenue. The wind had shifted and felt raw against their faces. Leo stopped and firmly pulled Timmy's woolen cap down over his forehead and ears.

"One of the guys in the eighth grade was walking to school this morning and some guy on a bike tried to grab his cell phone out of his hand. A policeman saw it and pulled the guy over," Timmy said.

It hadn't been an incident involving someone with blue eyes. Leo was ashamed to admit to himself how relieved that made him. Until Greg's killer was apprehended, he needed to know that Timmy and Laurie were safe.

Someday justice will be served, he vowed to himself.

This morning, as she hurried out to work seconds after he arrived, Laurie had said that she was going to hear the verdict on the reality show she was proposing. Leo's mind moved restlessly to that concern. He knew he would have to wait for the news until tonight. Over their second cup of coffee, when Timmy had finished dinner and was curled up in the big chair with a book, she would discuss it with him. Then he would leave for his own apartment a block away. At the end of the day, he wanted Laurie and Timmy to have their own space, and he was satisfied that no one would get past the doorman in their building without a phone call to the resident they claimed to be visiting.

If she got the go-ahead to do that series, it's going to be bad news, Leo thought.

A man with a hooded sweatshirt, dark sunglasses, and a canvas bag on his shoulder, seeming to come out of nowhere, darted past him on roller skates, almost knocking over Timmy, then brushing a very pregnant young woman who was about ten feet ahead of them.

"Get off the sidewalk," Leo shouted as the skater turned the corner and disappeared.

Behind the dark sunglasses, bright blue eyes glittered, and the skater laughed aloud.

Such encounters fed his need for the sense of power he felt when he literally touched Timmy and knew that on any given day he could carry out his threat.

3

Robert Nicholas Powell was seventy-eight years old but looked and moved like a man ten years younger. A full head of white hair framed his handsome face. His posture was still erect, although he was no longer over six feet tall. He had an air of authority that was instantly apparent to anyone in his presence. Except for Fridays, he still put in a full day at his Wall Street office, chauffeured back and forth by his longtime employee, Josh Damiano.

Today, Tuesday, March 16, Rob had made the decision to stay home and meet television producer Laurie Moran here in Salem Ridge instead of in his office. She had told him the reason for her visit and had couched it in an intriguing premise: "Mr. Powell, I believe that if you, your stepdaughter, and her friends agree to re-create the events of the Graduation Gala, the public will understand how incredible it is that any one of you could have been responsible for your wife's death. You had a happy marriage. Everyone who knew you knew that. Your stepdaughter and her mother were very close. The other three graduates had been in and out of Betsy's home from the time they were in high school, and then, when you and Betsy were married, you made them always feel welcome. You have a very large house, and with so many people at the party, there is every possibility that an intruder went undetected. Your wife was known to have beautiful and expensive jewelry. She was wearing her emerald earrings and necklace and ring that night."

"The tabloids turned a tragedy into a scandal." Robert Powell remembered his bitter retort to Laurie Moran. Well, she'll be here soon, he thought. So be it.

He was sitting at the desk in his spacious downstairs office. Large windows looked out over the back gardens of the estate. A beautiful sight in spring and summer and early fall, Rob thought. When it was snowing, that bare and naked view was softened and sometimes magical but on a damp, cold, sunless winter day in March, when the trees were bare and the pool covered and the pool house was shuttered, no amount of expensive planting could soften the stark reality of the winter landscape.

His padded desk chair was very comfortable, and Rob, smiling to himself, pondered the secret that he did not share with anyone. He was sure that sitting behind the impressive antique mahogany desk with the elaborate carvings on the sides and legs lent even more prestige to the image he had so carefully cultivated. It was an image that began the day he left Detroit at age seventeen to begin his freshman year as a scholarship student at Harvard. There, he referred to his mother as a college professor and his father as an engineer; in fact she was a kitchen worker at the University of Michigan and he was a mechanic at the Ford plant.

Rob smiled, remembering how in his sophomore year he had bought a book on table manners, purchased a box of battered silver-plated table settings, and practiced using unfamiliar utensils such as a fish knife until he was sure he was comfortable with them. Following graduation, an internship at Merrill Lynch began his career in the financial world. Now, despite a few rocky years along the way, the R. N. Powell Hedge Fund was considered one of the best and safest investments on Wall Street.

At precisely eleven o'clock the sound of the chimes at the front door announced the arrival of Laurie Moran. Rob straightened his shoulders. Of course he would get up when she was escorted into his office, but not until she had seen him seated at his desk. He realized how curious he was to meet her. It was hard to tell her age from her voice over the phone. There was a crisp, matter-of-fact note in the way she had introduced herself, but then her tone had become sympathetic when she spoke about Betsy's death.

After their conversation he had googled her. The fact that she was the widow of the doctor who had been shot in the playground and that she had an impressive background as a producer intrigued him. Her picture showed her to be a very attractive woman. I'm not too old to appreciate that, Rob thought.

There was a tap on the door, and Jane, who had been his housekeeper from the time he married Betsy, opened it and stepped into the room, followed by Laurie Moran.

"Thank you, Jane," Rob said, and waited until Jane had left, closing the door behind her, before he got up. "Ms. Moran," he said courteously. He extended his hand to Laurie and indicated the chair on the other side of the desk.

ROBERT POWELL COULD NOT KNOW THAT LAURIE was thinking, Well, this is it, as with a warm smile she settled in the chair. The housekeeper had taken her coat when she arrived. She was wearing a navy pin-striped pantsuit, white shell blouse, and navy leather boots. Her only jewelry was a pair of small pearl earrings and her gold wedding band. She had pulled her hair back and pinned it into a French knot, a style that made her feel more efficient.

Within five minutes she was sure that Robert Powell had already decided to go ahead with the program, but it took him ten minutes before he confirmed that fact.

"Mr. Powell, I'm thrilled that you are willing to let us re-create the night of the Graduation Gala. Now, of course, we will need the cooperation of your step-daughter and her friends. Will you help me persuade them to participate?"

"I'm happy to do that, although obviously I can't speak for any of them."

"Have you stayed close to your stepdaughter since your wife died?"

"No. Not that I haven't wanted to stay close. I was and am very fond of Claire. She lived here from the time she was thirteen until she was twenty-one. Her mother's death was a terrible shock for her. I don't know how much you studied her background, but her mother and father were never married. He took off when Betsy became pregnant with Claire. Betsy was doing bit parts on Broadway and when she wasn't acting she worked as an usher there. It was hardscrabble for her and Claire until I came along."

Then he added, "Betsy was beautiful. I'm sure she could have easily married someone along the way, but after her experience with Claire's father, I know she was gun-shy."

"I can understand that," Laurie said, nodding.

"I can, too. Never having had children, I thought of Claire as my own daughter. It hurt when she moved out so quickly after Betsy's death. But I think that between us there was too much grief to hold under one roof, and she sensed it immediately. As I'm sure you know, she lives in Chicago and is a social worker there. She never married."

"She never came back here?"

"No, and never accepted my offer of generous financial help. She returned my letters torn up."

"Why do you think she did that?" Laurie asked.

"She was fiercely jealous of my relationship with

her mother. Don't forget, it was just the two of them for thirteen years."

"Then do you think she'll refuse to take part in the program?"

"No, I don't. Every so often an enterprising reporter has written about the case, and some of them have quoted Claire or one of the other girls. What they have said has been uniform. They all feel as though people look at them with questions in their eyes, and they'd all like an end to it."

"We're planning to offer each of them $50,000 for being on the program," Laurie told him.

"I've kept track of all of them. There isn't one who couldn't use financial help. In order to ensure that they accept, I authorize you to say that I am prepared to pay each one of them a quarter of a million dollars for their cooperation."

"You would do that?" Laurie exclaimed.

"Yes, and tell me anyone else you will want to interview on your program."

Laurie said, "Of course, I will want to interview your housekeeper."

"Give her the $50,000 you're giving the others and I'll give her another $50,000. I'll make sure she does it. It is not necessary that she be paid the same as the others. I am seventy-eight years old and have three stents in the arteries leading to my heart. I know that, like the girls, I am under suspicion—or do you call it a 'person of interest' these days? Before I die, I want to sit in a courtroom and see Betsy's murderer sentenced to prison."

"You never heard any sound from her room?"

"No. As I'm sure you're aware, we shared a suite. The sitting room was in the middle, our bedrooms on either side. I confess I am a heavy sleeper and snore very loudly. When we said good night, I went to my bedroom."

THAT EVENING LAURIE WAITED UNTIL TIMMY WAS deep in his Harry Potter book before she told her father about her meeting with Powell.

"I know I shouldn't make any judgment yet, but I heard the ring of truth in Powell's voice when he was talking," Laurie said. "And his offer to pay the girls a quarter of a million dollars is wonderful."

"A quarter of a million dollars plus what you pay them," Leo repeated. "You say that Powell knows all four women could use the money?"

"Yes, that's what he said." Laurie realized that she sounded defensive.

"Has Powell helped any of them out along the way, including his stepdaughter?"

"He indicated that he didn't."

"I think it's a question you should look into. Who knows what his real motive may be to hand out all that money." Leo couldn't help but question these people's intentions. It was the cop in him. And the father. And grandfather.

With that, he decided to finish his coffee and go home. I'm getting too jumpy, he thought, and that won't do either Laurie or Timmy any good. Even the way I shouted at that guy on skates. I was right, he could have hurt someone; but it was the fact that he actually brushed against Timmy that scared me. If he'd had a gun or a knife, even with my hand in Timmy's, I couldn't have protected him from an attack fast enough.

Leo knew the grim reality that if a murderer had a grudge against someone, no order of protection or vigilance could keep them from satisfying his need to kill his target.

4

Claire Bonner settled at a table in the Seafood Bar of The Breakers Hotel in Palm Beach. She was facing the ocean and watched with detached interest as the waves crashed against the retaining wall directly below the Bar. The sun was shining but the winds were stronger than she had expected in Florida on an early spring day.

She was wearing a newly purchased zippered jacket in a light shade of blue. She had bought it when she noticed that it carried the name of THE BREAKERS on the breast pocket. It was part of the fantasy of spending this long weekend here. Her short ash-blond hair framed a face that was half-hidden by oversized sunglasses. The glasses were seldom off, but when they were, Claire's beautiful features were revealed, as well as the tranquil expression that had taken her years to achieve. In fact, a discerning observer might have realized that the expression was caused by the acceptance of reality rather than peace of mind. Her slender frame had an aura of fragility as though she had been recently ill. The same observer might have guessed her to be in her mid-thirties. In that case he would have been wrong. She was forty-one.

In the past four days she had had the same polite young waiter and now was greeted by name as he approached her table. "Let me guess, Ms. Bonner," he said. "Seafood chowder and two large stone crabs."

"You have it," Claire said as a brief smile touched the corner of her lips.

"And the usual glass of chardonnay," he added as he jotted down the order.

You do something for a few days in a row and it becomes the usual, she thought wryly.

Almost instantly the chardonnay was placed on the table before her. She picked up the glass and looked around the room as she sipped.

All of the diners were dressed in designer casual clothes. The Breakers was an expensive hotel, a retreat for the well-heeled. It was the Easter holiday week, and, nationwide, schools were closed. At breakfast in the dining room she had observed that families with children were usually accompanied by a nanny who skillfully removed a restless toddler so that the parents could enjoy the lavish buffet in peace.

The lunchtime crowd in the bar was composed almost totally of adults. In walking around she had noticed that the younger families gravitated to the restaurants by the pool, where the choice of casual fare was greater.

What would it have been like to vacation here every year from childhood? Claire wondered. Then she tried to brush away the memories of falling asleep each night in a half-empty theatre where her mother was working as an usher. That was before they met Robert Powell, of course. But by then Claire's childhood was almost over.

As those thoughts went through her head, two couples, still in travel clothes, took the table next to hers. She heard one of the women sigh happily, "It's so good to be back."

I'll pretend I'm coming back, she thought. I'll pretend that every year I have the same oceanfront room and look forward to long walks on the beach before breakfast.

The waiter arrived with the chowder. "Really hot, the way you like it, Ms. Bonner," he said.

The first day, she had asked for the chowder to be very hot and the crabs to be served as the second course. The waiter had also committed that request to memory.

The first sip of the chowder almost burned the roof of her mouth and she stirred the rest of it inside the soup bowl that was a scooped-out loaf of bread to cool it a bit. Then she reached for her glass and took a long sip of the chardonnay. As she had expected, it was crisp and dry, exactly as it had tasted for the last few days.

Outside an even stronger wind was churning the breaking waves into clouds of cascading foam.

Claire realized that she felt like one of those surges of water, trying to reach shore but at the mercy of the powerful wind. It was still her decision. She could always say no. She'd said no to returning to her stepfather's house for years. And she passionately didn't want to go now. No one could force her to go on a national cable television show and take part in reenacting the party and sleepover twenty years ago when the four of them, best friends, had celebrated their graduation from college.

But if she did take part in the show, the production company would give her fifty thousand dollars, and Rob would give her two hundred fifty thousand dollars.

Three hundred thousand dollars. It would mean that she could take a leave of absence from her job in Chicago's youth and family services. The bout of pneumonia she had survived in January had come close to killing her, and she knew her body was still weak and tired. She had never accepted Powell's offer of money. Not a single cent. She had torn up his letters and returned them to him. After what he did.

They wanted to call it the "Graduation Gala." It had been a beautiful party, a wonderful party, Claire thought. Then Alison and Regina and Nina had stayed overnight. And sometime during that night, my mother had been murdered. Betsy Bonner Powell, beautiful, vivacious, generous, funny, beloved Betsy.

I thoroughly despised her, Claire thought quietly.

I absolutely hated my mother, and I loathed her beloved husband, even though he kept trying to send me money.

5

Regina Callari was sorry she had gone to the post office and picked up the registered letter from Laurie Moran, a producer at Fisher Blake Studios. Take part in a reality program that would reenact the night of the Graduation Gala! she thought, dismayed—and, frankly, shocked.

The letter upset her so much that she knew she had lost a sale. She had to fumble for the features of the house she was showing, and in the middle of the walk-through the prospective client said, abruptly, "I think I've seen enough; this is not the house I'm looking for."

Then, after she got back to the office, she had to phone the owner, seventy-six-year-old Bridget Whiting, and tell her that she had been wrong. "I was sure we had a good prospect but it just didn't happen," she apologized.

Bridget's disappointment was palpably evident in

her voice. "I don't know how long they'll keep that apartment for me in the assisted-living home, and it's *exactly* what I want. Oh dear! Regina, maybe I built up my hopes too much. It's not your fault."

But it is my fault, Regina thought, trying to keep raw anger out of her voice as she swore to Bridget that she was going to find her a buyer and fast, and then, knowing how difficult that would be in this market, said good-bye.

Her office, a one-room former garage, had once been part of a private residence on the main street in St. Augustine, Florida. The bleak housing market had improved, but not sufficiently for Regina to do more than eke out a living. Now she put her elbows on her desk and pressed her fingers to the sides of her forehead. Wisps of curly hair reminded her that her midnight-black hair was growing with its usual annoying rapidity. She knew she would have to make an appointment for a trim. The fact that the hairdresser always insisted on talking a blue streak was what had kept her from making the appointment—that, and the cost.

That silly fact made Regina annoyed at herself and her own always present impatience. So what, she told herself, if for twenty minutes Lena yak-yak-yakked away? She's the only one who knows how to make this unruly mop look decent.

Regina's dark brown eyes traveled to the picture on her desk. Zach, her nineteen-year-old son, smiled back at her from it. He was just completing his sophomore year at the University of Pennsylvania, an education fully paid for by his father, her ex-husband. Zach had phoned last night. Hesitantly, he had asked if she would mind if he went backpacking through Europe and the Middle East this summer. He had planned to come home and get a job in St. Augustine, but jobs were hard to find there. It wouldn't cost all that much, and his father would finance him.

"I'll be back in time to spend ten days with you before the term starts, Mom," he had assured her, his tone pleading.

Regina had told him that it was a wonderful opportunity and that he should jump at it. She hadn't let the keen disappointment she felt sound in her voice. She missed Zach. She missed the sweet little boy who used to come bounding into the office from the school bus, eager to share every single moment of his day with her. She missed the tall, shy adolescent who would have dinner waiting if she was out late with a client.

Since the divorce, Earl had been skillfully carving out ways to separate her from Zach. It had begun when, at age ten, Zach went to sailing camp in Cape Cod for the summer. The camp was followed by the shared holidays when Earl and his new wife took Zach skiing in Switzerland or to the South of France.

She knew Zach loved her, but a small house and a tight budget could hardly compete with life with his wildly rich father. Now he'd be gone for most of the summer.

Slowly, Regina reached for the letter from Moran and reread it. "She'll pay fifty thousand, and the mighty Robert Nicholas Powell will pay each of us two hundred fifty thousand," she murmured aloud. "Mr. Benevolence himself."

She thought of her friends and former co-hosts of the Graduation Gala. Claire Bonner. She was beautiful, but always so quiet, like a faded shadow next to her mother. Alison Schaefer, so smart she put the rest of us to shame. I thought she'd end up the next Madame Curie. She got married the October after Betsy died, and then Rod, her husband, was in an accident. From what I understand, he's been on crutches all these years. Nina Craig. We called her "the flaming redhead." I remember even as a freshman if she got mad at you, watch out. She would even tell a teacher off if she thought she didn't get a good enough mark on an essay.

And then there was me, Regina thought. When I was fifteen I opened the door of the garage to put my bike away and found my father swinging from a rope. His eyes were bulging and his tongue was lapping over his chin. If he had to hang himself, why didn't he do it in his office? He knew that I'd be the one to find him in the garage. I loved him so much! How could he have done that to me? The nightmares have never stopped. They always started with her getting off her bike.

Before she called the police, and the neighbor's house where her mother was playing bridge, she had taken the suicide note her father had pinned to his shirt and hidden it. When the police came they said that most suicide victims leave a note for the family.

Sobbing, her mother had searched the house for it, while Regina pretended to help.

The girls were my lifeline after that, Regina thought. We were such close friends. After the Gala and Betsy's death, Claire and Nina and I were Alison's bridesmaids. That had been such a stupid move. It was so soon after Betsy died; the tabloids had made a spectacle of the wedding. The headlines were all a rehashing of the Graduation Gala murder. That was when we realized that all four of us would continue to be under suspicion; maybe for the rest of our lives.

We never got together again, Regina lamented. After the wedding we all went out of our way to avoid any contact with each other. We all moved to different cities.

What would it be like to see them again, to be under the same roof? We were all so young then, so shocked and frightened when Betsy's body was discovered. And the way the police questioned us, together, then separately. It's a miracle one of us didn't break down and confess to smothering her, the way they hammered at us. *"We know it was somebody inside that house. Which one of you did it? If it wasn't you, maybe it was one of your friends. Protect yourself. Tell us what you know."*

Regina thought of how the police had wondered if Betsy's emeralds might have been the motive. She left them on the glass tray on her dressing table when she went to bed. They suggested that she woke up while she was being robbed and whoever was there panicked. One of her earrings was on the floor. Had

Betsy dropped it when she took it off, or had someone, wearing gloves, panicked and dropped it when
she woke up?

Regina got up slowly and looked around. She tried
to visualize having three hundred thousand dollars
in the bank. Almost half of that would go to income
tax, she warned herself. But even so, it would be an
unimaginable windfall. Or maybe it would bring
back the days when her father had been so successful, and they, as well as Robert and Betsy Powell, had
the big house in Salem Ridge with all the trimmings,
housekeeper, a cook, a landscaper, a chauffeur, a top
New York caterer for their frequent parties . . .

Regina looked around her one-room real estate
office. Even with the Sheetrock walls painted light
blue to coordinate with her white desk and the white
armchairs with blue cushions for potential clients, the
room looked like what it was: a brave effort to hide
a thin budget. A garage is a garage is a garage, she
thought, except for the one luxury I installed when I
bought this property after the divorce.

The luxury was down the hall past the unisex restroom. Unmarked and always locked, it was a private
bathroom with a Jacuzzi, steam shower, vanity sink,
and wardrobe closet. It was here that sometimes, at
the end of the day, she would shower, change, and
then meet her friends or go out to a solitary dinner
followed by a movie.

Earl had left her ten years ago, when Zach was
going on nine. He hadn't been able to put up with
her bouts of depression. "Get help, Regina. I'm sick

of the moods. I'm sick of the nightmares. It's not good for our son, just in case you haven't noticed."

After the divorce, Earl, a computer salesman at the time, whose hobby had been writing songs, had finally sold a collection of his music to a major recording artist. His next step had been to marry budding rock singer Sonya Miles. When Sonya hit the charts with the album he wrote for her, Earl became a celebrity in the world he coveted. He took to that life as a duck takes to water, Regina thought as she walked over to the row of files on the far side of the room.

She took an unmarked package from the bottom of the locked file. Buried under miscellaneous real estate advertisements, it was a cardboard box that contained all the newspaper coverage of the Graduation Gala murder.

I haven't looked at it in years, Regina thought as she carried the box back to her desk, laid it down, and opened it. Some of the newspapers had begun to crumble at the edges, but she found what she was looking for. It was the picture of Betsy and Robert Powell toasting the four graduates—Claire, Alison, Nina, and herself.

We were all so pretty, Regina thought. I remember how we went shopping for dresses together. We all had done well in college. We had our plans and hopes for the future. And they were all destroyed that night.

She put the newspapers back in the box, carried it over to the file, and dropped it in the bottom drawer, carefully concealing it below the ads. I'm going to take his damn money, she thought. And that producer's as well. Maybe if I do, I can take hold of my life. I do know I can use some of the money to take Zach on a fun vacation, before he goes back to school.

She slammed the drawer, put the CLOSED sign in the window of the office, turned out the lights, locked the door, and went back to her private bath. In it, as the water ran in the Jacuzzi, she stripped and looked at herself in the full-length mirror on the door. I've got two months before the show and I need to lose twenty pounds, she thought. I want to look good when I get there and tell what I remember. I want Zach to be proud of me.

An unwanted thought crept into her mind. I know Earl always wondered if I was the one who killed Betsy. Did he ever plant that suspicion in Zach's mind?

Regina knew she didn't love Earl anymore, didn't want him anymore, but even more than that, she didn't want to have any more nightmares.

The Jacuzzi was filled with water. She stepped into it, leaned back, and closed her eyes.

As her curly black hair became straight and sleek around her face, she thought, This is my chance to convince everyone that I wasn't the one who killed that rotten slut.

6

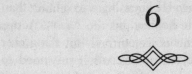

Rod Kimball signed for the certified letter and opened it while his wife, Alison, was busy filling a prescription. When the customer left she hurried over to take it from him.

"Who's sending a registered letter?" she asked, her tone worried, as without breaking stride she took it from him, turned, and went back to the pharmacy area of their drugstore, giving him no chance to warn her of the contents. Dismayed, he watched as her face flushed, then paled as she read the two-page missive. Then she dropped it on the counter. "I can't go through that again," she cried, her voice trembling. "My God, do they think I'm crazy?"

"Take it easy, love," Rod cautioned. Trying not to grimace with pain, he slid off the stool behind the checkout counter and reached for his crutches. Twenty years after the hit-and-run accident that had crippled him, pain was always a fact of life for him. Yet some days, like this one, cold and wet in late March in Cleveland, Ohio, it was more severe than others. Pain was etched into the lines around his eyes and the resolute set of his jaw. His dark brown hair had turned almost completely gray. He knew he looked older than his forty-two years. He hobbled over to Alison. Across the counter from her, his six-foot body towering over her petite frame, he felt an overwhelming need to protect her. "You don't have to do anything you don't want to do," he said firmly. "Tear up that letter."

"No." Shaking her head, Alison opened the drawer beneath the counter and shoved the letter into it. "I can't talk about it now, Rod," she said.

At that point the jingling sound that signaled the opening of the door told them that a customer was coming into the store, and Rod made his way back to the checkout counter.

He had been a rookie quarterback for the New York Giants when he and Alison were married. He was raised by a single mother who worked as a caretaker for an invalid to support him. His father, a hopeless alcoholic, died when he was two. The sportswriters were unanimous that a brilliant career was ahead of him when he had signed his first big contract. He and Alison were both twenty-two then, and he had been crazy about her since kindergarten. In fact, when they were in kindergarten together he had announced to the class that he was going to marry her someday.

Alison's family had never had any money. Her father was the produce manager in a grocery store. Alison went to college on a mix of student loans and working part time. She had lived in a modest section of Salem Ridge, not far from where Rod Kimball had lived. She had missed out on a scholarship to graduate school.

He officially proposed the day he was offered the big contract with the New York Giants. That was two months after Betsy Powell's murder. An important part of the proposal was that he knew Alison wanted to go to medical school and then into research. He promised to pay for her education, to tiptoe around the house when she was studying, and to delay having children until she obtained the degree she wanted so badly.

Instead, three weeks after the wedding, he had been in the accident, and Alison had spent the better part of the next four years at his bedside helping him to heal. The money he had saved from his one season with the Giants was soon exhausted.

At that point Alison had taken out more loans and gone back to school to become a pharmacist. Her first job came about because her elderly childless cousin had hired her to work with him in his drugstore in Cleveland. "Rod, there's a job for you as well," he had said. "My assistant is leaving. She does the ordering of everything except for the drugs, and she handles the cash register."

They had both been glad to get out of the New York area, where they always seemed to encounter speculation over Betsy Powell's death. A few years after they moved to Cleveland, the cousin retired and they took over the store. Now they had a wide circle of friends, and no one ever asked them about the Graduation Gala murder.

The nickname "Rod" had come about because in his college years on the football field, a sportswriter had commented that he moved as fast as a lightning rod. After the accident, Thomas "Rod" Kimball had managed not to let that nickname become a source of bitter irony.

The morning was fairly quiet, but in the afternoon business was brisk. They had two part-time assistants, a semiretired pharmacist and a clerk who stocked the shelves and helped at the cash register. Even with their help it was an exceptionally busy day, and by the time they closed at 8 P.M., he and Alison were both bone tired.

By then it was raining hard, a cold driving rain. Alison insisted that he use the wheelchair to get out to the car. "We'll both be drowned if you try to use the crutches," she said, an edge in her voice.

Many times over the years he had sought the courage to insist that she leave him, that she meet someone else and have a normal life. But he had never been able to bring himself to utter those words. He could not visualize a life without her now, any more than he could have visualized it all through his growing years.

He sometimes thought of an observation his grandmother had made long ago. "In most marriages, one of the couple is more in love than the other, and it's best if it's the man. The marriage will have a better chance of going the whole way."

Rod did not need to be told that with Alison, he was the one who loved the most. He was almost sure that she would not have accepted his proposal if he had not offered to send her to medical school. And then, after the accident, she was too decent to walk out on him.

Rod didn't let himself drown in that kind of speculation often, but the letter today brought back so much—the Graduation Gala, the pictures of the four girls plastered all over the newspapers, the circus the media had made of their wedding.

When they reached the car, Alison said, "Rod, let me drive. I know you're hurting."

She was shielding him with the umbrella as she opened the door, and without arguing he slid into the passenger seat. It was impossible for her to hold the umbrella and fold the wheelchair at the same time. He watched regretfully as the rain pelted her face and hair until she was finally settled behind the wheel. Then she turned to him. "I'm going to do it," she said. Her tone was defiant, as if she expected him to argue with her.

When he said nothing, she waited for a long minute, then started the engine. "No comment?" Now he detected a slight tremor in her voice.

He was not going to tell her what he was thinking—that with her long brown hair wet on her shoulders, she looked so young and so vulnerable. He knew she was frightened. No, he thought. Make that terrified.

"If the others agree to take part in the program and you don't, it wouldn't be good," he said quietly. "I think you have to go. I think we have to go," he corrected himself quickly.

"I was lucky last time. This time I may not be so lucky."

They were both silent for the rest of the trip. Their ranch-style home, designed to accommodate his disabilities, was a twenty-minute drive from the pharmacy. They were spared any further exposure to the downpour because a door from the garage opened into the kitchen. Once inside, shaking off her wet raincoat, Alison sank into a chair and buried her face in her hands. "Rod, I'm so scared. I never told you but that night when we all went up to bed all I could think of was how much I hated Betsy and Rob Powell." She hesitated and continued haltingly, "I think I was sleepwalking that night and I might have gone into Betsy's room."

"You thought you were in Betsy's room that night!" Rod dropped his crutches as he pulled a chair closer to Alison and eased himself into it. "Do you think there is any possibility that anyone saw you?"

"I don't know."

Alison pulled away from his embrace and turned to face him. Her large, expressive light brown eyes were her dominant feature. Now with tears streaming from them, they looked haunted and defenseless. Then Rod heard a question he never expected to hear from his wife's lips.

"Rod," she asked, "isn't it a fact that you have always believed that I killed Betsy Powell?"

"Are you crazy?" he asked. "Are you absolutely crazy?"

But even to his own ears, he knew that his protest sounded hollow and unconvincing.

7

"**W**ell, have you made up your mind if you're going?"

That was the question Nina Craig heard as she pushed open the door of her condo in West Hollywood. Oh God, she's in one of those moods, Nina thought, and bit her lip to keep from making a sharp reply to her sixty-two-year-old mother. It was five-thirty, and it was clear to her that Muriel Craig had started her private cocktail hour well before her usual five o'clock with a pitcher of apple martinis or a bottle of wine.

Muriel was still in her nightgown and robe, which meant that whatever time she had woken up, it was in the cloud of depression that so often enveloped her. It's going to be a long night, Nina thought resentfully.

"No response from the Academy Award winner?" her mother asked sarcastically as she refilled her glass from the almost empty bottle.

Ten years ago Nina had given up the hope of becoming a successful actress one day and had joined the guild for extras, the background people who worked on a day-by-day basis. Arriving at 5 A.M., she'd spent all day on the set of a film about a revolution and had been one of the hundreds of extras who held up banners. The set was in the desert near Palm Springs, and it had been mercilessly hot.

"I don't know what I'm going to do, Mom," Nina said, trying to keep her tone even.

"Why not go? Three hundred thousand dollars is pretty good money. I'll go with you. I wouldn't mind getting an in-person look at good old Robert Nicholas Powell again."

Nina looked at her mother. The hair that, like her own, had once been a natural deep red was now dyed a bright fire-engine shade and looked harsh against Muriel's face. Years of smoking had left deep lines around her lips and cheeks, and her skin was mottled with brown spots. Her shoulders slumped as she leaned forward on the couch, her two hands encircling the glass.

It was hard to visualize the beautiful woman who at one time had been one of those rarities, an actress who worked steadily. *She* had talent, Nina thought bitterly, not like me. And now look at her!

Don't you go into all that again, Nina warned herself. It's the end of the day, and you're hot and fed up with everything. "Mom, I'm going to shower and get into something comfortable," she said. "I'll join you for a glass of wine when I get dressed."

"Take the three hundred thousand." Her mother spat the words out at her. "Use it to buy me my own condo. You don't want me living with you any more than I want to be here."

Muriel had followed Nina to California after the acting jobs became fewer and fewer in New York. A year earlier, she had barely escaped being burned to death when her carelessly dropped cigarette had ignited the carpet in the living room of her apartment in a two-family house in Los Angeles. The people who owned the house where she had rented had refused to let her return after the damage to the apartment was repaired. "The same thing could happen in the middle of the night," the owner told Nina. "I'm not taking any more chances."

Her mother had been living with Nina for almost a year now. Now she, too, worked as an extra, but too often did not feel up to responding to a potential job.

I can't take it much longer, Nina thought as she closed and locked the door of her bedroom. In her mother's present frame of mind, it would not be unusual for her to follow Nina in to continue the discussion about the letter from the producer.

The room was cool and inviting. White walls, polished floors with white throw rugs on either side of the bed, narrow apple-green draperies at the windows. The white bedspread was accentuated by apple-green and white pillows. The four-poster bed and matching dresser were left over from her ten-year marriage to a mildly successful actor who had turned out to be a serial cheat. It was better that they had not had any children.

They'd been divorced for three years. I'm ready to find someone else, Nina thought. But I can't while I'm stuck with my mother. Who knows? I still look good. If I go on that program I might be able to parlay it into getting back into real acting, or even one of those reality shows. I can be a mad housewife with the best of them.

What would it be like to see Claire and Regina and Alison again? We were such kids, Nina thought. We were all so scared. The cops kept twisting what we were saying. Mom gave the performance of the year when she was asked if it was true that she had been seriously dating Powell before he met Betsy. "I was dating at least three people at that time," she said. "He was one of them."

That's not the way I heard it, Nina thought grimly. Her mother blamed her for introducing Betsy to Powell. She blamed me, and blamed me, and blamed me, Nina thought. It was all I ever heard from her. I ruined her life.

Muriel had turned down the part that would have made her a star because Powell didn't want her to be locked into a contract when they got married. Those were the exact words he used: "When we get married."

She'd thrown them at Nina often enough over the years.

Nina felt the white-hot anger that those memories evoked wash over her. She thought of the night of the Graduation Gala. Her mother had refused to come to the party. "I should be *living* in that house," she had said.

Betsy had made a point of seeking Nina out. "Where is your mother?" she had asked. "Or is she still a sore loser about Rob?"

I'm glad no one heard her ask me that question that night, Nina thought. It wouldn't have looked good when Robert Powell discovered his wife's body the next morning. But at that moment, if I had had that pillow, I would gladly have held it over her face.

I had much too much to drink that night. I don't even remember going to bed. I don't think I showed it, because no one mentioned it, including that nosy housekeeper who said that she thought Alison was drunk.

When she and the others got there Powell was collapsed on the floor, and the housekeeper pulled the pillow from Betsy's face.

Her mother was turning the handle of the door. "I want to talk to you," she called. "I want you to go on that program."

With a supreme effort Nina managed not to show how angry she was as she called back, "Mom, I'm stepping into the shower. It's all right. I *am* going to accept that offer. I'll be able to get you your own place."

Before I kill you, she added silently. And then wondered again what else she hadn't remembered about the night Betsy Powell was suffocated.

8

The agreements to participate in the reenactment of the events of the Graduation Gala had trickled in to Laurie's office one by one. The last of them had taken nearly two weeks, and it was from Nina Craig. The letter stated that she had consulted a lawyer and there were additional conditions she felt were appropriate. Robert Powell should put in escrow two hundred fifty thousand dollars for each of the four graduates, and it should be a net sum to each of them. Fisher Blake Studios must also offer fifty thousand net to the graduates. "Both Mr. Powell and Fisher Blake can well afford to compensate us fairly," Nina had written. "And now that I have contacted my longtime childhood friends, I realize that we have all suffered emotional damage from being in the Powell home the night Betsy Bonner Powell lost her life. I believe by once again exposing ourselves to the glare of publicity, we are surrendering our hard-earned anonymity, for which we should receive appropriate compensation."

Dismayed, Laurie reread the letter. "To net them that much money will mean we'd just about have to double what we're paying them," she said.

"I don't think Brett will go for it." Jerry Klein's flat tone did not match the disappointment that came over his face. He had signed for the certified letter from Ms. Nina Craig and carried it into Laurie's office.

"He's got to go along with it," Laurie said. "And I think he will. He's been talking the series up, and he won't want to pull back now."

"Well he won't be happy about it." The worried expression on Jerry's face deepened. "Laurie, I hope you haven't put yourself out on a limb with this *Under Suspicion* idea."

"I hope not, too." Laurie looked out the window toward the Rockefeller Center skating rink. It was a warm day for early April, and there were few skaters on the ice. Soon the rink would be gone, and the area it covered would be filled with tables and chairs for outside dining.

Once in a while Greg and I used to have dinner out there, she thought as a wave of longing for him swept over her. She knew why it had come at this moment. The show was about closure. Even though she had no intention of revealing her concern to either Jerry or Grace, she knew Jerry was right. After becoming openly enthusiastic about the project, her boss, Brett Young, would probably rather double the price he had agreed to pay the participants than back out.

"What about Robert Powell?" Jerry was asking. "Do you think he'll pony up and pay the taxes so they clear the two hundred and fifty grand?"

"I can only ask," Laurie said. "And I think I'd better do it in person. I'll call and ask if he can see me today."

"Shouldn't you check with Brett first?" Jerry suggested.

"No. There's no use in getting him going if it's a lost cause. If Powell doesn't agree to pay, our next move has to be for me to fly to Los Angeles and see if Nina Craig can be persuaded to accept our offer. The others all agreed to the original terms, but it's obvious she got them stirred up."

"What will you tell her?" Jerry asked.

"The truth. If necessary we'll do it without her, and that wouldn't look good for her. And don't forget that Betsy Bonner Powell was forty-two years old when she died. She'd be only sixty-two or sixty-three now. Today many people live well into their eighties. Betsy was robbed of half of the life she might have enjoyed if someone hadn't held a pillow over her face that night. The person who did that has woken up every morning since then and been able to enjoy a brand-new day while Betsy's body is in a casket in a cemetery."

Laurie knew her voice had become heated and angry and that it wasn't just about Betsy Bonner Powell. It was about Greg and the fact that his killer was a free man. Not only *free*, but a living, breathing threat to her and Timmy. Then she said, "Sorry, Jerry. I know that I have to be careful not to make this sound like a personal crusade."

She picked up the phone. "Time to make another appointment with Robert Nicholas Powell."

9

Rob Powell was on the three-hole golf course on the back lawn of his estate. The warm April day was conducive to getting out his clubs and practicing his swing before he joined a foursome at the Winged Foot Golf Club. Not bad, he thought as a well-struck putt rolled to the bottom of the cup.

Concentrating on his golf game had given him the opportunity to put aside the fact that he had not yet heard from the doctor. The chemo three years ago had seemed to take care of the nodules on his lungs, but he knew there was always a chance they would come back. He had had his semiannual checkup earlier in the week.

"Par for the course," he said aloud as he made his way back to the house, swinging his golf club.

Fifteen minutes until his guest arrived. What did Laurie Moran want? he asked himself. She'd sounded concerned. Is she going to tell me that one of them won't take part in the program? Rob frowned. I need to have them all here, he thought. No matter *what* it takes.

Even if Moran's report was favorable, Rob had a sense of time going by too swiftly. He needed closure, and when Laurie Moran had come to see him in March and proposed her concept of reenacting the night of the Graduation Gala, it had been the answer to a prayer. Except, Rob thought, I've never been much of one to pray. I left all that to Betsy.

At that thought he laughed, a mirthless sound that came out more like a bark, and was followed by a fit of coughing.

Why hadn't the doctor called with the results?

His housekeeper, Jane Novak, was opening the sliding glass door as he stepped from the cobblestone walk onto the patio. "Hole in one, Mr. Robert?" she asked cheerfully.

"Not quite, but not bad, Jane," Rob said, trying not to be annoyed that Jane always asked that after he had been on the greens. If there was one thing about Jane he wished he could change, it was her total lack of any sense of humor. She meant that question to be a joke.

Jane, a solidly built woman with steel-gray hair and matching eyes, had come to work for him shortly after he married Betsy. He had understood why Betsy was not comfortable with the previous housekeeper, who had been hired by his first wife and who had stayed with him after her death. "Rob, that woman *resents* me," Betsy had said. "I can *feel* it. Tell her it's not working out and give her a healthy severance check. I know just who I want in her place."

The person Betsy wanted was Jane Novak, who had worked backstage when Betsy was ushering in the theatre. "She's a marvelous organizer. She actually keeps the dressing rooms neat. And she's a good cook," Betsy had raved.

Jane was all of that. After entering the country on a green card from Hungary, she was overwhelmed with joy to be put in charge of the mansion, and, as Betsy had promised, she was fully up to the job. Exactly Betsy's age, Jane was now sixty-two. If she had any close friends or family, Rob had never seen them. Her very comfortable apartment was located behind the kitchen, and even on her days off, from what he could see, she seldom left it. Unless he was out of town, he knew that at seven-thirty every morning she would be in the kitchen ready to prepare his breakfast.

Over the years Rob had learned to see the slight nuances in Jane's placid expression that signaled any kind of distress. As he stepped inside the house, he realized he was seeing them now. "You said that Ms. Moran was coming, Mr. Rob," Jane said. "I hope you don't mind if I ask, but does that mean that the program is going to happen?"

"I don't mind you asking, but the answer is I don't know," Rob said. Even as he spoke, he realized that he *did* mind Jane asking, because there was a note of disapproval in her question.

He had just enough time to change into a long-sleeved sport shirt and go back downstairs before the doorbell chimed.

It was exactly four o'clock. He wondered if she had timed her arrival so precisely or if she had arrived a little early and waited in her car before coming up to the house.

It was the kind of totally irrelevant speculation that Rob Powell had found himself indulging in lately. "Woolgathering" is what they used to call it, he thought. He had even gone to the trouble of looking up the word in the dictionary. The definition was "indulging in idle fancies and daydreaming; absentmindedness."

Rob thought to himself, Snap out of it! and got to his feet. He had asked Jane to bring Laurie Moran into the library instead of his office. Betsy had liked the English custom of four o'clock tea. After her death he had gotten away from it, but today it suddenly seemed appropriate.

More woolgathering, he acknowledged as Jane came into the room, followed by Laurie Moran.

He had considered Moran to be an attractive woman when she came to the house last month, but now as she hesitated for a moment and stood framed in the doorway, he realized that she was beautiful. Her hair, a soft honey shade, was loose on her shoulders, and in place of the pin-striped suit she was wearing a long-sleeved print blouse and black-belted skirt that accentuated her small waist. Her black patent leather heels did not have the ridiculous stilts that were the fashion nowadays.

Once again, the seventy-eight-year-old appreciated her lovely looks.

"Come in, Ms. Moran, come in," he said heartily. "I won't bite you."

"I wasn't afraid of that, Mr. Powell," Laurie said, smiling as she crossed the room and sat on the couch opposite the roomy leather armchair where he was settling himself.

"I've asked Jane to prepare tea," he said. "You may serve it now, Jane, thank you."

"How kind of you."

It *was* kind of him, Laurie thought.

She drew a deep breath. Now that she was here, with so much at stake, it was difficult to appear calm. The four women, the stars of the Graduation Gala, would cost this man nearly two million dollars, instead of half that amount, to appear on the program.

Laurie marshaled her pitch to him, but before she started she waited for Jane's somewhat forbidding figure to turn and leave the room.

"I'm going to make this easy for you," Robert Powell said unexpectedly. "A problem has come up. I don't have to be particularly astute or a deep thinker to guess that it's about money. One of the four girls—women now—doesn't think we're paying enough to coax them to expose themselves to public scrutiny."

Laurie hesitated for the length of a few seconds, then said, "That's right."

Powell smiled. "Let me guess which one. It wouldn't be Claire. She has refused to let me help her since Betsy died. When she learns I have left her a substantial amount of money in my will it will not impress her. When the time comes, she might even give the money to charity.

"We were *very* close, but Claire was very close to her mother, too. The fact that Betsy died was overwhelming for Claire. Somehow it became my fault, not that she thought I had killed her mother, mind you. Angry as she was, she knew that was impossible, but I think that in her mind, she was begrudging me the time I had alone with Betsy." For a long moment he looked past Laurie.

"My guess," he added slowly, "is that Nina Craig is the one holding us up for more money. In that way she's very much like her mother. I actually dated Muriel Craig for a time. A very attractive woman, but with a touch of ruthlessness in her character. I didn't stop seeing her only because I'd met Betsy. It would have happened anyhow. It was just a coincidence that it happened at approximately the same time."

Jane carried in the tea tray, interrupting his reverie. She set it on the coffee table between the couch and Robert Powell's chair. "Shall I pour, Mr. Powell?" she asked. She was already holding the teapot and pouring it into Laurie's cup.

Robert Powell raised his eyebrows and cast an amused glance at Laurie. After Jane had offered cream or lemon and sugar or sweetener, and then left the room, he said, "As you can see, Jane asked a rhetorical question. She does that all the time."

Laurie realized she had skipped lunch and was starved. She made herself take only a nibble of the quarter-sized crustless salmon sandwich. Her first instinct was to pop it into her mouth whole and reach for another one.

But even as she made herself eat slowly, daintily, she had the feeling that Robert Powell was toying with her. Did he really guess that Nina Craig was the one looking for more money, or had Nina contacted him personally?

And did he know how much she was going to demand?

"Am I right about Nina?" Powell asked as he crossed his legs and began to sip his tea.

"Yes," Laurie said.

"How much does she want for all the graduates?"

"Two hundred fifty thousand dollars net each."

"She's even greedier than I remembered," Powell murmured. "So like her dear mother." The amused tone left his voice. "Tell her I'll pay it."

The abrupt change in his expression and tone shocked Laurie.

"Ms. Moran," he explained, "you need to understand something: like the four girls at the Gala, I have lived with the cloud of suspicion hanging over me for a long time. Today people are living to be one hundred, but many more don't live past eighty or eighty-five. Before I die, I want to have a chance for a wide audience to see the girls and me, and perhaps understand how big this house is, and how many people were in and out that night. How it could have been an intruder. As you know, we have extensive films of the party."

"I do know that," Laurie said. "I think I've read everything written about the case."

"Well, then, you can understand that except for some generous donations to charity and the schools Betsy, Claire, and I attended, I have a great deal of money to spend before I die, so the amount Nina is holding out for is quite insignificant.

"But do me a favor. When you write to say we accept the conditions of their appearance, please tell Nina that I hope her mother is planning to come east with her. It would be a pleasure to see her again."

He anticipated Laurie's protest. "Of course, I don't mean for her to stay as a guest in my home. I will reserve a room for her at the St. Regis."

He's going along with it. Laurie did not expect the tsunami of relief that swept over her. The possibility of the program had unexpectedly gathered momentum, and if Powell had flatly turned down Nina Craig's demand, the show could easily have been doomed, and her job along with it. Two failed series, then a rejected proposal, after intense media interest, would easily have meant her dismissal.

Brett Young did not tolerate failure.

She started to thank Powell, then realized he was looking past her out onto the patio beyond the glass doors of his den. Her eyes followed to see what he was looking at that had caused the sudden expression of disapproval.

She saw a landscaper standing on the patio outside the den, edging the grass around it with a clipper.

Powell looked from the man to Laurie. "Sorry," he

said, "but I find it annoying that they're working this late. I've made it clear that I want any work on the property completed by noon. If I have guests coming, I don't want those big trucks in the driveway."

OUTSIDE, BLUE EYES SAW THAT POWELL WAS looking at him. He finished clipping the last section around the patio and, without looking, carried his gardening equipment quickly back to the truck. It was his first day on the job for Perfect Estates. If Powell complained about him being there so late, Blue Eyes would say he stayed after hours to impress his new boss.

The Graduation girls won't be the only ones here when they are filming that show, he thought. I'll be here, too.

What a perfect scenario for him to take out Laurie Moran.

He had already prepared the sign he wanted to put on her body.

GOT GREG

GOT YOU

TIMMY'S NEXT

10

In June, preproduction for the "Graduation Gala" went into high gear. Laurie had already obtained all available film footage taken of the party, but then Robert Powell willingly turned over the extra footage other guests had captured that night.

It was like watching Cinderella's night at the ball. Only there were four Cinderellas, Laurie mused as she ran tape after tape.

After Betsy died, George Curtis, a member of the Winged Foot Golf Club in Mamaroneck, had brought to the police the footage he had taken that evening. But it was mostly a duplicate of what the police already had. The tape was copied and given to Robert Powell, who had requested it. "It's very similar to what I've already given you," he had told the detective in charge of the investigation, "but there are some scenes of Betsy and me that are particularly precious to me." He had pictures made of several of the frames in which he and Betsy had been together—one of them looking at each other, another of them dancing on the patio, another toasting the graduates.

"These films sure give us a look into the party," Laurie commented to Grace and Jerry as she played the copies over and over in the screening room of the office, trying to decide which scenes she wanted to include.

I start with the body being discovered and the cops arriving, she thought. That was at 8 A.M. Powell went in to wake up Betsy. He was carrying a cup of coffee for her. He always brought her wake-up cup at that time, even if she had had a late night.

Jane rushed in, screaming Betsy's name, and yelling for the others to dial 911.

We'll end the first segment with Betsy and Powell toasting the graduates. We'll have the narrator say, "At that moment, beautiful Betsy Bonner Powell had only four hours to live," Laurie decided.

GEORGE CURTIS KNEW THAT HE MIGHT BE caught on security cameras around the Powell estate, but it did not worry him. Half of Salem Ridge is driving past this house, he thought as he followed the stream of cars on the quiet road.

So what if the cops think I'm a voyeur? he thought. Practically everyone else on this road is, too.

He had chosen to drive the SUV rather than his red Porsche convertible. Unless security cameras photographed the license plate, he doubted very much that he would be recognized. Plenty of Salem Ridge residents had top-of-the-line SUVs. He was wearing a cap and dark glasses.

Sixty-three years old, tall, with a full head of gray hair, George Curtis had the trim appearance of a seasoned athlete. Married for thirty-five years and with college-age twins, he had been the scion and sole heir of a big chain of fast-food restaurants. After his father's death, when he was twenty-seven, he had taken over the business. A playboy until then, everyone expected him to sell the chain and live off his wealth. Instead he had married shortly afterward, and over time tripled the number of restaurants both in the United States and abroad until now the company boasted of serving a million meals a day.

Unlike Robert Powell, he had gone to Harvard as a fourth-generation legacy. The welcome mat had been laid out for him, as was his admission to Hasty Pudding, the student theatrical society at Harvard.

The fifteen-year difference in their ages had never interfered with his friendship with Robert Powell, even though, as he turned the car off Evergreen Lane, George thought, If he ever knew, if he ever guessed . . .

But Rob Powell had never suspected. George was sure of that. George had never given him reason to.

The phone rang, an unexpected and abrupt sound. He pressed the answering button on the steering wheel.

"George Curtis," he said.

"George, it's Rob Powell."

My God, was he looking out the window? George felt his face flush. No, he couldn't possibly have read the license plate, and certainly couldn't have recognized me just driving by.

"Rob, how are you, and when are we going to get together for a round of golf? I warn you, I broke eighty two Saturdays in a row."

"That means you'll never do it three weeks in a row! Tee-off time nine o'clock?"

"You're on. I'll make the reservation." George felt a palpable sense of relief as he turned left onto his own street. Rob Powell was not one to stay on the line longer than necessary. That's why when Rob said, "George, I have a favor to ask of you," he was startled.

"Whatever it is, the answer is yes," George said, sounding rattled to his own ears.

"I'll take all your franchises in Europe," Rob joked, then his tone became serious. "George, you can't have missed the news that the anniversary of Betsy's death in June is going to be the basis for a television program."

"No, I didn't miss that," Curtis said quietly.

"The point is that, besides the girls, they'd like to have one of the friends who was there that night to comment on the party between excerpts from the films. I suggested you, and they leaped at the prospect of getting you on camera. Of course I should have asked you first, but you can always say no to them."

Go on camera to talk about that night to a national audience? He could feel his hands turning sweaty on the steering wheel.

George Curtis found his throat constricting, but he kept his voice calm and warm as he said, "Rob, I told you a minute ago that whatever favor you wanted, it was yours. I meant it when I said it, and I mean it now."

"Thanks. It was hard for me to ask, and I'm sure hard for you to agree."

An abrupt click broke the connection. George Curtis realized that he was drenched with perspiration now. Was Rob Powell setting a trap for him? he asked himself as a feeling of dread engulfed him.

Now utterly distracted, he almost drove past his own driveway.

11

From the windows of the ornate and seldom-used living room, Jane Novak watched the stream of cars pass the house.

Today the television crew was upstairs in Betsy's bedroom.

I mean Mrs. Powell's bedroom, Jane thought sarcastically. Betsy had become "Mrs. Powell" to her the day she took over as housekeeper here twenty-nine years ago.

"Mr. Powell is quite traditional, Jane," she had said. "He told me that it was fine with him if I wanted to hire you, but that it was necessary for you to refer to me that way."

At the time, thirty-three-year-old Jane hadn't minded. She'd been thrilled to get the job. Mr. Powell had insisted on meeting her and sent his chauffeur to bring her up for an interview. He explained that because it was such a large house, two maids from a cleaning service came in four hours a day and would work under her supervision. She would prepare the meals. If they had a dinner party, their caterers would handle it. With two maids reporting to her, instead of having to clean dressing rooms after sloppy actors, Jane could spend most of her day cooking—a joy, not a task. She couldn't believe her good fortune.

By the time the first anniversary of working for the Powells had passed, Jane's heartfelt gratitude for the job had evolved.

She'd fallen passionately in love with Rob Powell.

She did not for a minute believe that she would ever have the slightest prospect of his looking at her as a man looked at a woman.

Providing for his comfort, glowing at his praise for the meals she served, hearing his footsteps as he came downstairs in the morning to get Betsy's wake-up coffee was enough. In the twenty years since Betsy's death, Jane had been able to live the fantasy that she was married to Rob.

Whenever he said, "I'm going out to dinner tonight, Jane," she would panic with fear and secretly look at the calendar he kept on his desk.

But women's names appeared only occasionally, and Jane had come to believe that, at his age, there would never be another Mrs. Powell.

One day last year he had been going over his will with his lawyer, who was also his close friend, and didn't put it away when they went outside to play on the golf course.

Jane had flipped to the end of the will and found what she was looking for—the bequest to her: three hundred thousand dollars for a condo in Silver Pines, the fifty-five-plus community where he knew Jane had formed a few friendships with residents she had met at her church. And an income of one thousand dollars a week for the remainder of her life.

Reading that made Jane's worship of Robert Powell even deeper.

But this program would start trouble. She knew it. Let sleeping dogs lie, she thought as she watched rubberneckers pass the house.

Jane shook her head and turned from the window and realized that the producer, Laurie Moran, was standing in the doorway.

"Oh," Jane said, startled out of her usual reserve.

Laurie sensed the housekeeper's resentment at her presence. "Oh, Ms. Novak, I'm sure you must be sick of us being here already, but I don't want to disturb Mr. Powell. I have just one question."

Jane managed to smooth her expression.

"Of course. What is it, Ms. Moran?"

"Mrs. Powell's bedroom is exquisite. Were the drapes and spread and carpet replaced after she died, or were they here the night of the murder?"

"No, Mrs. Powell had just had a decorator redo the room, then didn't like the effect. She said the colors were too bold."

The waste, Jane thought, not allowing herself to shake her head. The absolute waste of money.

"She'd ordered new draperies and a new headboard and a new carpet. After she died, Mr. Powell had them installed to honor her wishes. It's exactly as you see it now."

"It's beautiful," Laurie said sincerely. "Is it ever used?"

"It is *never* used," Jane said. "But it is always kept fresh. You'll never see the silver brush and comb on the dressing table not looking polished. Even the towels in her bathroom are replaced regularly. Mr. Powell wanted her room and bath to always look as if she were about to open the door and come in."

Laurie couldn't resist asking, "Does he spend much time in her room?"

Jane frowned. "I don't think so, but that's the kind of question I think you should ask Mr. Powell."

Now the disapproval was evident in the housekeeper's expression and tone of voice.

Oh boy, Laurie thought. I'd really hate to cross this one. "Thank you, Jane," she said soothingly. "We're all leaving now. We won't be back over the weekend. We'll see you Monday morning. And let me reassure you we will absolutely be finished on Wednesday after lunch."

It was nearly noon, which meant Robert Powell expected the crew from the production company to clear out. It was also a Friday, the day he worked from home. He had been in his office with the door closed since they'd arrived.

THREE DAYS, LAURIE THOUGHT LATER THAT DAY in her office as she went over her notes with Jerry and

Grace, who were with her every day of the shoot in Salem Ridge.

It was Grace who voiced what all three of them were thinking. "That place is gorgeous," she said. "In one way it makes me never want to come home to my five-story walk-up apartment that's not big enough to take three steps in without bumping into a wall." She paused, her expressive eyes even more mascaraed than usual, then finished, "On the other hand, it gives me the creeps. My grandmother used to say that a pigeon flying into the room was a sign of death coming to the house. Laurie, were you in Betsy Powell's bedroom today when a pigeon was flying around outside, trying to find a way to get in?"

"Oh, come on," Jerry said. "Grace, that's a stretch even for you."

Of course it's a stretch, Laurie told herself.

She was not about to admit to Grace and Jerry that the magnificent home where Betsy Powell had died also gave her the creeps.

12

At noon on Sunday Josh picked up the first arrival, Claire, at the Westchester Airport. Although she knew Josh, who had been hired shortly before Betsy's death, she gave him only a brief hello and did not engage in any conversation with him. As he drove her to the Westchester Hilton, she reflected on the plans for the next three days. On Monday they would meet for the first time over breakfast. They would be free for the rest of the day to reacquaint themselves with the house and the grounds. The individual interviews would take place on Tuesday. They had all agreed to sleep at the house Tuesday night in the same rooms they had been in twenty years earlier. Wednesday morning would be Robert Powell's interview, followed by their being photographed at the luncheon table. They would then be driven to their departing flights.

"While we are certainly aware of how painful this

will be for all of you, by your willingness to appear
on the program, you each are making a forceful statement to clear your names," was the conclusion of
Laurie's letter.

Clear our names! Claire Bonner thought bitterly
as she checked into the Westchester Hilton.

She was wearing a light-green summer pantsuit
she had bought at an expensive boutique in Chicago.
In the three months since the first letter had come
from Laurie Moran, she had let her hair grow and
had lightened it so that now it was a shining mane
around her shoulders. But today she had it tied in
a ponytail with a scarf over her head. She had also
practiced using makeup, but was wearing none today.
With makeup and hair combed as her mother had
worn it, she knew she bore a startling resemblance
to her. She did not want Josh to see that resemblance
and tell Powell until she met with him face to face.

"Your suite is ready, Ms. Bonner," the clerk said, and
waved to the bellman. Claire caught the long glance
he gave her and the hint of excitement in his voice.

Why not? It would be almost impossible to miss all
the newspaper articles about the upcoming program.
The gossip magazines were having a field day digging
up everything they could find about Betsy Bonner
Powell. USHERED TO A FATAL NEW LIFESTYLE was
a particularly grating one that had appeared on the
front page of the *Shocker*, a sensational weekly. The
article detailed the first meeting of Betsy Bonner and
Robert Powell. Betsy had taken her daughter, Claire,
to lunch at a restaurant in Rye for her thirteenth

birthday. Robert Powell, a widower, had been seated across the room with Claire's friend Nina and her mother. As Betsy and Claire were leaving, Nina had called to them. They walked over to Powell's table, where Nina introduced Betsy and Claire to the Wall Street hedge fund multimillionaire.

"The rest is, as they say, history," was the trite introduction to the final columns of that story. Robert Powell claimed it was love at first sight. He and Betsy Bonner were married three months later.

"Actress Muriel Craig put up a brave front, but insiders say she was furious and blamed her daughter, Nina, for making it a point to call out to Claire in the restaurant."

I know that's true, Claire thought as she followed the bellman to the elevator. Poor Nina.

The suite consisted of a large bedroom and living room, a full bath, and a powder room furnished in pastel shades. It was both attractive and restful.

Claire tipped the bellman, phoned room service, and unpacked her one suitcase. It contained the three outfits she had selected to bring with her, as well as her supply of new cosmetics.

In one of her e-mails, Laurie Moran had requested Claire's size and height, saying that she would have wardrobe changes available.

Wardrobe changes! Claire had thought when she read the e-mail. Why on earth would I need changes?

But then she had understood. Moran would provide gowns similar but not identical to the ones they had worn twenty years ago at the Gala.

They would reenact a few of the scenes in the films, like the one of the four of them clinking glasses or with arms around one another, posing for the cameras. And individually being questioned by the police.

I know I look good, Claire thought. Now I'm so like my dear mother.

A light tap at the door told her that room service had arrived with the chicken salad and iced tea she had ordered.

But as she nibbled at the salad and sipped the tea, Claire realized that she was not as brave as she had thought.

Something was telling her not to go forward with her plan.

Just nerves, she tried to reassure herself. Just nerves.

But it was more than that.

Like a drumbeat in her head, her inner voice was saying, *Don't do it. Don't do it. It is not worth the risk!*

13

It had been a long trip from Cleveland to Westchester Airport. A heavy rainstorm had caused their plane to sit on the tarmac for two hours, and even though they were flying on a small private jet, there was little space to move around. This made it very difficult for Rod's back. At one point, she suggested they just forget the whole thing.

"Alie, this is your chance to get the degree you always wanted. Between Powell and the production company, you'll net three hundred thousand dollars. It will pay for medical school and all the other expenses, but every cent counts. You know how desperately you have always wanted to be a doctor and then go into medical research," Rod had said in refusal.

Even if I can commute to school, I will have to be studying all the time. Where does that leave Rod? Or if I have to go away to school, does he leave his job at the pharmacy and come with me but then have nothing to do? she wondered. But if that happens, then the pharmacy loses both him and me, and we have to hire two new people. I don't know how that's going to work.

It was three o'clock by her wristwatch when they landed in Westchester. By then Rod's expression was sufficient proof of the pain he was in. After he hobbled on crutches from the cabin to his waiting wheelchair, Alison bent over him and whispered, "Thank you for making this trip."

He managed a smile as he looked up at her.

Mercifully the driver, a ruddy-faced man of about fifty with the build of an ex-boxer, was waiting for them in the terminal. He introduced himself to them. "I'm Josh Damiano, Mr. Powell's chauffeur. He wanted to be sure you had a comfortable ride from the airport to your hotel."

"How kind of Mr. Powell." Alison hoped that the contempt she felt did not show. Now that they were back in New York, a kaleidoscope of memories was flooding her mind. Neither one of them had been in New York in fifteen years. That was when the doctors had told Rod there would be no more operations.

By then their money was gone and Rod's family was taking out loans to support them, but Alison had managed to take the necessary courses at night for a year and get her license as a pharmacist. They had gratefully seized the opportunity to go to Cleveland and work in his cousin's pharmacy.

I loved New York, she thought, but I was happy to get away from it. I always thought that the minute people saw me, they wondered whether I'd killed

Betsy Bonner Powell. In Cleveland, for the most part, we have lived quietly.

"There are benches near the doors," Damiano said. "Let me get you settled comfortably and go for the car. I'll try not to be too long."

They watched as he collected the luggage from the pilots. He was back for them within five minutes. "The car's right outside," he said as he helped Rod with his wheelchair.

A shiny black Bentley was waiting at the curb.

When Damiano helped Rod out of the wheelchair and into the backseat, Alison felt her heart wrench.

He's in so much pain, she thought, but he never complains, and he never talks about the football career he would have had . . .

The big car began to move. "The traffic's light," Damiano told them. "We should be at the hotel in about twenty minutes."

They had chosen to stay at the Crowne Plaza in White Plains. The town was near enough to Salem Ridge, but far enough away from the hotels where the other three childhood friends who were on the program were staying. Laurie Moran made sure of that.

"You two okay?" Damiano asked them solicitously.

"I'm very comfortable," Alison assured him as Rod murmured his assent.

But then Rod leaned over and whispered, "Alie, I was thinking, when you're on camera, not a word about sleepwalking and possibly being in Betsy's room that night."

"Oh, Rod I never would," Alison said, horrified.

"And don't volunteer that you're hoping to go to med school unless they ask. It will remind everyone how disappointed you were when you didn't get the scholarship to medical school, and how furious you were that Robert Powell got the dean to throw it to Vivian Fields."

The mention of her heartbreak the day of her graduation from college was enough to make Alison's face contort with pain and rage. "Betsy Powell was trying to get into the Women's Club with the top-of-the-line socialites, and Vivian Fields's mother was the president of it. And of course Powell had leverage—he'd just donated a dormitory to the college! The Fieldses could have afforded to pay Vivian's tuition one hundred times over. Even the dean looked embarrassed when he called out her name. And then he muttered something about Vivian's academic brilliance. Right! She dropped out in her second year. I could have scratched Betsy's eyes out!"

"Which is why if they ask you what you'll do with the money, just say that we're planning to take a round-the-world ocean cruise," Rod counseled.

GLANCING INTO THE REARVIEW MIRROR, JOSH Damiano observed Rod whispering something to his wife and watched her shocked reaction and how upset she instantly became. He could not hear what they were saying, but he smiled inwardly.

It doesn't matter whether I can hear them, he thought. The recorder picks up everything that's said in this car.

14

Regina Callari's initial response upon learning that, between Fisher Blake Studios and Robert Powell, she would net three hundred thousand dollars for appearing in the program was one of relief and elation.

The crushing burden of living paycheck to paycheck, which translated to house sale to house sale in a terrible real estate market, had been lifted from her shoulders.

It almost gave her that warm, secure feeling she had felt in early childhood, until the day she found her father's body hanging in the garage.

Over the years she had had the same dream about her early life. In it, she woke up in her big bedroom, with the pretty white bed that had a spray of delicate pink flowers painted on the headboard, the night table, the dresser, the desk, and the bookcase. In the dream she could always vividly see the pink-and-white bedspread, the matching draperies, and the soft pink rug.

After her father's suicide, when her mother realized how little money they had, they had moved to a three-room apartment, where they shared a bedroom.

Her mother, who loved fashion, had gotten a job as a personal shopper at Bergdorf Goodman, where she had once been a valued customer. Somehow they'd gotten by, and Regina had proudly graduated from college on a financial-aid scholarship.

After Alison's wedding and all the gossip about Betsy's death, I moved to Florida to escape, Regina thought as she boarded the plane in St. Augustine. Some escape. Put it aside, she told herself. Don't keep dwelling or you'll drive yourself crazy.

A few hours earlier she had seen Zach off on his backpacking trip to Europe. He was meeting his group in Boston, and they were flying to Paris tonight.

Regina settled comfortably in the small private plane and helped herself to a predeparture glass of wine.

She smiled briefly at the memory of the visit she and Zach had just shared.

When he had arrived home from college two weeks earlier, she had put a CLOSED FOR VACATION sign up on the front door of the office and announced to Zach that they were going on a vacation together— a cruise through the Caribbean.

The closeness between them that she was so afraid was lost had been regained—even magnified—on that trip.

Zach purposely said little about his father and stepmother, but once she asked, he told her everything.

"Mom, I knew when Dad made money, lots of money, he should have given you more. I think he would have, except he was afraid of Sonya's reaction. She has a really bad temper."

Zach's father was writing the songs that made him rich when we were married, but the first one didn't sell until a year after we were divorced. I couldn't afford a lawyer to prove that he wrote it when he was married to me, Regina had thought bitterly.

"I think he regrets marrying Sonya," Zach had told her. "When they have an argument, the decibel level goes through the roof."

"I *love* it," Regina remembered telling Zach.

She warmed at the memory of Zach's compliments about her twenty-pound weight loss. "Mom, you look so cool," he'd said, more than once.

"I worked out at the gym a lot these past two months," she told him. "I realized that I'd gotten out of the habit of going there regularly."

On the cruise he asked her about her parents. "All you ever really told me was that Grandpa committed suicide because he had made some bad investments and was broke, and that Grandma was planning to live in Florida when she retired, but died in her sleep only a year after you moved here," he said.

"She never got over losing my father."

Zach looks so much like my father, Regina thought now as the plane took off. Tall, blond, and blue-eyed.

The last night they were at dinner on the cruise Zach asked her about the night Betsy died. He had overheard his father telling Sonya all about it and had googled it.

Regina had then told him about the note.

Was I wrong to tell him about it? she wondered now. I needed to talk to someone about it. I was always worried I had made a mistake by *not* showing it to my mother.

Don't dwell on it, Regina thought as she helped herself to a second glass of wine.

It was eight o'clock when she landed at Westchester. The driver who met her introduced himself as Mr. Powell's chauffeur, Josh Damiano. He told her that Mr. Powell wanted to ensure her comfort.

It was hard not to laugh out loud. When he opened the door of the Bentley for her, she could not resist commenting to him, "I guess Mr. Powell has outgrown the Mercedes?"

"Oh no," Damiano answered with a smile. "He has a Mercedes wagon."

"I'm so glad." Shut your mouth, Regina warned herself as she stepped into the car.

They were barely leaving the airport when her cell phone rang.

It was Zach. "We're about to board, Mom. Wanted to be sure you landed safely."

"Oh, Zach, how sweet of you. I miss you already."

Zach's tone changed. "Mom, the note. You told me you were tempted to shove it in Powell's face. Have you got it with you?"

"Yes. I have it, but don't worry. I won't be that

crazy. It's in my suitcase. I promise you, no one can find it."

"Mom, tear it up! If anyone found it, you could be in big trouble."

"Zach, if it makes you feel better, I promise I'll tear it up."

No I won't, she thought, but I can't let him get on that plane upset about me.

IN THE FRONT SEAT, JOSH DAMIANO HAD NOT expected to record Regina because she was traveling alone. When he heard her phone ring, he quickly turned on the recorder. Maybe I'll get lucky, he thought.

You couldn't be too careful when you worked for a man like Mr. Powell.

15

It had been a long day. Sitting in her office with Jerry and Grace, Laurie had gone over a myriad of details to ensure everything was in order for the first day of shooting.

She finally leaned back and said, "That's it, the die is cast, we can't do anything more now. The graduates are all here, and tomorrow we meet them. We start the day at nine A.M. Mr. Powell said that the housekeeper will have coffee and fruit and rolls prepared."

"It's amazing. They claim that not one of them has been in touch with the others all these years," Jerry observed, "but I bet they google each other once in a while. I would if I were one of them. My aunt always googles to see what her ex is up to."

"I would guess this meeting will be awkward for at least the first few minutes," Laurie said, a worried note in her voice. "But they were close friends for years, and they all went through hell being interrogated by the police."

"Nina Craig once told a reporter every one of them was accused of having been part of a plan to murder Betsy, and that the detective told her she'd better turn state's witness to get a lighter sentence," Jerry recalled. "That must have been pretty scary."

"I still don't get why any one of the graduates would have wanted to kill Betsy Powell," Grace said, shaking her head. "They're celebrating their graduation at a lavish party. They have their whole lives in front of them. They all look happy in the films of the party."

"Maybe one of them wasn't as happy as she looked," Laurie suggested.

"This is the way I look at it," Grace declared. "Betsy's daughter, Claire, certainly didn't seem to have any reason to kill her mother. They were always very close. Regina Callari's father lost his money in one of Powell's hedge funds, but even her mother admitted that Powell had repeatedly warned him that while he might make a lot of money, he should not invest more than he could afford to lose. Nina Craig's mother was dating Powell when he met Betsy, but unless you're really crazy you don't suffocate someone for a reason like that. And Alison Schaefer married her boyfriend four months after graduation. He was already a football star with a multimillion-dollar contract. What reason would she have had for putting a pillow over Betsy Powell's face?"

As she was speaking, Grace held up her fingers one by one to illustrate the point she was making.

"And that sour-looking housekeeper had been hired by Betsy," she continued. "My guess is it was as simple as a burglary gone wrong. The house is big. There are sliding glass doors all over the place. The alarm wasn't on. One door was unlocked. Anyone could have gotten in. I think it was someone who was after the emerald necklace and earrings. They were worth a fortune. Don't forget, one of the earrings was on the floor of her bedroom."

"Someone in the crowd may have been a party crasher," Laurie agreed. "Some of the guests asked to bring friends, and there are a couple of people in the films that no one could identify positively." She paused. "Well, maybe this program will bring that out. If so, Powell, the housekeeper, and the graduates will certainly be glad they participated."

"I think they're already glad," Jerry observed. "Three hundred thousand dollars net is a pretty nice number to put in your wallet. I wish I had it."

"If I did, I'd treat myself to a new apartment that's only a *four*-story walk-up," Grace said with a sigh.

"But if it turns out that one of them did it, she could always hire Alex Buckley to defend her," Jerry suggested. "With his fees, that three hundred thousand dollars would go up in smoke."

Alex Buckley was the renowned criminal lawyer who would be the host of the program and would conduct separate interviews with Powell, the housekeeper, and the graduates. Thirty-eight years old, he was a frequent guest on television programs discussing major crimes.

He had become famous by defending a mogul accused of murdering his business partner. Against tremendous odds Buckley had secured a not-guilty verdict, which the press had deplored as a miserable miscarriage of justice. Then, ten months later, the business partner's wife committed suicide, leaving a note saying that *she* had murdered her husband.

After watching countless videos of Alex Buckley, Laurie had decided he would be the ideal narrator of the Graduation Gala program.

Then she had to convince him.

She had called his office and made an appointment to see him.

A moment after she was ushered into his office he had taken an urgent phone call, and sitting across from his desk Laurie had had a chance to study him closely.

He had dark hair, blue-green eyes accentuated by black-rimmed glasses, a firm chin, and the tall, lanky build that she knew had made him a basketball star in college.

Observing him on television, she had decided that he was the kind of man people instinctively liked and trusted, and that was the quality she was looking for in a narrator who would also be on camera. That instinct was reinforced as she heard him reassuring the person he was speaking to that there was no reason to worry.

When he finished the phone call, his apologetic smile was warm and genuine. But his first question— "And what can I do for you, Ms. Moran?"—warned her not to waste his time.

Laurie had been prepared, succinct, and passionate.

She thought back to the moment when Alex Buckley leaned back in his chair and said, "I'd be very interested in taking part in the program, Ms. Moran."

"Laurie, I was sure you were going to get turned down flat that day," Jerry said.

"I knew that the money I could offer Buckley for being on the program wasn't enough to compensate him, but my hunch was he might be intrigued by the unsolved Graduation Gala case. Thank heaven it turns out that I was right."

"You were right on," Jerry agreed heartily. "He'll be great."

It was six o'clock. "Let's hope so," Laurie said as she pushed back her chair and got up. "We've labored in the vineyard long enough. Let's call it a day."

TWO HOURS LATER AS THEY SIPPED COFFEE, Laurie said to her father, "As I told Jerry and Grace today, the die is cast."

"What does that mean?" Timmy asked. Tonight he had not asked to be excused after he finished dessert.

"It means that I've done everything possible, and we start filming the people on the program tomorrow morning."

"Will it be a series?" Timmy asked.

"From your mouth to God's ear," Laurie said fervently, then smiled at her son. So like Greg, she thought, not just in looks, but in the expression he gets when he's thinking something through.

He always asked about any project she was working

on. This one she had described in the broadest terms as "a reunion of four friends who grew up together but haven't seen each other in twenty years."

Timmy's answer to that was, "*Why* didn't they see each other?"

"Because they lived in different states," Laurie answered honestly.

The last few months have been hard, she thought. It wasn't only the pressure of the enormous amount of preparation for the filming. Timmy had received his First Holy Communion on May 25, and she had not been able to keep the tears from slipping past her dark glasses. *Greg should be here. Greg should be here, but he'll never be here for all the important events in Timmy's life. Not his confirmation or graduations or when he gets married. Not any of them.* Those thoughts had sounded like a drumbeat in her head, repeating themselves over and over as she made a desperate effort to stop crying.

Laurie realized that Timmy was looking at her, a worried expression on his face.

"Mom, you look sad," he said anxiously.

"I didn't mean to." Laurie swallowed over the lump that was forming in her throat and smiled. "Why should I? I have you and Grandpa. Isn't that right, Dad?"

Leo Farley was familiar with the emotion he sensed his daughter was feeling. He often had moments of intense sadness when he thought of the years he and Eileen had been married. And then to lose Greg to some devil incarnate—

Leo stopped that thought. "And I have you two," he said heartily. "Remember, don't stay up too late, either one of you. We all have to get up early tomorrow."

In the morning Timmy was going away to camp for two weeks with some of his friends.

Leo and Laurie had wrestled with their abiding worry that Blue Eyes might somehow find out where Timmy was going, then realized that if they isolated him from activities with his friends, he would grow up nervous and fearful. In the five years since Greg's murder, they'd struggled to make Timmy feel normal—while keeping him safe.

Leo had gone upstate personally to look the camp over, and had spoken with the head counselor and been assured that the boys Timmy's age were under constant supervision, and that they had security guards who would spot a stranger in a heartbeat.

Leo told the counselor the words Timmy had been screaming: "Blue Eyes shot my daddy." Then he repeated the description the elderly witness had given the police. "He had a scarf over his face. He was wearing a cap. He was average height, broad but not fat. He was around the block in seconds, but I don't think he was young. But he could run really fast."

For some reason the image of the guy who had skated past them on the sidewalk in March ran through Leo's mind as he spoke the words "really fast." Maybe it's because he almost knocked over that pregnant lady who was ahead of us, he thought.

"A little more coffee, Dad?"

"No thanks." Leo had made himself stop telling Laurie that getting those people from the Graduation Gala under one roof again was too risky. It was going to happen, and there was no use wasting his breath.

He pushed his chair back from the table, collected the dessert dishes and coffee cups, and brought them into the kitchen. Laurie was already there, about to start loading the dishes into the dishwasher.

"I'll do those," he said. "You double-check Timmy's bag. I think I have everything in it."

"Then everything is in it. I never knew anyone so organized. Dad, what would I do without you?"

"You'd do very well, but I plan to be around for a while." Leo Farley kissed his daughter. As he said that, the words of the elderly woman who had witnessed Greg's death and heard the murderer shout to Timmy, *"Tell your mother that she's next, then it's your turn,"* rang in his head for the millionth time.

At that moment Leo Farley decided that he would quietly drive up to Salem Ridge for the days of the filming. I'm enough of a cop that I can do surveillance without being observed, he thought.

If anything goes wrong, I want to be there, he told himself.

16

Alex Buckley's alarm went off at 6 A.M., only seconds after his interior alarm made him stir in his sleep and open his eyes.

He lay quietly for a few minutes to collect his thoughts.

Today he would be in Salem Ridge for the first day of filming the Graduation Gala.

He pushed off the sheet and got up. Years ago, a client who was out on bail had come to his office. When he stood up to greet her, she had exclaimed, "My God, I never realized there's no end to you!"

Six foot four, Alex had understood the remark and laughed. The woman was only five feet tall, a fact that had not prevented her from fatally stabbing her husband during a domestic quarrel.

The woman's remark ran through his mind as he headed for the shower, but it quickly disappeared as he thought about the day ahead.

He knew why he had decided to accept the offer from Laurie Moran. He had read about the Graduation Gala when he was a sophomore at Fordham University and had followed the case with avid interest, trying to imagine which graduate had committed the crime. He had been sure it was *one* of them.

His apartment was on Beekman Place, by the East River, that was home to high-ranking UN delegates, as well as quietly wealthy businesspeople.

Two years ago he had happened to visit the apartment, and at the dinner table learned that the hosts were putting it on the market. He instantly decided to buy it. To him, its only downfall was the large, incessantly blinking red PEPSI-COLA sign on a building in Long Island City that marred the view of the East River.

But the apartment had six large rooms, as well as servant quarters. He knew he didn't need so much space, but on the other hand, he rationalized, the full dining room meant he could have dinner parties; he could turn the second bedroom into a den; and it would be handy to have a guestroom. His brother Andrew, a corporate lawyer, lived in Washington, D.C., and came up to Manhattan regularly on business.

"Now you won't need to go to a hotel," he had told Andrew.

"I'm willing to pay the going rate," his brother had joked, then added, "As it happens, I'm sick of hotels, so this will be great."

When he bought the apartment, Alex decided that

instead of a biweekly housekeeper it would be better to have one full-time employee who could keep the apartment clean, run errands, and prepare breakfast and dinner when he was home. Through the recommendation of the interior decorator who had furnished his new home with quiet good taste he had hired Ramon, who had been with one of her other clients but had chosen not to move to California with them. Ramon's former employers were an eccentric couple who kept erratic hours, and what they didn't wear they dropped on the floor.

Ramon happily settled in the studio-sized room and bath off the kitchen, which had been designed for a live-in helper. Sixty years old, born in the Philippines, he was long divorced, with a daughter in Syracuse.

Ramon had no interest in Alex's private affairs, and it would never have occurred to him to read anything Alex left on his desk.

Ramon was already in the kitchen when Alex, dressed in his usual business suit, white shirt, and tie, took his seat in the breakfast nook. The morning papers were next to his plate, but after greeting Ramon and skimming the headlines, he pushed them away.

"I'll read them when I get home tonight," he said as Ramon poured coffee into his cup. "Anything exciting in them?"

"You're on Page Six of the *Post*, sir. You escorted Miss Allen to the opening of a film."

"Yes, I did." Alex was still not used to the unwanted

publicity that accompanied the celebrity status he had achieved by his frequent television appearances.

"She is a very beautiful woman, sir."

"Yes, she is." That was something else. As an unmarried, prominent lawyer, he could not escort a woman to an event without being linked to her. Elizabeth Allen was a friend, and nothing more.

Alex made short work of the fruit, cereal, and toast Ramon set before him. He realized that he was anxious to get up to the home of Robert Powell and meet both him and the returning graduates.

They'd all be forty-one or forty-two by now, he thought, Claire Bonner, Alison Schaefer, Regina Callari, and Nina Craig. Since he had agreed to be the narrator of the program, he had done extensive research on each, and had read everything that had been in the media at the time of Betsy Powell's murder.

He had been asked to arrive at the Powell estate at nine o'clock. It was time to leave. "Will you be home for dinner tonight, Mr. Alex?" Ramon asked.

"Yes, I will."

"Do you plan to have a guest or guests?"

Alex smiled at the diminutive man who was looking so anxiously at him.

Ramon is a perfectionist, he thought, not for the first time. He did not like to waste food when it could be avoided, and he happily welcomed being informed when Alex was inviting friends for dinner. Alex shook his head. "No guests," he said.

A few minutes later Alex was in the garage of his

building. Ramon had phoned ahead, so his Lexus convertible was already parked near the exit ramp with the roof down.

Alex put on his sunglasses, started the car, and headed for the East River Drive. The questions he would ask the six people who were known to be in the house on the night that Betsy Bonner Powell had been suffocated in her sleep were already in his head.

17

Leo Farley gave his grandson a bear hug as he prepared to climb aboard the chartered bus from Saint David's School to Camp Mountainside in the Adirondacks. He was careful not to show any sign of his ever-present worry that Blue Eyes might ferret out Timmy's location.

He said, "You're going to have a great time with your pals."

"I know it, Grandpa," Timmy said, but then a frightened expression came over his face.

Glancing around, Leo could see that what was happening to Timmy was the same with all his friends. The moment of saying good-bye to parents or grandparents was causing a flicker of worry over *all* their faces.

"Okay, boys, all aboard," one of the counselors who were accompanying the campers called.

Leo hugged Timmy again. "You're going to have a

great time," he repeated as he planted a kiss on Timmy's cheek.

"And you'll take care of Mom, won't you, Grandpa?"

"Of course I will."

Laurie had had breakfast with Timmy at six o'clock before she was picked up by a Fisher Blake Studios car for the drive to Salem Ridge. Their goodbye had been tearful, but blessedly brief.

As Timmy turned and got on line for the coach, Leo could only think that the boy, who now had only an occasional nightmare about Blue Eyes, still retained his awareness of that terrible threat his father's killer had shouted.

And at eight years old, he was also worried that something would happen to his mother.

Not on my watch, Leo thought. After waving goodbye to the parting campers, he headed for the rented black Toyota he had parked a block away on Fifth Avenue. He had not wanted to risk Laurie catching sight of his familiar red Ford sedan. He turned on the engine and headed for Salem Ridge.

Forty-five minutes later he was on Old Farms Road as the limousine bringing the first of the graduates turned and entered the long driveway of the Powell estate.

18

Blue Eyes always followed his instincts. He had known that day five years ago that it was time to begin taking his revenge. He had followed Dr. Greg Moran and Timmy from their home in the Peter Cooper Village apartment complex on Twenty-first Street to the playground on Fifteenth Street that afternoon.

It had given him a rush of power seeing the two of them walking hand in hand to the place of execution. At the busy crossing on First Avenue, the doctor picked up Timmy and carried him. Blue Eyes laughed when he saw Timmy, his arms around his father's neck, a happy smile on his face.

For an instant he had wondered if he should kill both of them, but he decided against it. Then there would only be Laurie left. No, better to wait.

But now it was Laurie's turn. He knew so much about her; where she lived, where she worked, when she jogged along the East River. He had followed her sometimes onto the crosstown bus and sat next to her. *If you only knew, if you only knew!* It was hard not to say it out loud.

Blue Eyes adopted the "Bruno Hoffa" name after he was released from serving his five-year term. *It was really easy to change my name and get phony documents after my parole was completed,* he thought.

Most of the last six months, since he was released from prison for the second time, he'd been doing the kind of jobs where no one cares much about your background, like construction work and day labor.

He didn't mind hard work; in fact, he liked it. He remembered overhearing someone say that he looked and acted like a peasant.

Instead of being angry he had laughed at the remark. He knew he had the squat body and powerful arms people associate with someone who dug ditches, and that's the way he wanted it.

Even at sixty, he knew he could probably outrun any cop who tried to chase him.

In April he had read in the newspapers that Fisher Blake Studios was going to reenact the Graduation Gala murder and that Laurie Moran would be the producer.

That was when he knew he had to get a job somehow on the Powell estate to allow him to be there without arousing suspicion. He drove past Powell's property and observed the oversized truck with the PERFECT ESTATES sign on it. He looked up the company and applied for a job. As a kid he had worked for a landscaper and picked up everything he needed to know about the job. It didn't take a genius to mow a lawn or clip hedges and bushes or to plant flowers in the places pointed out by the boss.

He liked the job. And he knew Laurie Moran would be up there a lot when they started filming.

He had seen Laurie at the estate for the first time right after he got the job. He recognized her when she got out of her car and immediately grabbed a grass clipper to get close to the den, where Powell always met business guests.

He could have taken her out that day as she was walking back to her car, but he had decided to wait. He'd waited so long already, savoring her family's fear. Wouldn't it be better to wait until she was here with her film crew? he asked himself. Wouldn't the media coverage of her death be more dramatic when it was attached to the publicity around the Graduation Gala filming?

Powell had told Blue Eyes' boss, Artie Carter, that the filming would begin June 20th. Blue Eyes' concern had been that Powell would order all the planting and mowing and trimming be completed before the filming began.

That was why Blue Eyes spoke to Artie on the 19th, as they were wrapping up their final trimming and planting.

"Mr. Carter," he said, as he always did, even though the rest of the workers called him Artie. He had explained it was because he had been taught to respect the boss, and he sensed that Carter was pleased by it.

Actually, Artie Carter felt there was something not quite right about Bruno Hoffa. He never joined the other workers for a beer after work. He never entered debates about the baseball season when they were driving from one job to another. He never complained if the weather was lousy. In Artie's opinion, Bruno had one card missing from his deck, but so what? He was the best worker of all his crew.

As Artie finished inspecting the grounds, he was satisfied. Even the pain-in-the-neck client, Mr. Robert Powell, couldn't find anything to complain about.

It was then that Bruno Hoffa approached him.

"Mr. Carter, I have a suggestion to make," he said.

"What is it, Bruno?" It had been a long day, and Artie was ready to go home and have a nice cold beer. Or maybe a couple of nice cold beers.

Now Bruno, his narrow mouth extended into a forced smile, his lidded eyes fixed on Artie's neck, his tone unusually subservient even for him, hesitantly began his planned speech.

"Mr. Powell came out the other day when I was planting flowers around the pool house. He said that the flowers were beautiful, but he was really annoyed because he knew the film crew would crush the grass. He supposed it would be inevitable, but he wished he could do something about it."

"Mr. Powell is a perfectionist," Artie said. "And our biggest customer. From what I understand they'll be photographing outside all week. What are we supposed to do about that?" he asked irritably. "We've been told to stay off the property after today."

Blue Eyes began his carefully prepared pitch. "Mr. Carter, I was thinking. We couldn't have one of the trucks in the driveway, because Mr. Powell would have a fit. But maybe you could suggest I be stationed in the pool house. That way if the film crew tramples on the grass or makes holes with their heavy equipment, I could repair it the minute they leave the area. Also, the people who are in the film might decide to take a walk on the grounds, or maybe have lunch outside and leave litter behind them. I could take care of that, too. If he agrees, I'd have to be dropped off in the morning and picked up when they're finished shooting at the end of the day."

Artie Carter considered. Powell was such a perfectionist that this might appeal to him. And Artie knew that Bruno was so self-effacing that he wouldn't get in the way of anyone in the production company.

"I'll give Mr. Powell a call and suggest that you be around for the shooting. Knowing him, I bet he agrees."

Of course he will, Blue Eyes thought as he struggled to keep a triumphant smile off his face. Laurie, you won't have to grieve much longer for your husband, he told himself. That's my promise to you.

19

❖

Much to Nina Craig's dismay, there was a message for her mother waiting at the desk at the St. Regis when they checked in.

As she had feared, it was from Robert Powell, inviting Muriel to the 9 A.M. breakfast.

Muriel smiled with delight, then waved the note in Nina's face. "You thought he was toying with me," she snapped. "You don't, or won't, understand that Rob and I were deeply in love. The fact that his head was turned by Betsy Bonner doesn't mean he didn't care about me."

Nina realized that Muriel, having drunk a vodka and at least two glasses of wine on the plane, and after their argument in the car when she was screaming how much she hated Betsy, was out of control.

She could see the two desk clerks taking in the tirade. "Mother, *please . . . ,*" she began.

"Don't 'please' me. Read the reviews I got. You're nothing but an extra, a nobody. Didn't that woman stop me on the street and tell me how wonderful I was in the remake of *Random Harvest*?"

Muriel's voice was rising and her face was becoming flushed as she spat out the words. "As for you, you couldn't make it to first base as an actress. That's why you're an extra, a member of the crowd scenes."

Nina could see that the clerk had put the keys to the rooms in separate envelopes. She reached out her hand. "I'm Nina Craig," she said quietly. "I apologize for the scene my mother is making."

If Muriel had heard her, she did not indicate it. She was still finishing her sentence. ". . . and you're always trying to put me down."

The clerk was tactful enough not to offer any reply to Nina other than to murmur, "I'll have your bags sent up to your room."

"Thank you. I just have the large black one." Nina pointed to it, then turned and brushed past Muriel, who had finally stopped talking. Furious and embarrassed by the curious eyes of the onlookers who were in line at the desk, she walked rapidly to the elevator and managed to get in as the door was closing.

On the sixth floor she got out, and following the arrow to the odd-numbered rooms, hurried to get into 621 before Muriel arrived and tried to follow her into her room.

Once inside, Nina sat down in the nearest chair with her hands clenched and whispered, "I can't stand any more. I can't stand it any more."

Later she called for room service. It would have been typical of her mother, who was in the room next door, to phone her about dinner. But that didn't happen. Nina would not have agreed to meet with her, but was denied the satisfaction of saying the words that were crowding her throat. *Go ahead. Make a fool of yourself tomorrow. I tried to warn you. You're Muriel Craig, B-actress and a total failure as a mother and as a human being.*

HOPING TO HEAR MORE FROM THEM, JOSH HAD arranged the car service so that he was the one who picked them up in the morning and again taped their angry conversation.

That morning, Josh had arrived half an hour early for an eight o'clock pickup. But when he phoned Nina Craig, she had said, "We'll be right down."

Nina had thought that there was nothing else her mother could possibly do to upset her, but she quickly realized she was wrong. Muriel wanted to arrive at the breakfast early so she could have time with Robert Powell before the others arrived. At least this time they rode in silence.

When they arrived at the estate, the door was opened by Powell's longtime housekeeper, Jane. She eyed them up and down, greeted them by name, and said that Mr. Powell would be down at nine, and that the producer, Ms. Moran, was already in the dining room.

Nina watched as her mother hid her disappointment and became Muriel Craig, the actress. Her smile was gracious, her tone warm when she was introduced to Laurie Moran, and she thanked her for being invited to accompany Nina.

"Mr. Powell is your host, Ms. Craig," Laurie said quietly. "I can't take any credit for it. I understand that after the breakfast you'll be driven back to the St. Regis?"

Wonderful, Nina thought with satisfaction. As she extended her hand to Laurie, she realized how surprised she was that the producer of the program was so young. Mid-thirties, Nina thought enviously. Nina's forty-second birthday the previous week had made her keenly aware that her life was going nowhere, and this three-hundred-thousand-dollar windfall would only serve to buy her mother an apartment and get her out of her hair once and for all.

On the set of her last movie, Nina had been an extra in a ballroom scene, and the producer, Grant Richmond, had told her that she danced beautifully. "You put the others in the scene to shame," he had said.

Nina knew he was pushing sixty and recently widowed. Then, the other night, he had invited her to meet him for cocktails. He had taken the trouble to explain that he had promised to have dinner with the producer, but that "we'll make it another time." He sent her home in his car.

I wish my mother was right, that Robert Powell might still be interested in her, she thought. Then, as she accepted the housekeeper's offer of coffee, Nina appraised Muriel carefully. Her mother did look good. She was wearing a white suit—very expensive, and bought with Nina's American Express card—with white high-heeled shoes that showed off her long legs and excellent figure. At the pricey salon, she had accepted the beautician's tactful suggestion that perhaps her fiery red hair could be toned down a bit. Now it was an attractive rust shade and had been cut and shaped so that it was barely touching her shoulders. She had always been skillful at applying her own makeup. In other words, Nina thought, my beloved mother looks great.

How do I look? she wondered. Okay, but it could be better. I want space. I want to be able to go home to a neat, restful apartment that isn't choked with cigarette smoke and have a glass of wine on the deck looking over the pool by myself.

And be able to invite Grant Richmond in for a drink if he *does* invite me out for dinner, she thought.

With a cup of coffee in her hand, Muriel was telling Laurie Moran how vividly she remembered that terrible, tragic night twenty years ago when her dear, dear friend Betsy was viciously murdered. "My heart was broken," she was saying. "We were *such* good friends."

Disgusted, Nina walked to the windows overlooking the pool and, beyond it, the putting green.

The door of the pool house opened, and she could make out the figure of a man emerging onto the lawn.

Did Robert Powell have a guest staying there? she wondered, then realized something was dangling from the man's hand. As she watched, he began snipping at the bush nearest to the pool house.

Then the doorbell rang, and Nina turned from the window. One of the other suspects in the death of Betsy Bonner Powell had arrived.

20

George Curtis had become increasingly more nervous about why Robert Powell was drawing him into the Graduation Gala filming.

It was bad enough that he had been forced to agree to be on camera at some point, but why was he being invited to this breakfast, where, as Rob put it, "all the suspects will gather"? Then Rob quickly added, "Not that you're one of the suspects, George."

Now, as he parked his red Porsche in the driveway, George pulled out a handkerchief and patted his forehead dry, an unusual gesture for him. The convertible top was down and the air-conditioning was on. There was no reason to be sweating—except anxiety.

But George Curtis, billionaire, constant on the Forbes list, friend of presidents and prime ministers, at that moment acknowledged to himself that by the end of the week it was possible that he would be under arrest, in handcuffs. He dabbed at his forehead with his handkerchief again.

Taking a long minute to steady his nerves, he got out of the car. The June morning was, as one television weatherman was prone to saying, "A gift. A perfect day." And today he'd be right, George thought—blue skies, sun glowing warm, a soft breeze coming from nearby Long Island Sound. But he didn't care.

He started to cross the driveway to the front door, then waited as a limousine rounded the curve. The limo stopped to allow him to walk in front of it.

He did not ring the bell, but waited until the chauffeur opened the back door and the occupants stepped out. Even though it had been twenty years, he immediately recognized Alison Schaefer. She hasn't changed much, was George's immediate impression—tall, slender, the dark hair not quite so long on her shoulders as it used to be. He remembered that on the night of the Gala he had chatted with her for a few moments and had the impression that there was repressed anger in her when she said something about the lavish party. "The money could be put to better use," she said bitterly. Because it was such an unexpected statement coming from one of the honorees, George had never forgotten it.

Now Alison waited by the car until the other occupant got out with painfully slow movements. As George watched, Rod Kimball pulled himself to his feet and adjusted his crutches firmly under his arms.

Of course, George thought. Alison married the

rookie football player who was struck by a hit-and-run driver.

He rang the bell as the couple negotiated the one step to the wide entrance. With polite constraint, Alison and George greeted each other, and Alison introduced Rod.

Then Jane was opening the door for them. She greeted the three with what for her was warmth and said, unnecessarily, "Mr. Powell is expecting you."

AFTER ALEX BUCKLEY PARKED IN FRONT OF THE Powell mansion, he took a moment to study the massive stone house before he left his car.

What had Betsy Bonner thought when she saw this house? he wondered. She had been renting a modest condo in Salem Ridge in the hope of meeting someone with money.

She sure struck it rich for a lady born in the Bronx and making a living as an usher in a theatre, Alex thought as he got out of the car and walked to the front door.

He was admitted by Jane, and introduced to the group already in the dining room. He was relieved to see Laurie Moran had arrived before him.

"Well, here we go," she said when he walked over to her.

"Just what I was thinking," he replied, his tone equally low.

REGINA KNEW IT WAS DANGEROUS TO CARRY HER father's suicide note with her to the breakfast. If anyone opened her purse and found it, she would become the most logical suspect to have murdered Betsy Powell. They might as well stop filming the show, she thought.

On the other hand, she had an almost paranoid fear that if she left the letter in the safe at the hotel, someone would steal it. It would be just like Robert Powell to pull off something like that, she thought. I should know! At least I can keep my pocketbook with me.

Then she had folded the note so that it fit inside the small billfold that held her credit and insurance cards.

As her limo turned into the familiar driveway, she saw the front door being opened and three people going into the house. One of the men was on crutches.

That has to be Alison's husband, she thought. By the time she'd heard about the accident she'd been in Florida.

We were such dopes when we agreed to be her bridesmaids! she thought now. The press had had a field day taking pictures of Claire and Nina and me walking down the aisle in front of Alison. One of the captions read, "The bride and her fellow suspects."

Talk about a low blow!

Regina was so deep in her thoughts that for a moment she did not realize the car had stopped and the driver was holding the door open for her.

Taking a deep breath, she got out of the car and climbed the steps to the door.

How many times have I been in this house? she asked herself as she pressed the bell. She'd been close to Claire in high school.

But why did I keep coming after Daddy killed himself? Was it morbid curiosity to look at Betsy throwing her charm around? Or was it that I always planned to get back at both of them someday?

In the few moments she waited until the door was opened, she nervously reassured herself about her appearance.

She had lost the twenty pounds she vowed to drop when she received that letter asking her to be in the series. She had bought some new clothes for this trip, and she knew that the black-and-white jacket and white slacks flattered her reclaimed figure and complemented her midnight-black hair.

Zach kept telling me how good I look, she thought as the door opened and Jane, a perfunctory welcome on her lips, stepped back to admit her into the house.

Regina's unwelcome thought as she entered the mansion was to remember her promise to Zach to burn the letter before it provided a reason to suspect she had killed Betsy Bonner Powell.

CLAIRE HAD THOUGHT SHE WOULD BE NERVOUS and fearful at the meeting with her stepfather, Robert Powell. It had been years since they'd seen each other. Instead she woke from a troubled sleep alert with icy calm. Her room service order arrived promptly at seven, and she ate her continental breakfast sitting in the chair in front of the television, watching the news.

But instead of seeing the latest report on a series of muggings in Manhattan, she flashed back to the television coverage of her mother's body being carried out of the house.

We were all together, huddled in the den, she thought. We had robes on.

And then the police started to question us . . .

She turned off the television set and carried her second cup of coffee into the bathroom. There she drew a bath, and when the tub was nearly full, dropped the bath salts she had carried with her into it.

Dear Betsy's favorite, she thought. I want to smell just like her when I get there.

She was in no hurry. I want to be sure they're all there when I arrive. She smiled at the thought. Betsy was always late. It drove Rob crazy. He was a stickler for punctuality, no matter what the occasion.

I should know!

The outfit Claire had chosen was a sky-blue Escada cashmere and silk jacket and narrow gray slacks.

Betsy loved this color, she thought as she slipped on the jacket. She thought it brought out the color of her eyes. Well, let it bring out the color of mine.

The one piece of jewelry that she had taken when she left Robert Powell's house for the last time was the simple strand of pearls that had originally belonged to the grandmother whom she only vaguely remembered. But I *do* remember loving her, she thought. Even though I was only three when she died, I remember sitting on her lap while she read books to me.

At eight thirty the driver called to announce that he was downstairs.

"I'll be another half hour," she told him. She had calculated that that would bring her to the house about 9:20. Again she reassured herself that all the others would be gathered there.

Then Betsy Bonner Powell's daughter will make her entrance.

21

Laurie had known that this breakfast would be charged with tension, but had underestimated how electric the atmosphere in the room would become.

It hadn't taken a minute to know that Muriel Craig was a perpetual liar when she rattled on about how dear a friend Betsy Powell had been to her.

Everyone knew that at one time Muriel had been linked to Robert Powell, and that she had issued a statement after his sudden marriage to Betsy claiming that he was only one of three men she was dating.

What is she thinking when she looks around this house and knows it might have been hers? Laurie wondered. The dining room had a portrait of an aristocratic man with a disdainful expression, whom Jane had explained was Mr. Powell's ancestor, a signer of the Declaration of Independence, of course.

I'll check that one out, Laurie thought. She'd always heard Powell was self-made. That said, the dining room was beautiful, with its red walls and Persian carpet and splendid view of the back gardens. She watched as the film equipment was unloaded for the outdoor scene that would be one of the first shots of the program. They had already filmed the mansion from the front. Now Alex Buckley would begin his narrative as those clips were unrolling.

Jane had laid the juice, coffee, rolls, sweet buns, and fruit on the top of the antique sideboard.

The handsome table had been set for ten. The sterling flatware had the mellow glow of antique pieces, as did all the serving platters.

Powell is certainly making sure that this little breakfast get-together is a not-too-subtle reminder of who and what he is, Laurie thought as in quick succession George Curtis, Alison Schaefer and her husband, Rod, and Alex Buckley arrived. They were followed soon after by Regina Callari.

She watched with keen interest as .the three friends, who had not seen one another in twenty years, clasped hands and then exchanged spontaneous hugs.

"My God, it's been so long . . . You haven't changed a bit . . . I've missed you guys . . ." were the seemingly genuine expressions from the three graduates, while Muriel Craig, George Curtis, Rod Kimball, and Alex Buckley held themselves back from the reunion.

Promptly at nine o'clock Robert Powell entered the dining room. "Jane has told me that Claire is not here yet," he said. "In that way she is *exactly* like my dear Betsy."

Watching him closely, Laurie was sure that beneath the façade of being amused by Claire's absence, he was furious. He must have wanted to make an entrance with all four of the graduates here, she thought.

She watched as, one by one, Powell embraced each guest with an effusive welcome. He greeted George Curtis with a "Thanks so much for coming, George. We'd both be happier on the golf course." He turned to Rod with a warm "We never did meet, did we?" Finally he approached Muriel Craig.

"I saved you for last," he said tenderly as he put his arms around her and kissed her. "You're as gorgeous as ever. Have you been in a time capsule these twenty years?"

A radiant Muriel returned his embrace, then, as Laurie watched closely, shot a look at her daughter, who shook her head and turned away.

"I see you all have coffee," Rob said. "But you've got to at least sample the muffins Jane has baked for you. I can promise they're delicious. Then please sit down wherever you want, except that Muriel will sit next to me."

My God, he's laying it on, Laurie thought. The next thing, he'll be proposing to her on bended knee. She was surprised he was being so obvious. But of course, she *was* his old flame.

They all sat at the table, Alex Buckley choosing a seat between Nina Craig and Alison. Rod Kimball hobbled over to the chair on Laurie's left. "We're very grateful to you, Ms. Moran, for creating this opportunity for the girls—I guess I should say women—to try to clear themselves from the lingering suspicion that one of them was a murderer," Powell said.

Laurie did not say that there were two other people in the house that night: Robert Powell, Betsy's husband, who had been rushed to the hospital in a total collapse with third degree burns on his hands; and Jane Novak, Betsy's longtime friend and housekeeper.

Jane had arrived in the room seconds after Powell had become hysterical.

It would have seemed to me that he wouldn't want to keep her, but he did, Laurie thought. Since we've been around, it's obvious that her main purpose in life is to anticipate his every wish.

"I can only imagine what it would be like to never know when some journalist will rehash the story," Laurie said now.

"You don't need a journalist," Rod said grimly. "Everyone has a theory. There are wild rumors all over the Internet."

Laurie realized she had liked Alison's husband the minute she met him. His handsome face bore lines of the suffering he had endured after the terrible accident that had left him disabled and ruined his career, but she saw no trace of self-pity in his demeanor. It was obvious he was devoted to his wife. He had stood protectively at her side with his arm around her when she was greeted by Robert Powell. But why was that necessary? Laurie wondered.

"Well, let's hope that the program will give people an understanding that these young women were incidental to the tragedy. I know my two assistants have read everything there is to read about the circumstances, and both are convinced that an intruder, who may have crashed the Gala in evening clothes, slipped in through the unlocked door and was after Betsy's emeralds."

The sound of the doorbell hushed all conversation. Everyone turned to look at the entrance to the dining room.

Robert Powell pushed back his chair and stood up. They heard the sound of footsteps coming down the hall, and then she was there, Claire Bonner, stunning with her blond hair touching her shoulders, her blue eyes accentuated by carefully applied makeup, her slender figure elegant in a couture suit, a warm smile on her face as she looked from one face to the next at the table.

My God, she's the image of her mother, Laurie thought, then heard a strangled moan and the heavy thud of something falling on the floor.

Nina Craig had fainted.

22

❖

Leo Farley drove past Robert Powell's house at a normal speed. In no way did he want to attract attention, although if he were stopped for any reason, he had his NYPD retirement ID in his wallet.

That thought made him smile. *"Dad, every cop in the tristate area recognizes you; for years you were the one who talked to the media when there was a major crime."*

It was true, Leo acknowledged to himself. His boss, the then police commissioner, had preferred to be away from the glare of the media. "You do the talking, Leo," he always said. "You're good at it."

On his last drive-by he had noticed that the driveway next to Powell's had a chain across it to keep unwanted vehicles out. The shades of the mansion did not fully cover the windows, but were drawn very low. There were no cars in the driveway, and in general the entire property had an air of stillness about it that suggested the occupants of the house were away.

The name of the owner, J. J. Adams, was on the mailbox. Leo had googled and then looked him up on Facebook. It was a lucky hunch. A picture of Jonathan Adams and his wife was there, and their message to their friends was that they were in their villa in Nice and having a wonderful time. It was amazing what kind of information people volunteered, Leo thought. If he'd been a criminal, he could have used it to break into this house or worse.

Leo parked his car ten blocks away, near the railroad station, and then began to jog back to Old Farms Road. He had taken up jogging after he dropped Timmy off at school, and it was easy enough for him to get back to the place he had chosen as his observation post.

He was stopped at the corner by a squad car pulling up beside him. A veteran cop was next to the driver. "Inspector Farley, what are you doing here? I didn't know you set foot outside your territory."

It was a genial sergeant, whom Leo recognized as being a member of the bagpipe band that played on special occasions in Manhattan, such as the St. Patrick's Day Parade.

Leo did not believe in happenstance. His immediate question after greeting the sergeant was whether Ed Penn was still the chief of police in Salem Ridge.

"You bet he is," the sergeant confirmed. "He's retiring next year."

Leo considered. He had not planned to talk to the

local police, but suddenly it seemed like a good idea. "I'd like to see him," he said.

"Well, hop in. We'll take you to the station house."

Five minutes later, Leo was explaining to Chief Edward Penn why he was jogging on the streets of Salem Ridge.

"You know, of course, that my son-in-law, Greg Moran, was gunned down, and that the killer told my grandson his mother and he were next."

"I remember, Leo," Penn told him quietly.

"Did you know my daughter is the producer of the Graduation Gala program?"

"I did. She's an impressive woman, Leo. You must be proud."

"Call it a hunch, but I have a feeling that this program could be trouble."

"So do I," Penn said crisply. "Don't forget, I was around twenty years ago when we got the call from the housekeeper, screaming that Betsy Powell was dead. We thought it was a heart attack and called for an ambulance. Then we got there and the room was full—not just Robert Powell, but the four graduates and the housekeeper. It was a mess. And of course that meant that the crime scene was contaminated."

"What was Powell's reaction at that point?" Leo asked.

"White as a sheet, heart fibrillations, beyond shock. He always brought her coffee in the morning, so he was the one who found her, but I guess you read that in the papers."

"Yes, I did," Leo agreed, taking in the familiar

sights and sounds of the station house. First the squad cars parked outside as he got out of his ride, then the sergeant's desk, and then the hallway that he knew led to the holding cell and jail.

Leo missed being on the force in New York City. He had joined New York's Finest as soon as he graduated from college. It was the only career he ever considered, and he had loved every minute of it.

He also knew that had he not retired, when a new police commissioner was appointed last year, he would probably have gotten the job. But none of that was important compared to preventing Blue Eyes from carrying out his threat.

Ed Penn was saying, "We gave those four girls a pretty tough grilling, but not one of them broke. I always thought that one of them did it, but it is possible that an intruder got in. That was a big party, and someone in formal clothes could have mixed with the crowd. According to the housekeeper, she had locked all the doors before she went to bed, but someone opened the one from the den onto the patio and left it open. Turns out two of the girls, Regina and Nina, had gone out there a couple of times to smoke a cigarette."

It was everything that Leo had read. "You really think it was one of the girls who killed her?"

"They were too calm. Wouldn't you think they'd all be more upset? Even Betsy's daughter was mighty composed. I don't think I saw a tear shed by any one of them either in that bedroom or the whole next week."

"Would any one of them have had a motive?"

"Well, Betsy and her daughter, Claire, were so close that Claire drove back and forth to Vassar rather than boarding. Regina's dad went bust and hanged himself after investing in Powell's hedge fund. Regina was fifteen, and she found him hanging. But even her mother agreed that Powell had warned him strongly to invest only what he could afford to lose. Nina's mother, the actress Muriel Craig, had been dating Powell, but when she was asked about it, she said they were just friends and both were seeing other people when he met Betsy. That leaves only Alison Schaefer. She was going around with Rod Kimball, the football player, and married him four months later. No motive there. As for Robert Powell, by all accounts he was broken up by her death and he's never been linked to another woman."

"If it wasn't an intruder, that leaves the housekeeper," Leo suggested.

"No motive there, either. Betsy knew her from her ushering days. Knew what a good worker she was and that she was a good cook. Betsy wasn't comfortable with the previous housekeeper Powell had. She had been hired by Powell's ex-wife, so there was no love lost there. Jane went from cleaning dressing rooms in the theatre to living in a three-room apartment in a mansion and commanding a pretty big salary. Betsy was always saying how much she valued her."

"So that leaves an intruder," Leo said.

Chief Penn's expression became somber. "It doesn't mean that having all of those six people together might not bring something to light. If it was one of them, that person is going to make sure she doesn't raise any suspicion now, or that one of the others might know something that didn't come out before. I read in the papers that Alex Buckley, the big-shot defense lawyer, is going to question all of them on camera. The idea is for each of them to convince a national audience that she isn't guilty."

Leo sensed that it was time for him to reveal why he was jogging in Salem Ridge some twenty miles from his home. "I've always thought that getting those people together to, in essence, *relive* that murder was a bad idea. But you know how we cops have hunches."

"Sure I do. We'd be out of luck if we didn't have them."

"I have a hunch—make that a premonition—that my son-in-law's killer, 'Blue Eyes,' as my grandson described him, might think that this is the perfect time for him to try to kill my daughter."

Leo ignored the startled expression on the other man's face. "It's been five years. Laurie has had a lot of publicity about this program. Her picture has been in the media. On Twitter people have been giving their opinions of who might be guilty of Betsy Powell's murder. Wouldn't it make sense for the psycho-path who killed Greg and threatened Laurie and Timmy to make his move now? Can you see the headlines if he succeeded?"

"I can. But how do you plan to prevent it, Leo?"

"Have an observation post on the grounds of the

house next door. I checked, and the residents are away. I'll watch for someone trying to sneak in over the back fence of the property. From what I've seen, that would be the only way an intruder would get in."

"What if he tried to mingle with the television crew? Is that possible?"

"Laurie runs a tight ship. All the crew is on the lookout for the paparazzi. Any one of them would recognize a stranger in a minute."

"So what happens if you see someone climbing over the fence?"

"I'm there before he gets over it." Leo shrugged. "It's the best I can do. No one is going to get inside the house while they're filming there. Crew members will be guarding to make sure someone doesn't come in and spoil a scene. They wrap up at about six o'clock, and I'll take off. But I can't let Laurie know I'm around her. She'd be furious. This program will either enhance her career or, if it doesn't work, cost her her job." Leo was quiet, then said seriously, "So, Ed, now you know why I'm jogging through your town."

He saw a pensive look cross Penn's face.

"Leo, we're going to work with you. It won't seem unusual for a squad car to drive by the Powell estate every fifteen minutes or so on both the front and back roads. His property goes to the next street. If we see a car parked anywhere around the Powell place, we'll run the license plate. If we see anyone walking, if we don't know him, we'll check who he is."

Leo's heart surged with gratitude, and he stood up.

"And of course this may all be unnecessary. My son-in-law's murderer may be on another continent right now."

"And he may not be," Chief Edward Penn said. Then he rose from his chair, reached across his desk, and gripped Leo's hand.

23

Alex Buckley rushed to Nina and knelt over her, checking her heartbeat, making sure she was breathing.

After their initial shocked silence, the others pushed back their chairs. Muriel, genuinely pale, clutched Robert Powell's arm, then leaned over her daughter.

Nina's eyes fluttered.

"She's all right," Alex said. "But give her air."

"Betsy," Nina moaned. "Betsy."

Laurie's eyes turned to look at Claire, who had not moved from the doorway. It seemed to her that there was something of a triumphant expression on her face. Laurie had seen enough pictures of Betsy to guess that Claire had deliberately done everything possible to enhance her startling resemblance to her mother.

Alex picked Nina up, carried her into the den, and laid her on the couch. The others followed him as

Jane came running in with a cold towel, which, with expert fingers, she folded on Nina's forehead.

"Someone call a doctor!" Muriel screamed. "Nina, Nina, talk to me."

"Betsy," Nina murmured. "She came back." Then, as Nina looked around, Muriel swooped down and clasped her face with both hands. "Nina, baby, it's all right."

With a sudden, violent motion, Nina pushed her mother away. "Take your hands off me," she snapped, in a voice that was trembling with emotion. "Take your miserable hands off me!" And then she began to sob, "Betsy came back from the dead. She came back from the dead."

24

Blue Eyes watched with avid interest as Laurie Moran, clearly in charge now, directed the sequence of the filming.

She's very efficient, he decided, watching her check the cameras to see if the angle was what she wanted.

At one point she beckoned to him, and Bruno went scurrying over.

She smiled briefly and asked him to remove the extra plants he had put in early this morning.

"They're lovely," she said, "but they weren't here when we photographed last week."

Bruno apologized profusely, even while he felt the thrill of being so near his prey. She's so pretty, he thought. It would be a shame to spoil that beautiful face. He wouldn't do it.

But, as he was standing so close to her, a new and wonderful plan began to form in his mind.

Five months earlier he had hacked into Leo Farley's computer and phone, and since then he had known everything there was to know about his, Laurie's, and Timmy's activities. The computer courses he'd taken online had really paid off, he thought now.

He knew that Timmy was now in Camp Mountainside in the Adirondacks. And that it was only a four-hour drive from here.

Timmy's entire schedule of activities at the camp was on Farley's computer. And what was most interesting was that the hour between 7 and 8 P.M. was free time, when the campers were allowed to make or receive one phone call.

That meant that after 8 P.M., Laurie would not expect to speak to Timmy for another twenty-three hours.

How could he get the director of the camp to let him take Timmy away without arousing suspicion?

Blue Eyes pondered that question as he kept himself in the background, always ready to repair the slightest hint of damage to the lawn or shrubbery.

He even chatted a bit with the man and woman who were always close to Laurie.

Jerry and Grace. Young, both of them. The world ahead of them. He hoped for their sakes that they weren't too near Laurie when her time to die arrived.

Which it would. Oh, yes.

It was with regret that Blue Eyes watched the equipment be put away for the day. From the talk around him, he knew that they'd be back at eight o'clock tomorrow, and at that time they'd start filming the graduates.

Always anxious to stay under the radar, as instructed, he phoned the office of Perfect Estates and gave the secretary fifteen minutes' notice to pick him up.

When the van arrived, Blue Eyes was not pleased to see that Dave Cappo was behind the wheel. Dave was too nosy. "So, Bruno, where'd ya come from? Wuz ya always in landscaping? The wife and I would like to have you over for dinner any night at all. Up to ya." Big wink from Dave. "You and I know she'll squeeze your brains to hear everything about those four grads. Which one do you think did it?"

"Why don't we make it a day or so after they wrap up here?" Blue Eyes suggested.

By then, he thought, with any luck, I'll be gone, and you and your wife will have *plenty* to chew on.

25

"So other than that, how did the day go?" Leo asked. He and Laurie were having a late dinner together at Neary's, their longtime favorite restaurant on East Fifty-seventh Street. It was half past eight, and Laurie was visibly tired. She had just described the breakfast and Nina Craig's fainting spell to him, then Nina's reactions to her mother.

"It actually went all right," Laurie said wearily.

"Just all right?" Leo tried to sound casual as he reached for his glass and took another sip of wine.

"No, I should say it went well," Laurie said slowly. "We open with a view of the house as though we're coming down the driveway. Alex Buckley was definitely the right choice for narrator. Then we show some tape of the Graduation Gala from twenty years back with the four graduates, none of them looking particularly happy."

"How about Betsy Powell? Do you have much film of her interacting with the graduates?"

"Not that much," Laurie admitted. "Most of the frames with her show her with her husband or talking to other adults—not that the graduates were kids," she added hastily. "They were all twenty-one or twenty-two. But they were hardly ever with Betsy. We ran through the tapes with them today. I think they were all uncomfortable. Tomorrow we film them watching the excerpt we'll use on camera, then Alex starts talking with them about the Gala."

She sighed. "It sure has been a long day, and I'm starved. What about you?"

"I'm ready to eat," Leo admitted.

"What did you do all day now that your buddy is in camp, Dad?"

Leo was prepared for the question. "Nothing much," he said, biting his tongue over the lie. "The gym, picked up a couple of sport shirts at Bloomingdale's, nothing fancy." He hadn't meant to say it but involuntarily he added, "I miss Timmy, and it's only his first day away."

"Me, too," Laurie said fervently, "but I'm glad I let him go. He was looking forward to it so much. And as much as we miss him, he sounded great on the phone an hour ago."

"I don't know why they limit those kids to one phone call a day," Leo grumbled. "Haven't they heard about grandparents?"

Laurie realized that her father suddenly looked drawn and gray.

"Are you all right?" she asked anxiously.

"I'm fine."

"Dad, I should have thought to get home in time to share Timmy's call with you. I promise I will tomorrow."

They both sat thoughtfully, each with their own feelings about Timmy being so far away and without Leo's careful supervision.

Laurie glanced around the room. As usual, virtually every table was filled. The conversations were lively, and everyone looked as if they were having a good time. Are they all as free from stress as they seem to be? she wondered.

Of course they're not, she told herself. Scratch the surface and everyone has some sort of problem.

Then, determined not to voice her fear about Timmy, Laurie said, "I'm having liver and bacon tonight. Timmy doesn't like it, and I love it."

"I'll join you," Leo decided and waved away the menu when a smiling Mary, one of Neary's longtime waitresses, approached them.

"We both know what we want, Mary," he said.

Peace of mind, was Laurie's immediate thought. And that's not in the cards for us now, or maybe ever.

26

They were finally all gone. By the end of the day Jane could tell that Mr. Powell was sick of his "guests."

The minute the last car drove away he walked into the den, and Jane followed to ask if he wanted a cocktail.

"Jane, you read my mind," he said. "A scotch. And make it a strong one."

For dinner she had planned his favorite meal of salmon, asparagus, a green salad, and sherbet with fresh pineapple.

When he was home he liked to eat at eight o'clock in the small dining room. But tonight he did not finish his dinner, nor did he pay his usual compliment about how good it was. Instead he said, "I'm not very hungry, skip dessert." Then he got up and retreated back into the den.

Jane had the table cleared and the kitchen in its usual shining order in just a few minutes.

Then she went upstairs, turned down his bed, adjusted the air conditioner to sixty-five degrees, and placed a carafe of water and a glass on the night table.

Finally she laid out his pajamas, robe, and slippers, her hands moving tenderly over the clothing as she hung it in his bathroom.

Some nights when Mr. Powell was home he sat in the den for a couple of hours, watching television or reading. He enjoyed classic movies, and the next morning would comment to her about them. "Watched two of the Alfred Hitchcocks, Jane. No one could do suspense the way he did."

If he had had a hard day at the office, he would go directly upstairs after dinner, get changed, and read or watch television in the sitting room of his suite.

Other nights he invited six or eight people for cocktails and dinner.

It was a predictable pattern, making Jane's job quite easy.

The evenings that worried her were those when he went out and she saw in his appointment book that he was taking a woman to the club.

But that didn't happen very often, and he seldom saw the same woman more than two or three times.

All this was going through Jane's mind as she completed the nightly ritual.

Jane's final task of the day, when Mr. Powell was home alone, was to look in on him and see if there was anything else he needed before she retired to her apartment.

Tonight he was sitting in the big chair in his den,

his feet on the hassock, his elbows on the arms of the chair, his hands folded. The television was not on, and there was no sign of a book or magazine next to him.

"Are you all right, Mr. Powell?" she asked him anxiously.

"Just thinking, Jane," he said as he turned to face her. "I assume all the bedrooms are fresh?"

Jane tried not to bristle with annoyance at the suggestion that any room in the house wasn't in perfect order. "Of course they are, sir," she said.

"Well, just recheck them. As you know, I have asked all of the participants to stay overnight tomorrow night. We will have a celebratory brunch before we send them on their way."

He raised his eyebrows and smiled a secretive smile that he did not share with Jane.

"That should be very interesting, don't you think, Jane?"

27

Josh Damiano lived across town, just fifteen minutes from the Powell estate, but in an entirely different world.

Salem Ridge was a village on Long Island Sound adjacent to the wealthy town of Rye.

It had been settled in the late 1960s by people of medium income, moving into the Cape Cod and split-level houses developers had built.

But the unique location, only twenty-two miles from Manhattan and on Long Island Sound, attracted the interest of Realtors. Property values began to soar. The modest homes were bought and torn down, replaced by replicas of the kind of mansion Robert Powell had built.

A few owners held out. One of them was Margaret Gibney, who liked her house and didn't want to move. After her husband's death, when she was sixty, Margaret renovated the upstairs floor of her Cape Cod into an apartment.

Josh Damiano was her first and only tenant. Now eighty, Margaret thanked heaven every day for the quiet, pleasant man who took out the garbage unasked and even used the snowblower for her if he was home.

For his part, Josh, after a young marriage to his high school sweetheart that had lasted fourteen unpleasant years, was delighted with his living arrangement and his life.

He respected and admired Robert Powell. He loved his job of driving for him. Even more, he loved taping the conversations of executives when Mr. Powell sent him in the Bentley to pick up one or more of them for meetings or luncheons. Even if alone, a passenger's cell phone conversation was often helpful to Powell. When there was a particularly interesting conversation, like talking about insider trading, Josh would play it back for that executive and offer to sell it to him. He didn't do it much, but it proved to be very lucrative.

Over time, instead of listening to the tapes, Mr. Powell would merely ask Josh if there was anything interesting on the tapes. When Josh said "no," as he did with the graduates, Mr. Powell trusted him. "They all just said 'hello' and 'thank you,' sir," was what Josh had told him about his trips to pick up the graduates at the airport. A disappointed Robert Powell had just shaken his head.

At moments like that Josh remembered how he had almost lost his job. He had been working for Mr. Powell for only a few months when Betsy Powell died. His impression of her had been instantly unfavorable. Who does she think she is, the Queen of England? he would think as she waited imperiously for him to extend his hand and help her into the car.

A week before she died, he heard her say to Mr. Powell that she thought Josh was too familiar and lacked the dignity required of a servant. "Haven't you noticed how he slouches when he opens the door for us? He should know enough to stand up straight."

That rattled Josh, who had settled into his new job and liked it. It had been all he could do to act shocked and saddened by Betsy's demise. In fact he had breathed a sigh of relief that she was no longer around to fill Mr. Powell's ears about his supposed lack of dignity.

The day of the breakfast, Mr. Powell had had him pick up Claire Bonner. *Maybe I'll be lucky and she'll make a phone call.*

That hadn't worked. When he picked Claire up at the hotel, she got into the Bentley and promptly leaned back and closed her eyes—a definite signal that she was not going to be engaged in conversation.

Josh had been shocked to see how much Claire resembled her mother. He remembered her as a mousy-looking kid, young for her twenty-two years at the time.

That first day of filming, Josh had stayed at the mansion all day, helping Jane prepare sandwiches and dessert and serving them on the patio, where the breakfast group retreated between scenes.

When everyone left, Mr. Rob told him to go home and to pick up Claire again in the morning.

"Try to talk to her, Josh," Mr. Rob instructed. "Say how much you liked her mother, even though I know you didn't." At six o'clock Josh drove his own car home.

It was one of the nights when Mrs. Gibney was in a talkative mood and invited him to share the roast chicken that she had prepared.

That happened about once a week, and usually Josh was happy to accept—Mrs. Gibney was a good cook. But tonight he had things on his mind and he thanked her, saying he had had an early dinner. It was a lie, but he wanted to think.

In his pocket he had copies of the tapes he had made in the car of Nina Craig and her mother, Alison Schaefer and her husband, and Regina Callari on the phone with her son.

It was obvious that none of those women would want the tapes to be heard by either Mr. Powell or the police. They had agreed to come here to try to finally clear themselves from being under suspicion in Betsy's death, but each of the tapes revealed a motive for them to have killed Betsy.

They were all getting money for being on the program, a lot of money. Each would be horrified to know their motives were caught on tape, loud and clear. If they didn't trust him to stick to his side of the agreement, he has an answer prepared.

"I'll always have the master tape. You can destroy the copy I give you," he would say. "You don't want to go to Mr. Powell or the police with these tapes. Neither do I. Pay me and nobody will ever hear them."

He had figured out his suggested price—fifty thousand dollars. Only one-sixth of the three hundred thousand they would all be collecting.

It should work. They were all scared. He could sense it while he was serving them on the patio.

Josh wanted to build up his nest egg. He'd taken Mr. Powell to the cancer doctor a number of times. He had a hunch that Mr. Powell was sicker than anyone suspected. If anything happened to him, Josh knew he was in the will for one hundred thousand dollars. But adding $150,000 to that wouldn't hurt.

Now, if he could only get something on Claire!

28

George Curtis drove the four blocks to his home, outwardly composed but inwardly in a state of emotional exhaustion.

Rob Powell was toying with him. Rob knew about him and Betsy, George was sure of it. He thought about Laurie Moran, the producer, discussing the sequence of filming the next day. She had thanked him in particular for participating in the program.

"I know how busy you must be, Mr. Curtis," she said. "Thank you for giving up your day to be with us. I know there was a lot of waiting around while we set up for the shooting. Tomorrow we'll film you standing in front of the backdrop of clips of the Gala, then being interviewed by Alex Buckley about your memories of that night."

Memories, George thought as he turned into his driveway, memories. That was the night Betsy had given him an ultimatum. "Tell Isabelle you want a divorce like you promised, or pay me twenty-five million dollars to stay with Rob and keep my mouth shut. You're a billionaire; you can afford it."

And it was on the way to the Gala that Isabelle, her face radiant, had told him she was four months pregnant with twins.

"I waited to tell you, George," she had said. "After four miscarriages I didn't want to disappoint you again. But four months is a big milestone. After fifteen years of waiting and praying, this time we'll have a family."

"Oh my God," was all he could say. "Oh my God."

I was thrilled and terrified, George thought. I asked myself how I could ever let myself get involved with Betsy, my best friend's wife.

It had all started in London. George was there for a business meeting with the European director of the Curtis fast-food restaurant chain that his father had founded in 1940. Rob and Betsy Powell were in London at the same time, and they, too, were staying at the Stanhope Hotel, in an adjoining suite. Rob flew to Berlin overnight.

I took Betsy to dinner, then back at the hotel she suggested having a nightcap in my suite, George remembered. She never left that night. It was the beginning of a two-year affair.

Isabelle and I were growing apart, George thought as he parked the car in front of the house. She was taken up with volunteering for a number of charities, and I was all over the world opening up new markets.

When I was home, I didn't want to go to the charity dinners with her.

Because anytime Rob was away, I met Betsy somewhere.

But after a year it began to wear off. I finally saw her for what she was: a manipulator. And then I couldn't get rid of her. She kept hounding me to get a divorce.

At the Gala, Isabelle was telling her friends that she was pregnant.

When Betsy heard that, she told me she knew I wouldn't get a divorce. Instead she wanted that twenty-five million dollars to keep her mouth shut. "You can afford it, George," she had said, smiling, always aware of the audience around her. "You're a billionaire. You won't even miss it. Otherwise I tell Isabelle about us. Maybe the shock will cause her to miscarry again."

George was sickened. "If you tell Isabelle or anyone else, Rob will divorce you." George could hardly even manage to form the words. "And I know your prenup leaves you with almost nothing."

Betsy had actually smiled. "I know that won't happen, George, because you're going to pay me. And I'll keep living happily with Rob, and you and Isabelle will be in a state of bliss with your twins."

She continued to smile as George heard himself say, "I'll pay you, Betsy, but if you ever say anything to Isabelle or anyone else, I will kill you. I swear it."

"Here's to that agreement," Betsy said as she clinked her glass against his.

Twenty years later, George thought as he unlocked the door of the car. His mind switched to what Laurie Moran had told him about the rest of his part in the filming.

"And then we'll have you and Alex Buckley sitting together, and he'll ask you your overall impressions of the party and of Betsy Powell," Laurie had said. "Maybe you have some stories you could tell about Betsy. From what I understand, you were close friends of the Powells and frequently saw them socially."

I told Moran that I saw Rob more on the golf course at the club than socially, as couples, George thought as he walked up the three steps to the charming brick house that he and Isabelle had built twenty years ago. He remembered how the architect had come in with pretentious renderings of houses in which the entrance hall was big enough for a skating rink and twin staircases led to a balcony "where you could put a full orchestra."

Isabelle's comment was, "We want a home, not a concert hall."

And it *was* homey. Spacious but not overwhelming. Inviting and warm.

He opened the door and headed to the family room. As he had expected, Isabelle and the twins, Leila and Justin, who were home from college for the summer, were there.

George's heart swelled with love as he looked at the three of them.

And to think I almost lost them, he thought as he remembered his threat to Betsy.

29

When Claire got back to the hotel, the first thing she did was to put a DO NOT DISTURB sign on the door, then rush to wash her face.

All the carefully applied makeup vanished into the soapy washcloth as she checked and rechecked to be sure that every vestige of it was gone. Well, it served its purpose, she thought. I saw the look on all their faces, especially Rob Powell's, when they saw me. I'm not sure whether Nina pulled that faint or if it was genuine. She was a pretty good actress, even if she never did make it big.

But I think she upstaged Daddy Rob. He was just about to faint himself before she beat him to it. Well, didn't he used to brag that in high school he was voted best actor in the senior play? And he's perfected his act since then.

30

Nina could see the look of disappointment on her mother's face when Rob didn't extend an invitation to dinner. But in the car Muriel pointed out that he had referred more than once to the good times they had had together. That much is true, Nina acknowledged to herself.

As they got off the elevator in the hotel, Muriel asked, "Did you see the chandelier? It must be worth forty thousand dollars."

"How do you know?"

"I saw one like it when we were in Venice for background scenes."

Fitting, Nina thought. Now, as an actress, you're in the background again.

"Did you see how that housekeeper acted as if we were a bunch of intruders?"

"Mom, I remember her from the time when we were growing up. Jane always looked as if she disapproved of everyone except Betsy." Nina hesitated, then added sarcastically, "I mean 'Mrs. Powell.' That's what Jane was forced to call her, even though they'd worked together for years."

"Well, I certainly would have made her call me 'Mrs. Powell' instead of Muriel," her mother snapped. "If I had married Rob."

"I'm going to my room. I'll have dinner served there," Nina replied, rolling her eyes to heaven. As she walked rapidly away from Muriel, she thought, the greatest gift you ever received was that Betsy was out of your way, but even though you called Rob Powell any number of times after she died, he didn't want to see you again. And now it's obvious to me that he's just toying with you.

Will you ever learn?

31

Regina was barely in her hotel when she received a telephone call from Zach from London. He got directly to the point.

"Mom, please be honest, did you bring that letter with you?"

Regina knew there was no use in lying.

"Yes, I did. I'm sorry, Zach. I lied to you because I didn't want you to be upset."

"Then, Mom, I have to tell you. I destroyed the copy you had. I've been wanting to tear that letter up ever since you told me about it. I would have torn up the original, too, but I couldn't find where you put it."

"Zach, it's okay. I know you're right and after this week, I *will* destroy it. Or if you want, I'll let you burn it. That's a promise."

"Awesome, Mom, I'll hold you to that."

They both said, "I love you," then said good-bye.

Regina raced to the dresser where she'd left her

pocketbook, opened it, and with trembling fingers reached for her wallet. She had known when she arrived at the Powell estate that she should not have carried the letter with her.

She opened the secret flap in her wallet where she had carefully folded the letter.

It was empty.

Whoever had taken it must have suspected she might be carrying something important, or else had gone through all the pocketbooks that had been left on the patio table for the same reason.

And the letter provided the perfect reason for her to have murdered Betsy.

Frantically she dumped her pocketbook on the table and rummaged through the contents, hoping against hope that somehow she would find it. But it was not there.

32

Rod woke at four in the morning after hearing a door close. "Alie," he called. He turned on the overhead light. The door to the sitting room was open, and he could see Alison was not there. He bolted up and reached for his crutches. After all these years his arms and shoulders were powerful, and he could move swiftly on them. Was Alison sleepwalking again? He glanced into the bathroom and the dressing room. She was not in either of them. He reached the outer door of the room in seconds and threw it open. There was Alison, walking slowly down the long hallway.

He caught up with her at the top of the staircase to the lobby.

Once there, he reached for her hand and whispered her name. He watched her eyes blinking, and she turned her face to him.

"It's fine," he said soothingly. "It's fine. We're going back to bed."

When they were inside the room she began to cry. "Rod, Rod, I was sleepwalking again, wasn't I?"

"Yes, but it's all right. It's fine."

"Rod, the night of the Gala I was so angry. People were asking me if I was planning to go to medical school. I told them I was going to have to work for a year at least. Whenever I looked at Betsy all I could think was that she had stolen that scholarship from me so that she could get into a fancy club." Her voice a desperate whisper, she said, "I was sleepwalking that night of the Gala. I woke up leaving Betsy's room. I was so grateful she hadn't heard me. Or is it possible I killed her?"

Her words were drowned in sobs.

33

Leo Farley dropped Laurie off in a cab, then instructed her driver to wait until he had seen the doorman open the door into the lobby and close it behind her.

As safe as I can make her, he thought, then leaned back in the cab with a weary sigh. It had been a long day, made even longer by his anxiety about Timmy being away at camp.

He was so deep in thought that he did not notice when the cab pulled up at his apartment building on the next block.

Tony the doorman was there, waiting to open the door. Leo usually bounded out of the cab, but tonight, after he had paid the fare, he moved slowly and even reached for Tony's hand to help get him to his feet.

And then he felt it begin—the rapid pulsing of his heart that meant he was beginning to have an attack of cardiac fibrillation. As Tony waited attentively, Leo started to get out, then remembered that his doctor had warned him that he must not, absolutely *must* not ignore it when his heart began to beat like this—like a locomotive out of control.

"Get to the hospital right away, Leo," he had ordered. "A lot of people have this condition, but yours is much more serious than most. Your heart has to be slowed down immediately."

Leo looked up at Tony. "Just remembered I left something at my daughter's house," he fibbed, then added, "I may stay over with her."

"That's fine, sir. Good night."

Tony closed the door with a decisive click, and Leo reluctantly told the driver to take him to Mount Sinai Hospital.

At least it's only a few blocks way, he thought as he again checked his rapidly accelerating pulse.

34

Alex Buckley pondered the events of the day as he drove home from Salem Ridge to Manhattan. The four girls, now women, had been friends since their freshman year in high school, and it was obvious that their greetings to each other had been guarded, although as the hours wore on they seemed to be warming up.

Their reaction to Robert Powell was unmistakably hostile, even as they kept up a thin veneer of cordiality.

Years of interrogating witnesses had given Alex the ability to cut through the surface of what someone was saying and study their eyes and body language. What he concluded from all four graduates today was that they despised Robert Powell.

The question was, why? Alex would bet the animosity began more than twenty years ago.

Then why did they go along with the Graduation Gala? Even if my best friend wanted to share his graduation party with me, I wouldn't have done it if I hated his father, Alex thought. And that raised another question. How did they feel about Betsy Bonner Powell? If one of the four had killed her, there had to be a compelling motive for her to seize the opportunity to stay overnight at the Powell home.

These questions Alex began to sort in his head as he pulled the car into his garage and went to his apartment.

Ramon was quick to hear his key turn the lock in the door. He appeared in the foyer, a smile on his face. "Good evening, Mr. Alex. I hope you had a good day?"

"Let's call it an *interesting* day," Alex said, returning the smile. "I'm going to change right away. I certainly didn't need to wear a tie and jacket today. It was hot outside."

The apartment was comfortably cool, and as usual his closet was a masterpiece of precision, thanks to Ramon, who hung every jacket and shirt and tie in color groupings. Alex's trousers were placed in the same orderly pattern.

Now Alex changed into a short-sleeved sport shirt and khakis. Then he washed his hands, splashed water on his face, and decided that what he wanted was a cold beer.

As he passed the dining room, he saw that the table was set for two.

"Ramon, who's coming?" he asked as he opened the refrigerator door. "I don't remember inviting anyone."

"I didn't have a chance to tell you, sir," Ramon replied as he prepared a small plate of hors d'oeuvres. "Your brother should be here any minute. He has an appointment in New York in the morning."

"Andrew's coming, that's great," Alex said sincerely, although he had a fleeting moment of disappointment, since he had intended to jot down all his impressions of the day over dinner. But Andrew knew today was the beginning of the filming and would probably have lots of questions. Questions could be useful in drawing out facts. If anyone should know that, it's me, Alex thought.

His first sip of beer coincided with the sound of chimes announcing Andrew's arrival. He had his own key and was letting himself in when Alex walked into the foyer.

For a long time it had been just the two of them. Their mother had died when Alex was a freshman in college, and their father two years later. Alex had just turned twenty-one and had been appointed Andrew's guardian.

Like most brothers, they had had their squabbles growing up. Both were competitive in sports, and a victory over the other in golf or tennis was a source of great joy.

But competition had disappeared when it was just the two of them. They had only distant cousins in their extended family, none of whom lived in New York. They sold their home in Oyster Bay and moved into a four-room apartment in Manhattan on East Sixty-seventh Street, which they shared until Andrew had graduated from Columbia Law School and accepted a job in Washington, D.C.

Alex, by then five years out of NYU Law and a rising star in a litigation firm, had stayed in that apartment until he bought the one on Beekman Place.

Unlike Alex, Andrew had married six years ago and now had three children—a five-year-old boy and twin two-year-old daughters.

"How are Marcy and the kids?" was the first question Alex asked after giving his brother a brief hug.

Andrew, six two to Alex's six four, his hair slightly darker than Alex's, his eyes blue-gray, but with the same disciplined body, laughed.

"Marcy is jealous that I'm getting away overnight. The twins are living the concept of the terrible twos. Their vocabulary consists of one word: 'no.' Johnny, as usual, is a great kid. If he ever was a two-year-old like the girls, I don't remember it."

He looked at the glass in his brother's hand. "How about one of those for me?"

Ramon was already pouring the beer into a chilled glass.

They settled in the den, and Andrew hungrily reached for the plate of hors d'oeuvres. "I'm starving. I skipped lunch today."

"You should have ordered out," Alex suggested.

"That's profound wisdom. If only I had thought of it."

The brothers exchanged a brief grin, then Andrew asked, "And now for the sixty-four-thousand-dollar question. How did it go today?"

"Interesting, of course." Alex began telling him about the breakfast gathering. When he came to the fact that Nina Craig had fainted at the sight of Claire, Andrew interrupted.

"Was it a real faint or was she faking it?"

"What makes you ask that?" Alex said quickly.

"Well, don't forget, Marcy did a lot of acting before we were married. She lived in California for five years after college. When we knew that you were involved with all this and that the journalists were rehashing the case, she told me she had been in a play with Muriel Craig and that every night after the show Muriel would head for a bar, get drunk, and start telling people how she could have married Robert Powell except that her stupid daughter had dragged her friend's mother over to meet him. She'd rant on about how she and Powell were practically engaged and that right now she could be living in a mansion with a handsome, rich husband if it hadn't been for her stupid daughter, Nina. Apparently Nina was there one night, and after Muriel got finished, they almost came to blows!"

"Well, maybe that explains it," Alex said. "I think the faint was genuine, but as she was coming out of it, Nina screamed at her mother to take her miserable hands off her!"

"How long had Betsy been married to Powell when she was murdered?" Andrew asked. "Wasn't it six or seven years?"

"Nine years."

"Do you think there's any chance that Nina Craig

took the opportunity to get rid of Betsy by staying over at the house after the Gala and hopefully make Powell available for her mother again? From what Marcy told me, Nina can be a tough cookie."

Alex did not answer for a long minute, then said wryly, "Maybe you're the one who should have been the criminal lawyer."

Ramon was standing in the doorway. "Dinner is served if you are ready, sir."

"I hope we have fish," Alex commented as he stood up. "It's supposed to be brain food, isn't it, Ramon?"

35

Laurie had set the alarm for six o'clock but woke at five-thirty. A glance at the clock on her night table told her that she had the luxury of lying in bed for another half hour.

This was the hour when if Timmy woke up early, he would come into her room and snuggle against her in bed. She loved the feeling of putting her arm around him and having his head tucked under her chin. He was tall for his age, but he still seemed so little and vulnerable that a fierce need to protect him always filled her being. I would *kill* for you, she would think passionately when the threat Blue Eyes had shouted flooded her mind.

But today Timmy had just completed his first overnight away from her or her father since he was born. Whenever she had to go away on business, Leo moved in and stayed with Timmy.

Was Timmy enjoying camp? Was he homesick?

That would be natural, she told herself. All first-time campers are bound to feel that way for a day or two.

But I'm homesick for *him*, she thought as she threw back the light covers, knowing that it would be easier to get up than to lie awake worrying about Timmy.

She allowed herself to pick up the framed picture on her dressing table. It had been enlarged from a snapshot someone had taken of Greg, Timmy, and her when they had been with a group of friends at the beach in East Hampton.

It was the last picture of the three of them. Greg had been shot a week later.

Laurie ran the tip of her finger over Greg's face, a gesture that she had made hundreds of times in the last five years. She sometimes fantasized that one day instead of the flat surface of the print she would feel Greg's face, that she would run her finger along the outline of his mouth and feel it curve into a smile.

She thought of how one night a few months after Greg's death, her need for him had been so strong that she fell asleep whispering his name over and over again.

Then she dreamt so vividly of him, his expression troubled and sad, as if he were in distress that she was so aggrieved . . .

Shaking her head, she put the picture back on the dresser. Fifteen minutes later, her hair still wet from the shower, her cotton bathrobe covering her slender body, she went into the kitchen where the coffee had already brewed on the timer.

JERRY AND GRACE PICKED HER UP AT 7:45. THE rest of the crew would meet them at the Powell estate.

As usual, Grace was trying to pull herself awake. "I went to bed at ten o'clock," she told Laurie, "and then I couldn't sleep. I was trying to figure out which one of them might have killed Betsy Powell."

"What's your conclusion?" Laurie asked.

"Any one of them or all of them banded together—the four graduates, I mean. Like in *Murder on the Orient Express*. They all took turns stabbing the guy who had kidnapped the baby."

"Grace, even for you that's over the top," Jerry said flatly. "I say the housekeeper is guilty. She so obviously wishes we were all on Planet Mars that I think it's more than the fact that her usual routine is interrupted. I think she's worried. What about you, Laurie?"

Laurie was pulling out her cell phone. She had heard the faint sound that indicated she had received a text message.

It was from Brett Young. It read, "Laurie, the financial statements for the quarter indicate another drop in revenue. As I told you, the last two pilots you produced were expensive and disappointing. Make sure this one works."

36

Mr. Powell had awakened earlier than usual. By seven-fifteen he was finishing his second cup of coffee. From where he sat in the breakfast room he had a full view of the backyard, a sight that usually pleased him. But today, despite the fact that the rosebushes around the patio were in full bloom and the fountain was sending a spray of crystal water into the air and the plants around the pond made a display of color like the palette of an artist, the look on his face was one of displeasure. The film company had left two large vans pulled up to the side of the house in back, and Jane knew that the sight of them was as displeasing to Mr. Rob as it was to her.

Jane knew his moods. Last night he had seemed almost amused by the events of the day, like Nina Craig's fainting and Muriel's obvious and flirtatious reminders about dates they had shared before Betsy entered the picture.

How much did he know about George Curtis and Betsy? Jane wondered. She had been passing hors d'oeuvres at the Gala twenty years ago when she had sensed the palpable tension between Curtis and Betsy, and had managed to sidle close behind him in time to hear his threat to Betsy. Jane knew that if Betsy succeeded in getting $25 million from Curtis, she probably would have hidden the money, as she had the jewelry, and continued her life with Mr. Powell.

If you only knew how much I know about you, Jane thought as she firmly resisted the impulse to pat Mr. Powell on the shoulder. Should I remind him that he was the one who had agreed to all this and suggest he go to the office for the day, since from what I gather, he would not be needed on camera today? But she did not touch his shoulder or suggest he go to the office. She knew he would be appalled if she took either liberty. Instead she made the symbolic gesture of offering him more coffee, and after brusquely refusing, he quietly left the room.

Yesterday she had seen that sneak Josh go through the pocketbooks when the graduates were told to leave them on the table on the patio. He had removed something from one of them. She could not be sure which one, because he had been so quick about it. What had he found of interest? She had long known about his taping the people he was driving. She also knew that Betsy, "Mrs. Powell," she sneered to herself, didn't like his attitude. He wouldn't have lasted long in this job if she had lived, Jane thought.

What was it that he had taken from the pocketbook? She did know this—if it was something that would be beneficial to Mr. Powell, Josh would show it to him and, like a dog getting a friendly pat from his master, he would end up with a few hundred dollars extra in his pocket.

"Jane, I don't want to see anyone this morning," Mr. Powell said. "I will be spending a lot of time on the phone with the office. The production company is bringing their own food, so there's no reason to have an open kitchen for those people. The crew will be using the bathroom in the pool house. Let the others stay on the patio and come in and out through the kitchen to use the bathroom. I don't want any of them going upstairs or wandering through the house. Is that clear?"

What had changed so drastically from last night, when he had seemed to be enjoying himself? Jane wondered. Or was he dreading the one-on-one interview with that lawyer, Alex Buckley? Jane had read up on Buckley and had seen him on television discussing crimes. She knew that at some point he would be asking her questions about that night, too.

Well, I've managed to keep my thoughts to myself for almost thirty years, she thought. I'm pretty sure I can continue to keep secrets. Jane smiled to herself as she thought of the jewelry she had taken from Betsy's hiding place after her body was found. The earrings and ring and necklace George Curtis had given Betsy had of course never been worn around Mr. Powell. Betsy saved them for those quiet little get-togethers when he was out of town. Mr. Powell never knew about them, and George Curtis certainly wasn't looking to get them back.

I wonder if all these years, Curtis has been wondering if that jewelry would be found and traced to him? He did threaten Betsy that night, and he lives only a ten-minute walk away. Well, if any suspicion falls on either Mr. Powell or myself about Betsy's death, I can pretend that I just found them and let Mr. George Curtis be accused of her murder.

Satisfied with the reassuring presence of the jewelry well hidden in her apartment, Jane picked up the coffee cup that Robert Powell had put down when he left the room and, pressing it lovingly to her lips, finished the coffee he had left in the cup.

37

Claire had orange juice, coffee, and an English muffin sent up for breakfast. She was dressed and waiting long before the car arrived to pick her up and take her to the house where she had spent the nine most miserable years of her life.

She had deliberately dressed the way she usually dressed at home—a plain long-sleeved cotton shirt and black slacks. Today she did not put on makeup, nor, as was her custom at home, any jewelry. I've been fading into the background all of these years, she thought. When I was a child, my mother pushed me into it. Why should I change? Besides, it's too late for anything to change.

There was only one satisfaction in Claire's life—her job as a social worker dealing with domestic issues. She knew she was good at it, and it was only when she had helped to rescue women and children from unbearable circumstances that she had a sense of peace and fulfillment.

Why did I come back here? she wondered. What did I think I was going to get out of it? What did I think I was going to put to rest? By participating, each of the graduates risked revealing her own secret reasons for hating Betsy. Claire knew what those reasons were and sympathized with all of them. She remembered how the other three had been her strength during the high school years. When I was out with them, she thought, I could almost forget everything.

Now we're all afraid of what people might know about us. Will this program bring the truth to light, or will it simply be a messy rehash of painful memories and destroyed lives? She shrugged impatiently, then turned on the news to kill time until the car arrived. One of the items mentioned the filming of the show about the murder of Betsy Bonner Powell and how it was destined to be "the most highly anticipated event of the television season."

Claire pushed the remote control button and the screen darkened just as the telephone rang. From the lobby Josh Damiano asked in a cheery voice if she was ready to go.

Maybe I've been ready for twenty years, Claire thought as she picked up her pocketbook and slung it over her arm.

38

Chief Ed Penn had received a phone call from Leo Farley at nine o'clock on Monday evening. He could tell that Farley sounded fatigued but was shocked when Leo told him he was in the hospital. "They haven't been able to get my heart back to a normal rhythm," Leo told him. "And of course that means I'm not going to be around to keep an eye out for any potential problems."

Chief Penn's first reaction was that Leo Farley had been under the strain of the threat to his daughter and grandson for five years and was breaking under it. After pointing out what Leo already knew—that the film company had a guard at the gate of the Powell estate to keep out paparazzi and that the guard was checking everyone who attempted to get inside the grounds—Penn promised Leo he would station a squad car on the back road to be sure no one attempted to scale the fence.

Now that the program was actually being made, Penn had taken home the exhaustive file on the case and had once again been reading it through.

When Leo phoned, he had been examining the pictures of the crime scene with a magnifying glass, the beautifully appointed bedroom in the background and the incongruous sight of Betsy Powell's body, her hair loose on the pillow, her eyes staring, her satin nightgown curving on her shoulders.

The Chief read that the housekeeper had been in the kitchen when she heard the commotion upstairs and raced up to find Robert Powell gasping for breath on the floor by the bed, his hands burned from the coffee he had been carrying to Betsy.

The four graduates had rushed into the room when they heard Jane's shriek. According to them, Jane Novak had screamed, "Betsy, Betsy," even though she normally called her Mrs. Powell.

And immediately after pulling the pillow from the face of the victim, Jane admitted she had picked up the emerald earring from the carpet and put it on the night table.

"I guess it was because I almost stepped on it," she said. "I wasn't thinking about what I was doing."

What she had been doing was contaminating the crime scene, Penn thought. First by handling the pillow, then by picking up the earring.

"And then I ran over to Mr. Powell," Jane's statement continued. "He had passed out. I thought he was dead. I had watched someone do CPR on television and I tried it on him in case his heart had stopped beating. And by then the girls came in and I shrieked to them to phone the police and get an ambulance."

It was the collective calm of the four graduates that the Chief remembered noting immediately. Granted, they told him they had been up until 3 A.M. talking and had drunk plenty of wine. The lack of sleep and the excessive drinking might have numbed their immediate response to Betsy Powell's death. But it seemed to him that even allowing for the shock of it, Claire Bonner was surprisingly composed for a young woman whose mother was dead.

But then, so were the other graduates when they were interrogated.

I still don't think it was an intruder, Penn thought. *I have always believed that someone in that house killed Betsy Powell.*

The six people who had been there were Robert Powell, the housekeeper, and the four graduates.

They're all being questioned by Buckley, Penn thought. *He's supposed to be dynamite when he's cross-examining a witness. It will be interesting to compare their initial statements with what they say now on camera.*

Shaking his head, the Chief looked around his den. He felt that it was a stain on his department that the crime had never been solved. His eyes lingered on the wall with the many citations he and his department had earned over the years. There was another one he wanted.

It would be for solving the murder of Betsy Bonner Powell.

Then he glanced at his watch. It was ten minutes past nine. No more time for useless speculation. He picked up the phone to order that a squad car be stationed at the back of the Powell estate starting the next morning.

39

Bruno woke on Tuesday morning at six, aware that he was getting closer and closer to the moment of glory when he could take his final revenge.

He turned on the television as he prepared his spartan breakfast. He was allowed to keep a small refrigerator in his room. He plugged in the coffee-maker, then poured yogurt and cereal into a bowl.

After the hard news and a dozen commercials, he heard what he had been waiting to hear. "The pilot for the *Under Suspicion* series is presently being filmed at the estate of Robert Powell. Twenty years after the Graduation Gala the four honorees have gathered to appear on a television program to protest their innocence in the death of beautiful socialite Betsy Bonner Powell."

Bruno laughed aloud, a raspy, mirthless sound. Yesterday he had spoken with one of the surprisingly talkative television crew. He had said that they would be filming today and tomorrow. Tonight the graduates would stay overnight. They would be on camera, seated in the den as they had been twenty years ago. Then tomorrow morning they would be filmed at a farewell breakfast.

And while they were having breakfast, Bruno would emerge from the pool house with his rifle and take aim at her.

Bruno thought of that day long ago when, as a kid in Brooklyn, he had hung around the guys he knew were in the mob. He had a job as a busboy in the diner where some of them had breakfast every morning.

He heard a couple of them bragging about how they could shoot the apple off the head of William Tell's kid, but with a rifle, not an arrow. That was when Bruno bought a rifle and a pistol secondhand and started practicing.

Six months later, when he was clearing the table, he told the two guys who had been boasting that he'd like to show them how good a shot he was. They laughed at him, but one of them said, "You know, kid, I don't like people wasting my time with bragging. If you want to show off, I'll give you a try."

And that was how he was hired by the mob.

Bruno could take out Laurie Moran anytime, but he wanted to be sure the cameras would be rolling when she slumped over.

He slurped his coffee in anticipation of that moment.

The policeman in that squad car on the back road

would come rushing over the fence and run toward the dining room. The television crew, too. When they were all past the pool house Bruno would leave by the back door and be over the fence in seconds.

It would take him only four minutes to jog to the public parking lot at the train station. The lot was only a block from the room he was sitting in right now.

He had chosen the car he would steal, a Lexus station wagon whose owner parked it at seven every morning to get on the seven-fifteen train to Manhattan.

Bruno would be driving away before they had even figured out where the shot had come from.

The owner wouldn't report the car missing until Thursday evening.

Bruno was so busy going over his plan that he did not even realize his coffee cup was empty.

What were the possibilities of failure?

Of course there were a few. A policeman might not be able to scale the fence. In that case he'd be sure to challenge me, Bruno thought. I don't want to have to shoot him. The noise would bring the other cop back. But if I used the butt of the rifle, I'd have all the time I need . . .

The element of surprise, the confusion over Laurie slumping over, blood beginning to pour from her head—all of this would work in his favor.

I might be caught, Bruno admitted to himself, and that would permanently end any hope of eliminating Timmy. But if I get away with it, I'll take care of him fast. My luck won't hold out forever.

By hacking into Leo Farley's computer, Bruno knew that Timmy was at camp, and even knew which tent he was in and every detail of its layout. But even if he could get into the camp during the night and kidnap Timmy, Laurie would be notified in minutes, and he'd never be able to get near her. Timmy had to come second.

Bruno shrugged. He was sure that old lady had heard his threat, "Your mother's next, then it's your turn." He'd have to stick to that plan.

He hadn't checked Leo's phone since yesterday, not that Leo had much to say to anyone.

Bruno listened to the recording of Leo's call to the police chief last night. *Leo Farley was in Mount Sinai Hospital in intensive care.*

Bruno began to consider the possibilities this suggested.

Then he began to smile.

Of course, of course, it would work. It would have to work. He could pull it off.

When Laurie was at the farewell breakfast, Bruno would come out of the pool house holding Timmy's hand—and pointing a gun at his head.

40

Regina's hands were trembling so violently that she could hardly pull the T-shirt over her head. Laurie Moran had told them to dress simply. She had had replicas made of the outfits they had been wearing when the police arrived after Betsy's body was found. They had handed over their pajamas for evidence and been asked to wait in the den until they could be questioned.

Regina had been wearing a long-sleeved red T-shirt and jeans. The thought of wearing a similar outfit now was upsetting. She felt as if all the protective layers she had built around herself over twenty years were being peeled away.

Just thinking about that outfit made her remember how they had all sat huddled together, not allowed to go into the kitchen even to get a cup of coffee or a piece of toast. Jane, too, had been in the den with them, despite pleading to be allowed to go in the ambulance with Mr. Powell to the hospital.

Who had taken her father's suicide note from her pocketbook? And what would that person do with it?

If the police found it, they could arrest her for taking the letter from her father's body. She knew they always suspected that if he'd written a note, she'd taken it. She had lied over and over to them when they were investigating his death. Whoever had the note now could provide the police with everything they needed to indict her for Betsy's murder.

Regina's eyes filled with tears.

Her nineteen-year-old son, Zach, had had the brains to destroy the copy she made of the note and had tried to find the original, then begged her not to carry it with her.

What would it do to his life if she were arrested and indicted for Betsy's death?

She thought of the little boy who would come to the real estate office after school when he didn't have practice for one of his sports and want to help her by folding and mailing ads for the agency to the local communities. He was always thrilled when one of the ads resulted in a listing. They'd always been close. She knew how lucky she was on that count.

When Regina's breakfast arrived, she tried to drink the coffee and eat a bite of the croissant, but it stuck in her throat.

You've got to get a grip on yourself, she thought. If

you look too nervous when that lawyer, Alex Buckley, interviews you, you'll only make things worse.

Please, God, she thought, let me be able to pull it off. The phone rang. The car was here to take her to the Powell estate.

"I'll be right down," she said, unable to conceal the quiver in her voice.

41

Alison did not go back to sleep after the sleepwalking incident. Rod felt her tossing and turning in bed and finally put his arm around her and drew her close to him.

"Alie, you've got to keep reminding yourself that you were sleepwalking that night. Even if you believe you were in Betsy's room, it doesn't mean that memory is accurate."

"I was there. She kept a low night-light on. I even remember seeing the earring sparkling on the floor. Rod, if I had picked it up, my fingerprints would have been on it."

"But you *didn't* pick it up," Rod said soothingly. "Alie, you've got to stop thinking like that. When you're in front of the camera, you've got to just tell what you know—which is nothing. You heard Jane scream and rushed to the bedroom with the others. Like the others, you were shocked. When you're interviewed, just keep saying 'the others' and you'll be all right. And remind yourself that the reason you're doing this program is because you want to have the money to go to medical school. What is it I've been telling you since you got the chance to go back to school?"

"That one day you'll be calling me the new Madame Curie," Alison whispered.

"Correct. Now go back to sleep."

But even though she stopped twisting and turning, Alison did not go back to sleep. When the alarm went off at seven o'clock, she was already showered and dressed in the slacks and polo shirt that she would soon be exchanging for the T-shirt and jeans she had worn the morning after Betsy Powell's murder.

42

Laurie, Jerry, and Grace arrived at the Powell estate a few minutes after the crew, which included a hairdresser, makeup artist, and wardrobe assistant this morning. Two new vans were on the set for their use—one to serve as a dressing room, the other for hair and makeup for those who would be on camera.

Laurie had worked well with all three crew members before. "The first scene we're shooting will be of the four graduates and the housekeeper in the clothes they put on after the body was discovered. The makeup should be light, because they wouldn't have had the time or inclination to put any on. We have a picture taken that morning by the police. Study it, then try to make them look the way they looked twenty years ago. Obviously they don't have the long hair, but they've all aged very well."

Meg Miller, the makeup artist, walked over to the window of the van to get a better look at the photograph. "I can tell you this, Laurie: they all look scared to death."

"I agree," Laurie said. "My job is to find out why. Of course you'd expect that they would look shocked and grief-stricken, but why do they all look so fearful? If Betsy was killed by an intruder, then what are they afraid of?"

The scene would be shot in the den, where the police had directed the girls to wait that morning. Incredibly, none of the furniture or draperies had been changed, so the room bore an eerie sameness to the way it had looked twenty years ago.

On the other hand, Laurie reasoned, my guess is that only Robert Powell has ever used that room in all these years. According to Jane Novak, the living room and dining room are where he does his entertaining when he has guests. From what she says, when he's alone after dinner he either goes to the den and watches television or reads, or else he goes up to his suite.

With only him living here and the way Jane keeps this place up, it's no wonder there was no need to change the interior decorating.

Or, she wondered, did Powell *want* to keep his home frozen in time, just as his wife had left it? She had heard of people like that.

She shivered as she walked quickly back to the den and entered by the patio door. The crew was setting up the cameras. There was no sign of Robert Powell. Jane had told them that he was in his office and would be there all morning.

From the beginning Powell had told her there

was no need for him to equally compensate Jane. "I think I speak for her when I say we would both like a conclusion to this terrible business. Jane has always regretted the fact that after she locked all the doors for the night, the girls opened the one from the den, then when they came back in from smoking on the patio, they left it unlocked. If that had not happened, an intruder might not have been able to get in."

Maybe Powell and Jane are right, Laurie thought. After checking the cameras and the lighting, she went back out onto the patio and saw Alex Buckley getting out of his car.

Today he was wearing a sport shirt and khakis in place of the dark blue suit, shirt, and tie he had been wearing yesterday. The top of his convertible was down, and the breeze had ruffled his dark brown hair. She watched as with what was probably an instinctive gesture he smoothed his hair back and walked toward her.

"You're an early bird," he said with an easy smile.

"Not really. You should be around when we start shooting a program at daybreak."

"No thanks. I'll wait until I can push a button and see it on TV."

As he had in his office, he suddenly became businesslike. "Is the agenda still that we begin with me speaking to the graduates after you film them sitting in the den?"

"Yes. I'm doing this out of sequence because I have a strong hunch that they have all rehearsed what they're going to say to you. By starting with them all together, it may put them off guard.

"And don't be surprised at the way they're dressed. They're wearing replicas of the clothes they wore after Betsy's body was found, and then they were told to change into street wear."

Alex Buckley seldom allowed his face to register surprise, but this time he was so startled that he could not conceal it.

"You're having them wear replicas of what they wore twenty years ago?"

"Yes, for two scenes. The one in the den where they were herded with Jane as soon as the police arrived. And then one wearing gowns that are identical to the ones they wore to the Gala.

"We'll photograph the graduates against the background of films of them individually and together at the Gala. For example, when Robert Powell is toasting them, we'll have a picture of the four of them looking at him."

Alex Buckley's reply was interrupted by the limousines with the graduates arriving almost simultaneously. It was Laurie's turn to be astonished when Muriel Craig stepped out of the backseat of the second limo while her daughter, Nina, stepped out of the front passenger door. Muriel wasn't supposed to come today, she thought. Powell either called her or she's come on her own.

Either way, she's bound to make Nina edgy and angry.

Which might be good when Nina is being questioned.

43

On Tuesday morning Josh drove the Bentley to be hand-washed and detailed. Mr. Rob was very particular that it be kept in pristine order, Or *else*, Josh thought as he waited in the chair in the service center.

With a sense of satisfaction, Josh congratulated himself on solving the problem of how the graduates would be able to play the tapes he had recorded. He would put his cassette player in the powder room in the hallway next to the kitchen. There was a vanity table and bench in it for any guest who might want to touch up her makeup or hair. He would present the cassettes to Nina, Regina, and Alison and tell them they might be interested in hearing their conversations in the car, then suggest it might be worth fifty thousand dollars to have each copy destroyed.

They would be panicky, the three of them, he was sure of it. Claire hadn't said a word in the car when he drove her, so there was no cassette for her. And yet, of all of them, Josh would bet that she had the most to reveal.

He had the suicide note that Regina had hidden in her purse. Josh had debated whether to give it to Mr. Rob or try to find a better use for it. Then he found his answer: charge Regina one hundred thousand dollars, maybe even more, to get it back and tell her that otherwise he would go straight to the police. That note might take any suspicion of killing Betsy off Mr. Rob, Jane, and the other graduates.

And Josh would be a hero and good citizen if he turned it over to the police chief. But the police might ask what he was doing going through ladies' handbags. He did not have a good answer to that question, and he was hoping one would not be necessary.

Mr. Rob hadn't sent him to pick up any of the graduates this morning. Instead, sounding testy, he instructed him to come to the house after he left the service center, in case he decided to go into the office.

It was obviously unsettling for Mr. Rob to have all these people around. Not only must it bring up a lot of memories, Josh thought, but Mr. Rob must know that he's under suspicion, too, and want desperately to clear his name.

Like Jane, Josh had managed to sneak a look at Mr. Rob's will when it was on his desk. He had left $10 million to Harvard, to be used to fund scholarships for deserving students, and $5 million to

Waverly College, where he had received an honorary doctorate and had already had the library named after Betsy and him.

Alison Schaefer had gone to Waverly. Josh remembered how she was the best student of the four girls and had talked about going to medical school, but then married Rod Kimball instead four months after the Gala.

Josh had always wondered why she hadn't brought Rod to the Gala that night. You never know, he told himself, they might have had an argument.

As the service manager approached Josh to tell him the car was ready, Josh concluded his line of thinking. Mr. Rob is a very sick man trying to ensure his legacy before he dies, he decided.

But as Josh got into the Bentley and drove away, he could not help thinking that there might be more reasons for Mr. Rob going ahead with the program than met the eye.

44

Leo Farley's impatience at his hospitalization grew with every passing moment. Disdainfully, he looked at the needle inserted in his left arm and the bottle of fluid connected to it dangling overhead. He had a heart monitor strapped to his chest, and when he had tried to get up a nurse came rushing in. "Mr. Farley, you cannot go to the bathroom alone. You have to be accompanied by a nurse. However, you *can* close the door."

Isn't that wonderful, Leo thought mockingly, even as he realized it wasn't right to kill the messenger. Instead, he thanked the nurse and grudgingly allowed her to follow him to the door of the bathroom. At 9 A.M. when his doctor came in, Leo was loaded for bear. "Look," he said, "I can get away without calling my daughter. She saw me last night just before I came in here, so I know she won't look to speak to me until tonight. She has two more days to finish this program, and there's a lot of pressure on her to make sure it's successful. If I have to tell her I'm in the hospital, she'll be terribly upset and probably end up coming here instead of finishing the show."

Dr. James Morris, an old friend, was equally forceful. "Leo, your daughter will be a lot more upset if something happens to you. I'll call Laurie—she knows you get these fibrillations—make it very clear to her that you're stable now and I should be able to release you tomorrow morning. I can do it before you call this evening or after. You will do her and your grandson a lot more good by staying alive and healthy than by risking a major heart attack."

Dr. Morris's beeper sounded. "I'm sorry, Leo, I have to go."

"Don't worry. We'll finish this later."

After Dr. Morris left him, he reached for his cell phone and called Camp Mountainside. He was connected to the camp administrator's office, then the head counselor, whom he had met before. "This is the pain-in-the-neck grandfather," he said. "I just wanted to know how Timmy was doing. Any nightmares?"

"No," the counselor said firmly. "I inquired about him at breakfast, and the senior camper in his bunk said he slept for nine hours straight without stirring."

Relieved, Leo said, "Well, that is really good news."

"Stop worrying, Mr. Farley. We're taking good care of him. And how are *you* doing?"

"I could be better," Leo said ruefully. "I'm in Mount Sinai Hospital with heart fibrillations. I never like feeling that I'm not available for Timmy every minute of the day."

Leo could not know that the counselor was thinking that with the strain he had been under for the last five years, it was no wonder he was having fibrillations. Instead he heard and appreciated the counselor's assurances. "You take care of yourself, Mr. Farley. We'll take care of your grandson. I promise."

Two hours later, when Blue Eyes heard the recorded conversation, he thought excitedly, He has played into my hands. Now they'll *never* doubt me.

45

Jane Novak had worn the same-style plain black dress and white apron for the twenty-nine years she had been in the Powell household.

Her hair was also in the same style: combed back into a neat bun. The only difference was that it was now streaked with gray. Jane had never worn makeup and was scornful of Meg Miller's attempt to put even the lightest powder and eyebrow pencil on her. "Mrs. Novak, it's simply because the lights from the camera will wash you out," Meg said. But Jane would have none of it. "I know I have good skin," she said, "and that's because I never used any of that silly junk on it."

She did not know that even while Meg was saying, "Of course, as you wish," she was thinking that Jane indeed had a beautiful complexion and good features. Except for the droop at the end of her lips and the almost-scowling expression in her eyes,

Jane Novak would be a very attractive woman, Meg thought.

Claire was the next one who would accept only a minimum amount of makeup. "I never wore any," she said. Then she added bitterly: "No one would look at me anyhow. They had my mother to rave over."

Regina was obviously so nervous that Meg did her best to pat the light beads of perspiration from her forehead with a concealer, in case she continued to sweat.

Alison, very quiet, simply shrugged when Meg said, "We're only doing a little because of the lights."

Nina Craig said, "I'm an actress. I know what lighting does. Do the best you can."

There was little that Courtney, the hairdresser, could do except to style the graduates' hair as close to how it had looked in the twenty-year-old photograph.

While Laurie waited for her stars in the den, Jerry and Grace were ready to make any adjustments Laurie thought necessary.

An enlarged picture of the four graduates and Jane, taken twenty years ago by the police photographer, rested on an easel out of the range of the camera, a template for arranging the women for their interviews. The cameraman, his assistant, and the lighting technician had already placed the cameras accordingly. Three of the girls had been sitting on the long couch, giving the appearance of being huddled together. There were two armchairs on either side of the cocktail table in front of the couch. Jane Novak was in one of them, her face grief-stricken, her eyes shining with unshed tears. Claire Bonner was sitting opposite her, her expression contemplative, but without any visible sign of grief.

Busily observing the present activity, Alex Buckley sat near the door in the leather chair in which Mr. Rob often sat at the end of the day. "It's a recliner," Jane told Laurie. "He likes to adjust it so his feet are up. His doctor said it was good for circulation."

It's a beautiful room, Alex thought as he looked around appraisingly. The mahogany paneling on the walls was the background for the vivid Persian carpet. The wall-mounted television was in the center of the bookshelves and over the fireplace. The furniture had been broken into two seating groups; the couch and chairs where the graduates and Jane Novak were now seated, and the couch and armchair with the leather recliner. The sliding glass door to the patio was on the right side of the couch where the girls were sitting and was, according to Jane, the door they had gone in and out to have cigarettes the night of the Gala, leaving it unlocked.

According to the police report, the ashtrays on the patio table had been filled to overflowing that morning. Jane indicated that at least three empty bottles of wine were in the glass disposal unit, left after she and the caterers had cleaned up after the party.

Alex listened as Laurie explained the photo shoot to the girls. "As you know, we simply want this shot of you to set the scene, with you in virtually the same outfits and in the same places as you were that morning. Then, separately, Alex Buckley will interview you in the spots where you are sitting now, to get your reflections on what you were thinking and feeling that morning. Were you talking to each other? From the old picture it doesn't look as if you were."

Nina answered for them. "We almost didn't say a word. I guess we were all in shock."

"I can understand that," Laurie said soothingly. "So just sit the way you did that morning, and we'll start taking pictures. Don't look at the cameras. Look at the picture and try to re-create the same poses."

From his vantage point behind one of the cameras, Alex Buckley could feel the tension in the room, the same kind of tension that he sometimes felt in a courtroom when an important witness was called to the stand. He knew Laurie Moran was going for dramatic impact by having the two pictures incorporated into the film, but he also knew that her goal was to unsettle the graduates and Jane until one or more of them gave a statement that contradicted what was on record. Alex watched as Meg, the makeup artist, came quietly into the den, a compact in her hand. He knew she was there in case the camera revealed anyone's face to be too shiny.

He marveled at the graduates' youthful appearances and how they all had stayed slender, and he thought that Nina, who didn't look thirty, had probably had some work done. It had been a shock to see Claire Bonner, who just yesterday had looked so glamorous and so like the pictures of her mother, by comparison look shockingly plain today. What kind of game is she playing? he wondered.

"All right, let's get started," Laurie was saying. "Grace, that pillow behind Nina, it's too far to the right." Grace adjusted it. Laurie checked the camera again and nodded to the cameraman. Alex watched as picture after picture was taken with an occasional comment from Laurie.

"Alison, try not to turn to the left. Nina, sit back the way you were in the original, otherwise you look as if you are posing. Jane, turn your head a little this way."

It was thirty-five minutes before Laurie was satisfied with what she saw in the camera's viewfinder. "Thanks very much," she said briskly. "We'll take a short break and then Alex will start interviewing you. Claire, he'll start with you. We'll be back in the den and you two will sit opposite each other in the chairs you and Jane are in now. The rest of you will have some downtime. There are newspapers and magazines in the dressing rooms. It's such a beautiful day, I imagine you will want to sit on the patio?"

One by one they all got to their feet. Jane was the first one to head for the door. "I'll put the snacks out and you can help yourselves," she said. "You can have them outside or in the breakfast room. We'll be having lunch at one-thirty."

46

Chief Ed Penn did not realize how much Leo's abiding worry about his daughter's safety while the *Under Suspicion* program was being filmed had affected him.

Even though he had ordered the squad car for the back road, he decided to take a look at the site himself. He was admittedly very curious to see how the graduates looked twenty years later.

It was around ten o'clock when, after having checked the squad car, the Chief decided to go onto the grounds and meet Laurie Moran. Of course he would not tell her of her father's concern, but on the other hand she was with six people who had been in the house on the night of Betsy Powell's murder. Penn was convinced that one of those six people was the murderer.

Robert Powell had been in a state of collapse with his hands badly burned from the steaming cup of coffee he had been carrying to his wife. He still could have killed her and figured that burns on his hands were a small price to pay for the appearance of innocence, Penn thought.

Chief Penn well knew that Regina's father had committed suicide because of the investment he made in Powell's hedge fund. A grieving daughter might very well have resented Powell for being the indirect cause of his death. The Chief was sure Regina had been lying when she claimed there was no suicide note. She had been only fifteen then, but she had withstood intense questioning, which suggested to him a steely resolve beyond her years.

Claire Bonner was a puzzle. Was it shock that made her so calm after her mother's death? He had been at the funeral. While tears streamed down Robert Powell's face, Claire had been cool, calm, and collected, as the expression went.

Nina Craig he knew less about—only that her mother constantly castigated her for introducing Betsy Bonner to Robert Powell.

Alison Schaefer seemed to be the one least likely to have a grudge against Betsy. She got married four months after Bonner's death, and, at that time, Rod had a brilliant future in football.

Penn had wondered if the paparazzi would try to get on the set. But there was no evidence of that. The guard at the gate let the Chief's car pass through, and his driver, a young policeman, parked behind the vans. "I won't be long," Penn told him and walked toward the patio, where people were gathered for lunch.

Laurie came to meet him and escorted him back to the group, where Penn immediately recognized the four graduates. They were sitting at the same table with Alison's husband and they all looked up as he approached. They all seemed startled, then defensive, but Regina was the only one who seemed to recoil as if from a blow.

He addressed her first. "Regina, I don't know if you remember me," he said.

"Yes, of course I remember you," she replied.

Chief Penn continued. "How have you been? I was sorry to hear about your mother's death right after she moved to Florida."

It was on the tip of Regina's tongue to say that her mother died of a broken heart because she never got over her husband's death, but that might open up the subject of the suicide note. Or is the police chief here because he already has it? she wondered. Hoping her hand would not tremble, Regina picked up her glass of iced tea and began to sip it as the police chief greeted the other graduates.

He turned to the table where Laurie, Alex Buckley, Muriel Craig, Jerry, and Grace were sitting.

"In a few minutes Alex will be talking with Regina about her memory of that night and the next morning," Laurie said. "Tomorrow evening when it gets dark, we will be filming the graduates in evening dresses against the background of the film of the party taken that evening. If you would like to come by and see that scene, you are welcome to come back."

It was at just that point that Robert Powell came

out to the patio. "I've been working in my office," he explained. "Anyone who runs a hedge fund cannot take his eyes off the market for even a minute. Ed, how are you? Are you here to protect us from each other?"

"I don't think that's necessary, Mr. Powell."

Even though he was smiling and seemed at ease, Penn could see the fatigue around Robert Powell's eyes and the overall weariness in his body as he sat down at the table and shook his head when Laurie offered him a sandwich from the platter Jane had placed there. Muriel, who had been complaining she had nothing to do, suddenly came alive.

"Rob, dear," she said, "you've worked enough today. Why don't you and I go over to the club for a round of golf? I used to be a pretty good golfer, you know. I'm sure I can rent clubs, and I put golf shoes in my tote bag, just in case I could persuade you."

Laurie expected to hear a flat refusal, but Powell smiled. "That's the best idea I've heard all day," he said. "But I'm so sorry to say I must take a rain check. I have a lot of work to do in my office." He paused, then looked at Laurie. "You don't have anything for me to do today, I gather?"

"No, Mr. Powell. Alex will be interviewing the girls one by one. And then Jane, if we have time today."

"How long will the interviews take?" Powell asked. "I expected them to be about ten minutes each."

"They'll be cut to that time," Laurie said. "But Alex is planning to speak with each of them for about an hour. Isn't that right, Alex?"

"Yes, it is."

"Mr. Rob, are you sure that you don't want to have a snack?" Jane asked. "You hardly touched your breakfast."

"Jane takes such good care of me," Powell told the others. "In fact, sometimes she's almost like a mother hen."

Not exactly a compliment, Laurie thought. She could see from the flush on Jane's face that she didn't think so, either.

"Familiarity breeds contempt," Muriel snapped, staring at Jane as Robert Powell pushed back his chair and went into the house.

Wordlessly, Jane turned away from the table and went to where the graduates and Rod were seated. They all declined more coffee, and seeing that, Laurie pushed back her chair. "If you didn't know it before, I guess you know it now. There's a lot of waiting around in this business. Alex will start by interviewing Claire. When she is finished she can go back to the hotel, and then the same for each of you. Figure about an hour apiece."

Chief Penn stood up. "Any sign of the paparazzi or anyone trying to get in here while you're filming," he told Laurie, "give me a call immediately." He handed her his card.

Rod said to Alison, "It's getting warm out here. I guess we're not invited to sit in the living room," he added sarcastically, "and the den is being used for filming. But I suppose we can sit in the breakfast room. The chairs look comfortable there."

Laurie stood up and said to Claire, "I do think you should have a little more makeup on. With your blond eyebrows and lashes you'll end up looking terribly washed out on camera. You really need a little touch-up." She looked toward the door of the makeup van. "They're ready for you now," she said. With a brief nod, she walked over to the door that led to the den and opened it.

Chief Penn signaled to his driver and walked over to his car. He happened to glance at Bruno, who was meticulously searching for any scrap of paper or matted grass that might be disrupting the serene beauty of the grounds. Penn barely caught a glimpse of Bruno's profile, but as he got into the car he realized that something in his subconscious was bothering him. A little voice was saying, *I should know this guy, but why?*

As Alex Buckley followed Laurie into the den, he had exactly the same thought about Bruno. *I should know that guy, but why?* Alex hesitated, then reached into his pocket for his phone and snapped a photo. He made a mental note to get the landscaper's name and forward it to his investigator.

And then, for the first time, the four graduates were alone, and Josh, who had been helping Jane serve coffee, saw his chance. "I have a present for the three of you," he said, "except Claire." He looked at Claire. "I tried to talk to you in the car, but you were having none of it." Josh looked at the other three graduates. "Here is a tape I think each one of you will find very interesting. You especially, Regina. Maybe you've mislaid something I found?"

He handed separate envelopes to Regina, Alison, and Nina, then said, "There is a cassette player in the drawer of the vanity in the restroom by the kitchen. Why don't we talk after the three of you have a chance to listen to the tapes?"

Then Josh picked up the coffee cups in front of him and said: "See you all later," in a confident voice, with just the slightest undertone of threat.

47

❖

Because his office was next to the den, where all the activity was taking place, Robert Powell chose to go back upstairs to the bedroom suite he had shared with Betsy for the nine years of their marriage. At his curt request Jane followed him with a fresh pot of coffee. Then, sensing his irritable mood, she closed the door to his bedroom so she could make up the room quickly and quietly. She skipped her usual vacuuming because she knew the sound of it would annoy him. Then she left by the bedroom door to go downstairs.

Robert was wondering once again whether he had made a drastic mistake by inviting these girls—women, he corrected himself sarcastically—to reenact what had happened twenty years ago. Had his doctor's prognosis been the reason for it? Or was it because of a perverse need to see them again, to toy with them as Betsy had toyed with them all those years ago? Had he absorbed so much of Betsy's personality that he no longer had anything left of his own, even twenty years later? Each graduate had a reason to kill Betsy, he knew that. It would be interesting to see if one of them broke down under Alex Buckley's questioning. He was sure Buckley was capable of detecting prepared answers.

Powell would bet that all the graduates had carefully practiced what they would say in their one-on-one interview with Buckley. He was sure they would start with their first impressions of what they saw when they ran into Betsy's room after hearing him shout.

It seemed like only yesterday that he had walked into her bedroom carrying the cup of coffee that she had always insisted be red-hot "to get the flavor through the coffee beans."

Rob looked down at the angry scars on his hands that had resulted from walking into Betsy's room and seeing the pillow covering her face. Betsy's long blond hair had spilled out from under it, her hands still clutching the pillow's edges. She had obviously been struggling to push the pillow away from her face.

He remembered shrieking her name and trying to keep the coffee cup from spilling before his knees buckled under him. He remembered Jane leaning over him and attempting some clumsy CPR while the girls stood around the bed like ghostly wraiths. The next thing he remembered was waking up in the hospital, conscious of nothing but the pain in his hands, and calling out for Betsy.

Robert Powell leaned back in his chair. It was time to go downstairs and make some business calls. But he hesitated for a moment as he stopped to reflect on what Claire would be telling Buckley.

He realized that what had been amusing to him was no longer amusing. All he wanted now was to have these women out of this house and to resume what little time was left of his quiet and pleasant life.

48

Alex looked at Claire Bonner across the table from him in the den. Claire had once again resisted Meg Miller's suggestion to touch up her lashes and eyebrows. Now, as Alex looked at her, he found it incongruous to compare her with the beautiful woman who had walked into this house yesterday.

It was easy to see what had made the difference. Claire's long lashes and well-shaped eyebrows were very pale, as was her complexion. She wore no lip coloring, and he could swear that she had washed the gold highlights out of her hair. I'll find out what she's up to, he thought and smiled encouragingly at her when Laurie said, "Action," and the camera's red light went on.

"I'm here in the home of Wall Street financier Robert Nicholas Powell," he began, "whose beautiful wife, Betsy Bonner Powell, was murdered twenty years ago following a Graduation Gala for Betsy's daughter, Claire, and Claire's three closest friends and fellow graduates. Claire Bonner is with me now. Claire, I know this has to be extraordinarily difficult for all of you to be here today. Why did *you* agree to come on the program?"

"Because the other girls and I, and to a lesser degree my stepfather and the housekeeper, have been under suspicion as 'persons of interest' in Betsy's death, which is the new way of saying it, for the last twenty years," Claire declared passionately. "Can you have any idea of what it's like to be in a supermarket and see your own picture on the cover of some trashy magazine with the question 'Was she jealous of her beautiful mother'?"

"No, I can't," Alex replied quietly.

"Or maybe there would be a picture of the four of us lined up, as if we had had mug shots taken of us by the police. That's why we're here today, to make the public realize how unfairly we four young women, who were traumatized beyond belief and bullied by the police, have been treated. That's why I'm here now, Mr. Buckley."

"And I assume that's why the other girls are here, too," Alex Buckley said. "Have you done much catching up with them?"

"We actually haven't had very much time to visit," Claire said. "I know it's because you people didn't want us to put our stories together. Well, let me tell you something: we have *not* boned up on each other's stories, and I think you will find that out. They'll be pretty much the same because we were together at the moment when everything was happening."

"Claire, before we discuss your mother's death, I'd like to go back in time a little. Why don't we start with your mother's meeting with Robert Powell? I understand you had only lived in Salem Ridge a short while. Is that right?"

"Yes, it is. I had graduated from grammar school in June, and my mother wanted to move up to Westchester County. Quite frankly, I know she wanted to meet a rich man. She found a rental in a two-family house, and I can assure you there aren't many two-family houses in Salem Ridge.

"I started my freshman year in high school that September, and that's when I became friends with Nina and Alison and Regina. My birthday is in October, and Mother splurged and took me to La Boehm in Bedford. Nina Craig and her mother were there. Nina spotted us, and asked us to come over and meet her mother. Of course we also met Robert Powell, who was at the table. I guess it was love at first sight for both of them, my mother and Robert. I do know that Nina's mother has never gotten over the fact that 'Betsy stole Rob from me when we were on the verge of becoming engaged,' as she put it."

"Your own father had abandoned you and your mother when you were only an infant. How did your mother manage to look after you and still work fulltime?"

"My grandmother was alive until I was three years

old." Tears began to shine in Claire's eyes as she mentioned her grandmother. "Then there was a series of babysitters, one after the other. If they failed to show up, Mother would bring me to the theatre and I'd sleep in an empty chair, or sometimes it would be in an empty dressing room if the play had a small cast. One way or the other we managed. But then Mother met Robert Powell, and of course everything changed."

"You and your mother had been very close, I gather? Were you ever jealous of the fact that Robert Powell came so suddenly into your life and claimed so much of your mother's time and attention?"

"I wanted her to be happy. He was obviously a very rich man. After the dinky little apartments we'd lived in all my life, it seemed like heaven to move into this beautiful house."

"*Seemed* like heaven?" Alex asked quickly.

"*Was* heaven," Claire corrected herself.

"That was quite a year for you, Claire, moving into a new area, starting high school, then your mother's wedding and moving into this house."

"It was all quite a change," Claire said with a faint smile. If you only knew, she thought. If you only knew!

"Claire, were you close to Robert Powell?"

Claire looked straight into Alex's eyes. "Right from the beginning," she said. Oh, I was close to him all right, she thought, remembering how she listened for the sound of her bedroom door opening.

Alex Buckley knew that behind Claire's smooth

answers there was a land mine of smoldering anger she was trying to conceal. It wasn't all sweetness and light in this house, he thought as he decided to change his questioning. "Claire, let's talk about the Gala. What kind of night was it? How many people were here? We have that information, of course, but I'd like to hear it from your perspective."

Alex had foreseen that Claire would begin answering him in carefully rehearsed sentences. "It was a perfect night," she said. "It was an absolutely balmy evening, about seventy-six degrees, I think. There was a band on the patio, and a dance floor. There were stations everywhere with all kinds of food. Near the pool a table was beautifully decorated. The centerpiece was a sheet cake with all of our names on it and the symbols of the four colleges we went to in their school colors."

"You chose to commute to Vassar, didn't you, Claire?"

Again Alex saw a look in Claire's eyes that he could not identify. What was it? Anger, disappointment, or both? He took a shot at what he surmised. "Claire, were you disappointed that you didn't go away to college as your other friends did?"

"Vassar is a wonderful college. I may have missed out on a part of the college experience by commuting instead of boarding, but my mother and I were so close that I was happy to stay home."

Claire's smile was more of a sneer, but then she recovered herself. "We all had a wonderful time at the party," she said. "Then, as you know, the other girls slept over. When everyone was gone we put on our pajamas and robes, went to the den, and drank wine. Lots of wine. We gossiped about the party, as girls do."

"Were your mother and Mr. Powell with you in the den?"

"Rob said good night to us right after the last guests left. My mother sat with us for a few minutes, but then she said, 'I want to get comfortable, the way you all are.' She went upstairs and came back down in her nightgown and robe."

"Did she stay long?"

For a moment there was a real smile on Claire's lips and in her eyes. "My mother wasn't a drunk, never think that, but she *did* love to have a couple of glasses of wine in the evening. She had about three glasses that night before she went upstairs. She hugged and kissed us good night, which is why we all had DNA from her hair on our pajamas or robes the next morning."

"The other girls were very fond of your mother, weren't they?"

"I think they were in awe of her."

Alex knew that what Claire didn't say was that each of the girls had a reason to hate Betsy Powell. Nina, because her mother tortured her about having introduced Robert to Betsy. Regina, because her father had lost all his money in one of Robert Powell's investments. Alison, because she had lost out on a scholarship that she should have won but Betsy Bonner directed elsewhere. Robert Powell had donated a load of money to Alison's college. That donation was not forgotten when the graduate scholarship was awarded to the daughter of a woman who chaired a club Betsy was desperate to join.

"After your mother said good night to all of you, did you see her again?"

"Do you mean did I see her again alive?" Claire did not wait for an answer. "My last memory of seeing my mother alive was when she turned and smiled and blew a kiss to all of us. Of course it's a vivid memory. She was a very beautiful woman. She always wore beautiful matching nightgowns and robes. That night she was wearing a pale-blue satin set, edged in ivory lace. Her hair was loose on her shoulders, and she seemed so happy about how successful the party had been. The next time I saw her, either Rob or Jane had taken the pillow off of her face. Her eyes were wide open and staring. One hand was still clutching the pillow. I know she must have been sleepy because of all of the wine she had drunk, but I always had the feeling she put up a fight."

Alex listened as Claire spoke in a voice that seemed to be suddenly without emotion. Her hands were now clasped together, and her face had turned even paler than it had been.

"How did you know that something was terribly wrong?" Alex asked quietly.

"I heard the most terrifying shriek coming from my mother's room. I later learned that it was Rob, who was bringing my mother her usual cup of morning coffee. I think all of us girls were in a heavy sleep—

we had talked and drunk until three A.M. We all got to the room at about the same time. Jane must have heard Robert's shout. She got to my mother's room first. She was on her knees bending over Robert, who had collapsed and was writhing in pain. I guess he must have rushed to grab the pillow away from my mother's face, and the hot coffee had spilled all over his hands. The pillow was to the side of my mother's head and had coffee stains on it."

Alex saw that Claire's expression suddenly turned cold. It was a startling difference from the way she had reacted to his questions about her grandmother.

"Then what happened, Claire?" he asked.

"I think it was Alison who picked up the phone and dialed 911. She shouted something like 'We need an ambulance and the police! Betsy Bonner Powell is dead! I think she's been murdered!'"

"What did you do while you waited for them?"

"I don't think it was more than three minutes later that both the ambulance and the police arrived. Then it was chaos. We were literally chased out of her room. I remember the police chief ordering us to go back to our bedrooms and change our clothes. He had the nerve to say that he could see what we were wearing and we shouldn't try to switch what we had slept in. Later we realized that those clothes would be tested for DNA as potential evidence."

"So you changed into jeans and T-shirts similar to the ones you were photographed in this morning?"

"Yes. When we had changed we were escorted downstairs here to the den and told to wait until the police questioned us. They wouldn't even allow us to go to the kitchen to make a cup of coffee."

"You're still very angry about that, aren't you, Claire?"

"Yes, I am," she said, her voice trembling with rage. "Think about it. We were all barely twenty-one. Looking back, I realize that even though we thought we were all grown up, having just graduated from college, in reality we were just frightened kids. The interrogation they put all of us through that day, and for weeks afterward, was a travesty of justice. They called us in to the police station over and over again. That's the reason that the press began to refer to us as 'suspects.'"

"Who do you think killed your mother, Claire?"

"There were three hundred people at that party. Some of them we can't identify from the photos and film we have of that night. People were going in and out of the house to use the bathrooms. Jane had put a rope across the landing at the bottom of the staircase, but anyone could have sneaked up the stairs. My mother was wearing her emeralds that night. Anyone could have picked out her bedroom and even hidden in one of those walk-in closets. I think someone waited until he thought she would be in a deep sleep, then picked up the emeralds from her dressing table. Who knows if she started stirring and he panicked and tried to put them back? One emerald earring was found on the floor. I believe she woke up. Whoever was in that room tried to keep her from calling for help the only way that was available to him."

"And that person, you believe, is your mother's murderer?"

"Yes, I do. And remember, we had left the patio door open. The four of us were smokers, and my step-father absolutely forbade smoking in the house."

"Is that why you resent the media coverage of your mother's death?"

"That is why I am telling you that none of us here—not Rob, nor Jane, nor Nina, Regina, or Ali-son—had a thing to do with my mother's death. And obviously neither did I." Claire's voice became shrill. "And neither did I!"

"Thank you, Claire, for sharing your memory of that terrible day when you lost the mother you loved so dearly."

Alex reached across the table to shake Claire's hand.

It was drenched in perspiration.

49

❖

On Tuesday morning, George Curtis got up at six thirty as was his custom and brushed Isabelle's forehead softly with his lips, trying not to wake her. He felt a desperate need to touch her. He had woken often during the night and put his arm around her. Then the guilty memory would flood his brain: *Betsy always wore satin nightgowns, too.* Inevitably his next thought was, Isabelle, I almost lost you. I almost lost the joyful life I have been living with you and our children for nearly twenty years.

That new life had begun the morning of the Gala when Isabelle told him that she was expecting twins. That incredible news was followed by Betsy demanding $25 million for her silence about their affair. I didn't mind paying her, George thought, but I knew it would be only the beginning of her threats to go to Isabelle.

These were the thoughts that were running

through his head as he showered, dressed, and went down to the kitchen to make a cup of coffee. He carried the cup out to the car, placed it in the holder, and was on his way to his office, the international headquarters of Curtis Foods, ten miles away in New Rochelle.

He loved his early morning hour-and-a-half alone time in the office. It was when he could concentrate on important mail and e-mails from his district managers all over the world. But today he could not concentrate. After going over the highly favorable earnings reports, his only reaction was that he could easily have found a way to pay Betsy and bury the payment without raising any suspicion.

But I couldn't have trusted her, was the refrain that ran through his head.

When the office began to fill up just before nine, he greeted his longtime assistant Amy Hewes with his usual cordiality and crisply began to go over some e-mails he wanted answered immediately. But he knew he was too distracted to concentrate. At eleven-thirty he called home. "Any plans for lunch?" he asked Isabelle when she answered.

"Not one," she said promptly. "Sharon called and asked me to meet her for golf, but I'm too lazy today. I'm stretched out on the patio. Louis is preparing gazpacho and a chicken salad. How does that sound?"

"Perfect. I'm on my way."

As he passed Amy's desk and told her he wouldn't be coming back this afternoon, she looked surprised. "Don't tell me that you, the sought-after speaker who always wows the audience, is nervous about being interviewed this afternoon?"

George tried to smile. "Maybe I am."

The short drive seemed interminably long to him. He was so impatient to see Isabelle that he left his car in the circular driveway, bounded up the steps, threw open the door, and rushed down the long hallway to the rear of the house. Before he opened the glass door to the patio he stopped and looked out. Isabelle was sitting in one of the padded chairs, her feet on a hassock, a book in her hands. Sixty years old on her last birthday, her hair was now completely silver. She wore it in a new shorter length and with bangs. The style framed her face perfectly, with her classic features that were the product of generations of fine breeding. Her ancestors had come over on the *Mayflower*. Her slender body was already tanned. She had kicked off her shoes, and her ankles were crossed.

For a long minute George Curtis studied the beautiful woman who had been his wife for thirty-five years. They had met at a dance given by the senior class at Harvard. Isabelle had attended it with friends from Wellesley College. The minute she walked into the room, I made a beeline for her, George thought. But the first time I met her parents, I know they were underwhelmed. They would have preferred that our family had made its money on Wall Street, not by selling hot dogs and hamburgers.

What would her mother and father have thought had they known I was having an affair with my best friend's wife? They'd have told Isabelle to get rid of me.

And if Isabelle had ever known, even though she was pregnant with our twins, she would have dropped me, too.

And still would, George thought grimly as he slid open the patio door. Hearing the sound, Isabelle looked up and smiled warmly. "Was it me or the menu that inspired you to join me for lunch?" she asked as she got up and kissed him warmly.

"It was you," George replied fervently, returning her kiss and putting his arms around her.

Louis, their chef, came out onto the patio carrying a tray with two iced teas.

"Good to have you home for lunch, Mr. Curtis," he said cheerfully.

Louis had been with them for twenty-two years. He had been working as a chef in a nearby restaurant when one evening as they were having dinner there, he came to the table. "I heard that you are looking for a new chef," he had said quietly.

"Yes, our current chef is retiring," George had verified.

"I would very much like to try out for the job," Louis said. "We serve mostly Italian food here, but I am a graduate of the Culinary Institute in Hyde Park, and I promise I can offer you a wide selection of menus."

And so he had, George thought, including preparing fresh baby food every day when the twins were born and letting them "help" him in the kitchen when they were little.

George sat in a chair near Isabelle, but as Louis

placed the glass next to him, he said, "Louis, will you put my tea on the table and bring me a Bloody Mary?"

Isabelle raised an eyebrow. "That's not like you, George. Are you nervous about the interview with Alex Buckley?"

He waited until the patio door closed behind Louis, then answered, "Uncomfortable rather than nervous. To me the whole idea of this program seems bizarre. I get the feeling that this is not about proving people innocent as it is proving that someone in the group was guilty of Betsy's death."

"Someone like *you*, George?"

George Curtis stared at his wife, his blood running cold. "What do you mean by that?"

"I overheard that interesting conversation you had with Betsy the night of the Gala. Even though you had pulled away from the crowd, I followed you. I was on the other side of those palms they had brought in for decoration. You didn't realize how much you had raised your voice."

George Curtis knew that the nightmare he had feared was happening. Was Isabelle going to tell him, now that the twins were raised, that she wanted a divorce? "Isabelle, I'm sorrier than you can possibly imagine," he said. "Please, please forgive me."

"Oh, I already have," Isabelle said promptly. "Did you think that I was too stupid to suspect you were having an affair with that slut? When I overheard the two of you, I decided I wasn't about to lose you. I realized we had grown apart, and I knew that some of it was my fault. I wasn't going to forgive you too easily, but I'm still glad I made that decision. You've been a wonderful husband and father, and I love you dearly."

"I was so terribly worried and guilty all these years," George Curtis said, his voice breaking.

"I know you were," Isabelle said crisply. "That was my way of punishing you. Oh, here's Louis with your Bloody Mary. I'll bet you're ready for it now."

My God, I thought I knew my wife! George Curtis exclaimed to himself as he reached for the glass Louis was putting in front of him.

"Louis, I think we're ready to have lunch now," Isabelle said as she took a sip of her iced tea.

When Louis went back to the kitchen, Isabelle said, "George, when you warned Betsy that if she ever told me about your affair with her you would kill her, I may not have been the *only* one who heard you. Like I said, you didn't realize how loud you were speaking. Then, after we came home and went to bed, I fell asleep in your arms. When I woke up at four A.M. you weren't in bed, and it was more than an hour before you returned. I just assumed that you were downstairs watching television. You always do, if you wake up and can't go back to sleep. When I heard Betsy had been smothered, I begged God that if you had killed her, you didn't leave any evidence that would lead to you. If anything comes up during the filming of this program, I'll swear that you never left our bed that night."

"Isabelle, you don't believe . . ."

"George, we live only a few blocks away from

them. You could have walked to their house in five minutes. You knew the layout. And frankly, I don't *care* if you killed her. I know we can afford it, but I see no reason why you should have paid twenty-five million dollars in blackmail to that tramp."

As George held her chair for her at the table, Isabelle said, "I love you so dearly, George, and the twins adore you. Don't say anything to spoil that. Now here comes Louis with the salad. I'll bet you're hungry, aren't you?"

50

"Okay, guys, that was great. Take a break now. Alison Schaefer is next. We'll start in half an hour," Laurie said briskly. Jerry, Grace, and the camera crew knew that was Laurie's way of saying, "Get lost." It was clear to them that she wanted to talk to Alex Buckley alone. As they filed out, they closed the door of the den without asking. Then Alex suggested, "Why don't I get a cup of coffee for both of us? I know you like yours black, no sugar."

"Sounds wonderful," Laurie admitted.

"I'll be right back," he said as he unfolded his long legs and stood up.

When he returned five minutes later, coffee cups in hand, Laurie was seated in the chair where Claire had been and was busy scribbling notes. "Thanks so much," she said as he placed the cups on the table between them. "Are they all out there? I mean, is Claire talking to them about her interview with you?"

"I don't know where Claire is, but there's some-thing funny going on with the rest of them," Alex Buckley replied. "Regina is white as a ghost, and Nina and her mother are obviously having an argu-ment on the patio. No surprise there. Alison and Rod are taking a walk near the pool. The way he has his arm around her, I think she's terribly upset. She's holding a handkerchief and dabbing her eyes."

Astonished, Laurie asked, "What could have brought all that on?"

"When you and I left them, Claire followed only a few minutes behind," Alex said, his brow furrowed. "We left the other three waiting for Josh to bring more coffee. I'm telling you, Laurie, something hap-pened that upset all of them. Maybe I can get it out of Alison when I interview her." His tone became crisp. "I know you want to talk to me about the interview with Claire."

"Yes, I do," Laurie said. "Why did you ask her so much about her relationship with Robert Powell?"

"Laurie, think about it. She and her mother had obviously been very tight for the first thirteen years of Claire's life. Then Robert Powell enters the picture. No matter how glamorous it may have been for her to move into this mansion, there is no doubt from everything I have read that Claire's mother and Pow-ell were virtually inseparable. And why didn't Claire go away to college as her friends did? Claire must have been home alone a lot of nights. From what I gathered, Betsy and Powell were out almost every night on the social scene. Why couldn't Claire board at Vassar? Didn't you hear and see the way Claire's expression changed when she talked about Powell? I'm telling you right now that something was going on there," Alex said vehemently.

Laurie stared at him, then nodded.

Alex smiled. "You caught it, too. I was sure you would. Whenever I'm preparing a case for trial, I have my investigators dig into the backgrounds of the people I'm defending as well as the ones who are on the witness stand testifying either for or against my client. One of the first things I learned was to dig below the obvious. If you ask me, Claire Bonner was not as heartsick at her mother's death as she claims to be."

"At first I was attributing her reaction to shock," Laurie admitted. "Then I felt the same way. She only talked about her anger over the way the police treated her and the other girls. Not one word about grieving for her mother." Laurie changed gears. "Now, before Alison Schaefer comes in, let me give you my first impressions of her."

Alex sipped his coffee as Laurie continued. "Rod Kimball and Alison Schaefer were married four months after the Gala, and yet she hadn't even invited him as her date that night. Was she rushing into a situation because of the way they were all grilled after Betsy's death? The only other thing that I can see was that she lost out on a scholarship. It was awarded to the girl whose marks were second to hers but who happened to be the daughter of Betsy's friend. Did the fact that Powell donated a ton of money to Alison's college influence the scholarship award? Yes, I think it was the kind of scholarship donated by an alumnus, and the dean chose the winner at his discretion."

Alex nodded. "You've done plenty of your own digging, I see."

"Yes, I have," Laurie agreed. "And I've wondered whether the fact that Rod had just signed a great contract with the Giants had anything to do with Alison suddenly marrying him. But if so, when he had that accident, she certainly stuck by him, didn't she? Apparently he had always had a crush on her, from way back when they were in kindergarten. At the time they were married, he had a brilliant future as a quarterback. Even if the attraction was the fame and fortune of pro football, there had to be more to her feelings than that. The last twenty years are proof of it."

"Or is it possible she was so upset about losing the scholarship that she smothered Betsy and confessed it to Rod? That would certainly have been his hold over her for all of these years," Alex suggested.

There was a knock on the den door, and the cameraman looked in. "Laurie, are you ready for us yet?"

Laurie and Alex looked at each other. It was Alex who answered. "You bet we are. Please ask Alison Schaefer to come in now."

51

Later that morning, Leo Farley stared at the ceiling as his doctor and longtime friend checked his heartbeat. "There's nothing the matter with me," Leo said, his tone icy.

"That's your opinion," Dr. James Morris replied mildly, "but believe me, this is where you're going to stay until I discharge you. And before you ask me why again, let me explain again. You were still having heart fibrillations yesterday evening. If you don't want to have a heart attack, you'll stay put."

"All right, all right," Leo said with angry resignation. "But Jim, you don't get it. I don't want Laurie to know I'm here, and I can tell she's already guessed. She never calls me on the way to work, but she did today. She was so persistent asking me where I was last night . . . I can't have her worrying about me while she's doing this program."

"Do you want me to phone Laurie now and reassure her?" Dr. Morris asked.

"I know Laurie. If you call, it would upset her even more."

"When do you usually talk to her?"

"After she gets home from the studio. I got away with it last night, but tonight she'll expect me to go out and at least grab a hamburger with her. I don't know what my excuse will be," Leo Farley said, his voice somber but no longer angry.

"Look, Leo, I can tell you this. You had two episodes of fibrillation yesterday. If you don't have any tonight, I will discharge you tomorrow," Dr. Morris promised. "And don't forget, I still know how to reassure my patients' relatives about their health. If you let me tell Laurie that, barring any more fibrillations, I'm discharging you tomorrow morning, I think that would be the best way to go. So think about it. She can always stop in here tonight and see you. Doesn't Timmy call her between seven and eight?"

"Yes. She has him call at quarter to eight so she's sure to be free to talk."

"Then why not have her here in time to take the call, and the two of you can talk to him together? From what you tell me, he can only make one phone call every evening."

Leo Farley's face cleared. "As usual, you have a good idea, Jim."

Dr. Morris knew of Leo Farley's desperate worry about the threat to his daughter and grandson. And it won't be over until that Blue Eyes guy is rotting in prison, he thought.

He touched Leo's shoulder, but managed to close his lips before he uttered the two most useless words in the English language, "Don't worry."

52

After Josh handed the three of them the tapes, Alison was the first to go into the bathroom, take the cassette player from the vanity drawer, insert the tape, and listen to it. Aghast, she heard her conversation with Rod about her sleepwalking into Betsy's room. Near hysteria, she grabbed the tape and rushed outside. Rod had seen her from the window and hurried as fast as possible to join her.

Now, his crutches beside him, he sat on the bench near the pool with his arm around her, their backs to the production crew outside. She had managed to stop crying, but her lips were still trembling.

"Don't you see, Rod?" Alison said. "That's the reason Powell had Josh pick all of us up at the airport in that fancy Bentley at two-hour intervals, except for Claire, who arrived the night before. Powell wouldn't have done that except for one reason. The Bentley was bugged. Rod, don't you remember we talked about my sleepwalking into Betsy's bedroom?"

"Shh," Rod cautioned, then looked around. There was no one within hearing distance. My God, I'm getting paranoid around this place, he thought.

He tightened his arm around Alison's shoulder. "Alie, if they bring it up, say of course you were disappointed about the scholarship, but then it didn't matter. You'd had a secret crush on me from the time we were in kindergarten." He paused, then thought ruefully, at least that part was true for me.

"And you asked me to marry you, even though you believed I had been angry enough to kill Betsy Powell," Alison said flatly. "You can't deny that for all these years you have believed I might have killed her."

"I know how much you hated her, but I never really believed that you could kill her."

"I did hate her. I've tried to get over it, but I can't. I still hate her. It was so unfair," Alison said passionately. "Powell donated a ton of money to Waverly because Betsy was desperate to get into that fancy club. When the dean gave the scholarship to Betsy's friend's daughter, don't you think I had a good reason to kill her? Did I mention that my fellow student flunked out her second year?"

"I think you may have mentioned it once or twice," Rod said quietly.

"Rod, when everything you ever worked for and prayed for and dreamed about falls apart . . . I was half out of the chair to accept that award when the dean announced her name. You can't imagine it!"

Then she looked at him, seeing the lines of pain on his handsome face, the crutches next to him. "Oh, Rod, how stupid of me to say that, to you of all people."

"It's all right, Alie."

No it isn't, she thought. It isn't all right at all.

"Alison, they're ready for you."

It was Laurie's assistant Jerry who was approaching them.

"Rod, I'm frightened I'm going to fall apart," Alison whispered frantically as she stood up and bent to brush a kiss on his forehead.

"No, you're not," Rod said firmly as he looked up at the woman he loved so dearly. Her light-brown eyes, the most prominent features in her thin face, were ablaze. The tears had left her eyelids slightly swollen, but he knew the makeup artist would repair that.

He watched Alison as she walked to the house. In twenty years, he had not seen her so emotional. And he knew why—because she had a second chance at the career she wanted so desperately, the one that had been stolen from her.

A random thought hit him. Alie had let her hair grow longer, and now it was brushing her shoulders. He liked it that way. The other day she had said she was going to have it cut soon. He regretted that, but would never dream of saying so. There were so many things he had not told her over the past twenty years . . .

If she got through this program and received the money, Rod couldn't help but worry, would it be her ticket to freedom—from him?

53

Nina was the second one who listened to her cassette. When she came back to the table her expression was almost triumphant. "This is more for you than it is for me," she told her mother. "Why don't you go in there and dwell on every word? And when you do, I don't think you'll be sobbing so much to Rob Powell that Betsy was your closest and dearest friend."

"What are you talking about?" Muriel snapped as she stood up and pushed back her chair.

"The cassette player is in the center drawer of the vanity in the hall bathroom," Nina said. "You should be able to find it."

The contented expression Muriel had been wearing turned into one of uncertainty and worry. Without answering her daughter, she hurried to the hallway. A few minutes later the slamming of the bathroom door signaled her imminent return.

When she came out her face was set in hard angry lines. Her head jerked in Nina's direction. "Come outside," she said.

"Well? What do you want?" Nina demanded as soon as the door to the patio closed behind them.

"What do I want?" Muriel hissed. "What do I want? Are you crazy? Did you listen to that tape? It makes me sound terrible. And Rob asked me to have dinner tonight. Everything is going so well, the way it was before . . ."

"Before I ruined everything for you by introducing Rob Powell to Betsy when you were practically engaged to him," Nina finished for her.

Muriel's expression became hard and calculating. "Do you think Rob has heard those tapes?"

"I don't know. I would guess he has, but that's just a guess. The chauffeur may be blackmailing us as his own little game and not telling Rob."

"Then give him the fifty thousand dollars."

Nina stared at her mother. "You have got to be joking! Rob Powell is making a fool out of you with this sudden attention. If he'd wanted you, why didn't he call you twenty years ago when Betsy died?"

"Pay that chauffeur," Muriel said flatly. "Otherwise I will tell Rob and the police that you confessed to me you killed Betsy to give me another chance at Rob. I'll say that you thought I'd be very generous to you when I became Mrs. Robert Nicholas Powell."

"You would do that?" Nina asked, white-lipped.

"Why not? It's true, isn't it?" Muriel sneered. "And

don't forget that Rob's million-dollar reward for information leading to the arrest and conviction of Betsy's murderer can always be my consolation prize if you're right about his interest in me *not* being genuine. He posted that reward twenty years ago and it's never been withdrawn."

54

After she'd seen Alison rush outside and Muriel ordered Nina to go with her to the patio, Regina knew she had to listen to her own tape.

On the way to hear it, she thought, Josh must be the one to have that letter. The cassette player was on top of the vanity. She inserted the tape, then numb with fear, pressed the button. The sound of her conversation with her son, Zach, was crystal clear, even though he was calling from England.

It's as bad as it can get, Regina thought wildly. Now what happens if I don't admit that I saved Daddy's suicide note? Josh can produce it at any time. Then I could be arrested for lying to the cops when they questioned me for hours on end. He'd have both the tape and the letter to show as evidence.

Knowing she had no choice but to pay Josh whatever he was demanding, she went back to the table and pushed away her coffee, which was cold now.

Sour-faced as always, Jane promptly appeared with a fresh pot of coffee and a new cup. Regina watched as the steaming cup of coffee replaced the one she had ignored.

As Regina began to sip, the familiar nightmare replayed itself in her head. Riding her bike in the driveway of the beautiful home with the priceless view of Long Island that she had lived in for fifteen years. Tapping the switch that raised the garage door. Seeing her father's body as it swayed in the breeze that rushed in from the Sound. His jaw had slackened, his eyes were staring, his tongue was protruding. A paper was pinned to his jacket. One hand was clenched around the rope. At the last moment had he changed his mind about dying?

Regina remembered how she had felt numb and emotionless, how she had reached up for the note, unpinned it as his body moved under her touch, read it, and, shocked, stuffed it in her pocket.

In it, her father had written that he had been having an affair with Betsy and bitterly regretted it.

Betsy had told him that the hedge fund Rob had begun was about to explode in value and to invest everything he could in it. Even then, at age fifteen, Regina was sure Betsy was doing that at Powell's direction.

I couldn't let my mother see that note, Regina thought now. It would have broken her heart, and I knew her heart would be broken enough by Daddy's death. And my mother *despised* Betsy Powell. She knew what a phony she was.

Now *someone* had that note. It almost had to be Josh, who was hanging around all day helping Jane. What can I do? she asked herself. What can I do?

At that moment Josh came into the room, a tray in his hands, to clear the table. He looked around to be sure they were alone.

"When can we talk, Regina?" he asked. "And I must tell you, you should have taken your son's advice to burn your father's suicide note. I've been thinking it over. No one has a stronger motive for killing Betsy Powell than you do. Don't you agree? And don't you think that the quarter of a million dollars you're getting from Mr. Rob is little enough to assure that no one will ever see the note or hear the tape?"

She could not reply. Her face was frozen in a look of horror and self-reproach, and her eyes looked beyond Josh to something else—her father's neatly dressed body, swaying from the rope around his neck.

55

As if by instinct, Claire raced upstairs to her old bedroom after her interview with Alex Buckley.

She knew it had not gone well. She had rehearsed her answers to the questions about the Gala, from being in the den together after the party ended to rushing into her mother's bedroom early the next morning.

It had been easy enough to re-create that terrible moment: Rob on the floor writhing in pain, the coffee splattered on his hands, his skin already raised in angry blisters. Jane shrieking "Betsy, Betsy," and holding the pillow that had smothered the life from her mother. The hair that had looked so glamorous when her mother had said good night to them was brassy in the early morning light, the radiant complexion now gray and mottled.

And I was *glad*, Claire thought. I was frightened, but I was glad.

All I could think of was that now I was free—now I could leave this house.

And I did the day of the funeral. I moved in with Regina and her mother in that tiny apartment. I slept on the couch in the living room.

There were pictures of Regina's father all over the place. Her mother was sweet and kind to me, even though they had lost everything they had because he had invested in Robert Powell's hedge fund.

Claire remembered hearing Betsy and Powell joking that Eric, Regina's father, was so gullible. *"Now remember, Betsy, I don't like you doing this, but it's necessary. It's either him or us."*

And her mother's answer: *"Better he should go broke than us,"* and laughing.

The nights I lay awake on that couch thinking that if it weren't for my mother and stepfather, he would still be alive and they would still be living in that lovely house on the Sound.

And what about Alison? She worked so hard for that scholarship and lost it just so my mother could get into some club.

Claire shook her head. She had been standing at the window looking out over the long backyard. Even with the vans from the studio discreetly parked on the left side of the property, and Alison and Rod sitting on the bench near the pool, the scene seemed as still as a painted landscape.

But then she saw movement. The door of the pool house opened, and the swarthy figure of the man who had been puttering around the garden these last few days exited.

His hulking presence broke the sense of stillness, and sent a shiver through Claire. Then she heard the click of her bedroom door opening.

Robert Powell stood there, smiling. "Anything I can do for you, Claire?" he asked.

56

Chief Ed Penn did not sleep well on Monday night. The sense of urgency that Leo Farley had imparted to him made whatever sleep he did manage to get troubled and fretful. And he had strange dreams. *Someone was in danger. He didn't know who. He was in a big empty house and, with his pistol in hand, he was searching through it. He could hear footsteps, but he could not tell where they were coming from.*

At 4 A.M., Ed Penn woke up from that dream and did not go back to sleep.

He understood Leo's concern that it was potentially dangerous to have those six people together again after twenty years. Penn had no doubt that one of those six—Powell, his housekeeper, Betsy's daughter, or one of her three friends—had murdered Betsy Powell.

Sure, the door from the den to the patio was unlocked. So what? Sure, maybe a stranger mingled with the crowd.

But maybe not.

The thing he had noticed when he arrived that morning was that among those four girls, including the daughter, he had not sensed one bit of genuine grief at Betsy Powell's passing.

And the housekeeper had kept begging to be allowed to go to the hospital to see "Mr. Rob."

Then she realized how that looked and clamped her mouth shut, Penn thought.

Powell? Few men would deliberately scar themselves with third-degree burns on their hands. Spilling coffee may have been his cover, but it's not clear what his motive would have been.

The housekeeper? Entirely possible. Interesting that the four girls had all agreed that she was screaming "Betsy, Betsy!" and holding the pillow in her hand.

Not that anyone's first instinct wouldn't be to rip the pillow off Betsy Powell's face, but Jane shrieking "Betsy, Betsy!" was another matter. Ed Penn had learned that when Betsy became Mrs. Robert Nicholas Powell and hired her friend Jane as a housekeeper, she instructed Jane to call her "Mrs. Powell."

Had Jane been burning with resentment for the nine years she had spent reduced from friend to servant?

That landscaper guy? He didn't have a record. Maybe it was just that stupid name that made him stand out. What mother with a brain in her head would give her kid the name Bruno when his last name was Hoffa and the Lindbergh case was still front page news?

Well, I guess it's better than some of the handles people are sticking their kids with these days, Ed decided.

There was no more use lying in bed. The police chief of Salem Ridge might as well get on the job. Ed thought, I'll take a ride over to Powell's place around noon and probably catch all of them at lunch.

He sat up. Then, from the other side of the bed, he heard his wife say, "Ed, will you *please* make up your mind? Either get up now or go back to sleep. The way you've been bouncing around is driving me crazy."

"Sorry, Liz," he mumbled.

As he got out of bed, Ed Penn realized that he was torn between two wishes. One, that somehow one of them would trip and reveal himself or herself as Betsy Powell's killer. The other, equally ardent, was that the filming would be wrapped up tomorrow as planned and they would all go home. The unsolved crime had been a thorn in Ed Penn's side for twenty years.

The Powell place is a tinderbox, he thought, and I can only watch it burst into flames.

When he returned to headquarters in the early afternoon, after his visit to the Powell home, his impressions had not changed.

57

Laurie decided that she had to talk to her father again. The night prior he had looked so terribly tired, and his usually ruddy face had been pale.

When she called him on her way to work, he said he was just stepping into the shower, and that he was fine.

He's *not* fine, she thought.

Now she got up and moved back to the chair behind the camera. "I'm just going to make a quick call to my father before Alison gets here," she explained to Alex.

"Of course," he said amiably.

But when she dialed the number and waited, he could sense her mounting nervousness.

"He's not answering," she said.

"Leave him a message," Alex suggested.

"No, you don't understand. My father would take a call from me if he was kissing the pope's hand!"

"What do you think he might be doing?" Alex asked.

"Maybe he's heard something about Blue Eyes and doesn't want to tell me," Laurie said, her voice trembling. "Or getting heart fibrillations again."

Alex Buckley looked compassionately at the young woman who had suddenly lost all her professional veneer of authority. Until now he had been surprised that, with her husband's murder unsolved and the threat hanging over her son and herself, she had still been able to do this program on an unsolved murder, but now he could see the degree to which she was acutely dependent on her father.

He had looked up the accounts of Greg Moran's murder. The picture of the thirty-one-year-old widow with her father's arm guiding her from the church behind her husband's casket flashed in his mind.

He knew the father had resigned abruptly from the police force to watch over his grandson.

If anything happened to Leo Farley now, any protection Laurie felt from Blue Eyes would be destroyed.

"Laurie, who is your father's doctor?"

"His cardiologist's name is Dr. James Morris. He's been my father's friend for the last forty years."

"Then phone and ask him if your father has been seeing him."

"That's a good idea."

There was a tap on the door. Alex sprang to his feet. When Grace looked in, the question she had been about to ask—"Ready for us?"—died on her lips. She saw the troubled look on Laurie's face as she held the phone to her ear and heard Alex's "Give her a minute," then closed the door.

58

"You're right, Laurie was terribly upset when I told her you were in the hospital," Dr. Morris told Leo Farley. "But I managed to calm her down. She's coming to see you straight from the filming, and as I suggested, the two of you can take Timmy's call together."

"It's a relief to know I don't have to try to figure out how to lie to her," Leo Farley said. "Did you tell her that I'm getting out of here tomorrow?"

"I told her that, barring any more fibrillations, I'll discharge you in the morning. I also told her that in forty years of practicing medicine, you're the crankiest patient I have ever had. I promise you that's what reassured her, Leo."

Leo Farley laughed a relieved laugh. "Okay, I believe that. But I'm only cranky because I feel helpless with all of these damn monitors pinning me to this bed."

Dr. James Morris took care not to let sympathy

manifest itself in his voice. "Let's both hope that you don't get any more fibrillations, Leo. And I suggest that if you can force yourself to stay calm and maybe watch some game shows on television, you will be on your way home tomorrow morning."

BRUNO LISTENED WITH GLEE. HACKING INTO Leo's phone had been a brilliant idea. Leo had already called the head of the camp and told him that he was in the hospital. And now Bruno knew that both Laurie and her father would be on the phone with Timmy tonight.

If Leo and Laurie speak to Timmy around eight o'clock tonight, they'll be reassured and not expect to speak to him again until tomorrow night, Bruno thought.

I'll put on my police uniform and get up to the camp at ten o'clock, Bruno thought. I'll tell whoever is in charge up there that the kid's grandfather has taken a turn for the worse. If they call Mount Sinai, they'll confirm that he's a patient, but won't say anything about his condition.

It will work. Bruno was so sure of it that he began to make preparations for his little guest. In the utility room of the pool house he laid out blankets and a pillow. It would be far too dangerous to put Timmy in the bedroom in the pool house. He would have to tie him up and put a loose gag on him. He knew that it was necessary to follow the routine and have Perfect Estates pick him up in the landscaping truck and drop him off again tomorrow morning. He would bring in some Cheerios and orange juice for Timmy. He always brought his lunch in a grocery bag, so having one would not seem unusual.

The production crew had left copies of the schedule all over the place. He knew that tomorrow Powell would do the last individual interview and then everyone would be photographed at the breakfast table, as they had been for the opening segment.

That's when Timmy and I make our entrance, he thought. I'm holding his hand and have a gun to his head. I call Laurie to come out or I shoot him. Any good mother would come running out to save her little boy.

He laughed, a deep rumbling sound, then opened the door of the pool house. The graduate with the husband on crutches was sitting on the bench near the pool.

Bruno began to studiously examine the plantings around the pool house for any sign of imperfection.

Tomorrow they'll be stained with blood, he thought gleefully. Mother and son. How appropriate that they'll die together, even if I don't get away.

59

"I was right," Laurie whispered as she turned off her phone. "Dr. Morris said that they're doing an angiogram on Dad right now, that it's just a precaution. But can I *believe* that?"

"Laurie, what exactly did the doctor say?" Alex asked.

"That Dad had heart fibrillations last night." In a halting voice Laurie explained what the doctor had told her. "I know the reason for the fibrillations. Dad was afraid of my doing this program," she said. "He thinks that one of these six people is a murderer, and could explode under pressure."

He may be right, Alex thought. "Look, Laurie," he said, "when you're finished here tonight, let me take you straight to the hospital. You don't have to wait for the company van. Let Jerry and Grace wrap up here."

Then he added impulsively, "I'll wait downstairs at

the hospital until you have your visit, then we'll get something to eat, unless you have other plans."

"My plan for tonight was to have a hamburger with Dad. As ex-cop number one, he'll want to know every detail of what went on today."

"Then give him your report in the hospital and have a hamburger with me afterward," Alex said firmly.

Laurie hesitated. Given the circumstances, she could not picture going out alone to a restaurant. *Alex Buckley is a reassuring presence,* she thought. *And besides, I can talk to him about the interviews we'll be doing.*

"Thanks, I'll take you up on that." She smiled faintly, then, as Alex watched, she called, "Jerry, will you please tell the crew and Alison Schaefer to come in?" Her voice was crisp and authoritative again.

60

A grim-faced Regina went looking for Josh Damiano. She found him vacuuming the huge living room. She remembered how Betsy had grandly referred to it as "the salon." *"Until the time she married Richard Powell, the only salon she ever walked into was a beauty salon."* That's what Mother used to say about Betsy, Regina remembered.

Josh looked up and, when he saw her, turned off the vacuum. "I knew you'd be looking for me, Regina," he said with a cheerful smile.

Regina had turned on her iPhone and was recording every word they exchanged. "You have different jobs, I see, Josh. Chauffeur-housemaid-blackmailer. Obviously there is no limit to your talents."

The smile vanished from Damiano's face. "Be careful, Regina," he said evenly. "The only reason I'm helping in the house is because Mr. Powell canceled the usual maintenance service until Thursday, when everyone has gone."

"The housekeeper label isn't one you like, is it, Josh?" Regina asked. "How about embezzler? Are you sensitive about being called that?"

Josh Damiano did not blink. "I prefer to think that I am defending you from being accused of murdering Betsy Powell. Your father's suicide note gives you the greatest motive to kill her, and remember, you lied to the cops over and over again that you had not found a suicide note on or near your father's body."

"I did, didn't I?" Regina agreed. "On the other hand, I also did Robert Powell a great favor by not revealing that. Have you considered that? The note details how he let his wife have an affair with my father so she could feed him an inside tip about Powell's hedge fund. The result was that my father lost his entire fortune, and by doing so, he bailed the Powells out."

"So what?" Damiano asked.

"So I lied to my son in the conversation you taped in the car. I have another copy of my father's note. Now I'm giving you an alternative: give me back the original and we call it quits. Otherwise I take the copy and my recording of this conversation today to Police Chief Penn, and *you* land behind bars. I *assume* you taped everyone else. I'll bet they'll all produce those tapes, if pressed hard enough."

"You're joking."

"No, I'm not. I was fifteen years old when I found

that note. As it was, my father's suicide was the start of my mother's slow decline. She would have gone quicker if she had known he was having an affair with Betsy as well."

Josh Damiano attempted a laugh. "All the more reason you jumped at the chance to spend your first overnight in this house, to get revenge on Betsy."

"Except that Betsy Powell wasn't worth sacrificing the rest of my life in prison. I'm a bit claustrophobic. I hope you're not."

Without waiting for a reply she left the room. Once she was in the hallway, she began to tremble violently.

Would it work? It was her only hope. She went up to the bedroom where she would spend the night, locked the door, and checked her phone.

The battery was dead.

61

Alison went into the den, outwardly calm but inwardly frantic with worry.

I was in Betsy's room that night, was the uppermost thought in her mind.

She tried to remember Rod's reassurances, but, oddly, all she could think of was that she had told him he couldn't know what it was like to want something so badly and lose it.

He couldn't? she asked herself.

She remembered the blazing headlines when he was signed by the Giants. The speculation about his brilliant future.

All the time she had spent studying, he had spent practicing football.

From kindergarten on, Rod had always been there for her.

But I was planning to marry a scientist, she

thought. We'd be the new Dr. and Madame Curie. "Dr. and Dr." Curie, she corrected herself.

The arrogance of me. And Rod accepted it. He proposed to me and I accepted because of his promise to send me to medical school.

While he was so sick, I did manage to become a pharmacist, but I couldn't leave him. Underneath, I've always begrudged him the fact that I felt obligated to stay.

And even now, I'm thinking that if I had come here alone, I wouldn't have been talking in the car. No recording would *exist*.

"Come right in, Alison," Laurie Moran invited.

Alex Buckley stood up.

My God, he's tall, Alison thought as she took the seat across the table from him. Her body felt so rigid that she worried some part of her would break like glass if she moved too quickly.

"Alison, thank you so much for being with us on this program," Alex began. "It's been twenty years since the Graduation Gala and Betsy's Powell's death. Why did you agree to be on this program?"

The question was friendly. Rod had warned her against letting her guard down. Alison chose her words carefully now. "Do you know, or can you imagine, what it's like to be under suspicion of killing someone for *twenty years*?"

"No, I don't, and I couldn't even imagine it. As I'm a criminal defense lawyer, I have seen persons of interest live with an ax swinging over their head until a jury declared them not guilty."

"Until a jury declared them not guilty," Alison repeated, and he could hear the bitterness in her voice. "But don't you see? That's the problem. No one has formally accused any one of us, and so we are *all* treated as if we were guilty."

"You *still* feel that way?"

"How could I not? This last year alone there were two major articles in syndicated newspapers about the case. I can always tell when a new one comes out. Someone comes into the pharmacy and buys something insignificant like toothpaste and looks at me as though I were a bug under a microscope."

"Alison, that's an interesting comparison. Have you been feeling like a bug under a microscope all these years? You had hoped to earn a medical degree, didn't you?"

Be careful, Alison warned herself. "Yes, I did."

"You had every expectation of being awarded a scholarship, isn't that true?"

"I was in contention," Alison said evenly. "I came in second. It happens."

"Alison, I've done some research. Isn't it a fact that just before your graduation, Robert Powell pledged some ten million dollars to your college for a new dormitory to be named 'The Robert and Betsy Powell House'?"

"I know he did."

"Is it true that the recipient of the scholarship was the daughter of a friend of Betsy Powell's?"

Alison, you're bitter. You can't let the bitterness show.

It was as though Rod were shouting in her ear.

"Of course I was disappointed. I earned that scholarship and everyone knew it. Throwing it to Vivian Fields was Betsy's way of getting into the club Vivian's mother ran.

"But you see, all regret stopped right there. Rod had just signed a big contract with the Giants, and the first thing he did was to propose to me. We were engaged, and his wedding present to me was going to be sending me to medical school."

"Then why didn't you invite Rod to the Gala, if you were engaged to him?"

Alison attempted a smile. "Actually, it was just prior to our engagement. Rod thought I was very foolish to go to the Gala after what Betsy pulled on me."

It sounds all right, she thought. I didn't invite him because I wasn't in love with him. But then when he signed with the Giants and promised to send me to school, I agreed to marry him . . . She fought to keep control of herself.

Alex Buckley's eyes bored into her. "Alison, I would like you to close your eyes and visualize the moment you walked into Betsy's room after you heard Jane screaming."

His tone was almost hypnotic. Obediently, Alison closed her eyes.

She was in Betsy's room. She stepped on the earring, and that startled her. She heard a door open and slipped into the closet behind her. She saw someone come in and take the other pillow from Betsy's bed. Then that shadowy figure leaned over Betsy.

Through a crack in the door she watched as Betsy's body twisted and turned as the pillow suffocated her. Her muted groans were quickly stifled.

Then the figure slipped away. Was I dreaming, Alison asked herself, or did I really see a face?

She didn't know. Her eyes snapped open.

Alex Buckley saw the startled look on her face. "What is it, Alison?" he asked quickly. "You look frightened."

Alison burst out: "I can't stand this anymore! I absolutely can't stand it. I don't care what people think about me. Let them wonder if I killed Betsy. I did *not*, but I will tell you this: when I ran into that room and saw she was dead, I was *glad*! And so were the others. Betsy Powell was evil and vain and a whore, and I hope she's rotting in hell."

62

Jane was next. She was not a heavy woman, but her broad shoulders and straight carriage gave her a formidable appearance. Her constant uniform of black dress and crisp white apron seems almost a caricature, Alex thought. Except for during formal dinners, none of his friends had their help dressed like that.

She sat in the chair vacated by Alison. "Ms. Novak," Alex began. "You and Betsy Powell worked together in the theatre?"

Jane smiled thinly. "That sounds very glamorous. I cleaned the dressing rooms and mended the costumes. Betsy was an usher, and when a play closed, we would both be transferred to another theatre."

"Then you were good friends."

"Good friends? What does that mean? We worked together. I like to cook. I'd ask her and Claire to dinner some Sundays. I was sure everything they ate was takeout. Betsy was no cook. And Claire was such a sweet child."

"Were you surprised when Betsy moved to Salem Ridge?"

"Betsy wanted to marry money. She decided living in a wealthy community was her best chance. Turns out she was right."

"She was thirty-two when she married Robert Powell. Wasn't there anyone before that?"

"Oh, Betsy dated, but no one had enough money for her." Jane smirked. "You should have heard what she said about some of them."

"Was there anyone who was especially close to her?" Alex asked. "Someone who might have been jealous when she married?"

Jane shrugged. "I wouldn't say so. They came and they went."

"Were you upset when she asked you to call her 'Mrs. Powell'?"

"Was I upset? Of course not. Mr. Powell is a very formal man. I have a beautiful apartment of my own here. A cleaning service comes in twice a week, so I do no heavy work. I love to cook, and Mr. Powell loves gourmet food. Why would I be upset? I came from a little village in Hungary. We had only the barest modern conveniences—running water, sometimes electricity."

"I can see why you have been very content here. But I understand that when you rushed into Betsy Powell's room that morning, you screamed 'Betsy, Betsy!'"

"Yes, I did. I was so shocked, I didn't know what I was doing or saying."

"Jane, do you have any theory about who killed Betsy Powell?"

"Absolutely," Jane said firmly, "and in a way I blame myself for her death."

"Why is that, Jane?"

"It is because I should have known those young women would have been in and out, smoking. I should have stayed up and made sure the door was locked after they went to bed."

"Then you think it was a stranger who came in?"

"Either through the unlocked door or else during the party. Betsy had two walk-in closets. Someone could have hidden in one of them. She was wearing a fortune in emeralds, and don't forget, one of the earrings was on the floor."

Behind the camera, watching and listening, Laurie found herself wondering whether Jane was right. Claire had suggested the same thing. And from what she could see, it was entirely possible that someone might have slipped upstairs during the party.

Jane was telling Alex that she had put a velvet rope across both the main and back staircases of the first floor. "There are four powder rooms on the main floor," she concluded. "There would be no need for anyone to go upstairs, unless he or she was planning to steal Betsy's jewelry."

It's as if they all put their heads together and decided on that story, Laurie thought.

Alex was saying, "Thank you for talking to us,

Ms. Novak. I know how difficult it is to relive that terrible night."

"No, you don't," Jane contradicted him, her voice even and sad. "To know how beautiful Betsy looked that night, then to see her face covered by that pillow and know she was dead, and to hear Mr. Powell moaning in pain . . . You don't and can't understand how hard it is to relive it, Mr. Buckley. You just can't."

63

❧

Nina kept a frosty distance from her mother for the rest of the morning. When Alison went in for her interview with Alex Buckley, she joined Rod on the bench near the pool.

"Mind if I sit with you for a while?" she asked.

Rod looked startled, but then attempted a smile and said, "Of course not."

"Are you and Alison sorry you got into this situation?" Nina asked as she sat next to him.

At Rod's surprised look, she said, "Look, I got a tape, too, and so did Regina. I don't know about Claire.

"I could see that Alison was terribly upset when she played hers. So was Regina. Do you think that Josh Damiano made those tapes for himself, or do you think Rob Powell ordered him to make them?"

"I don't know," Rod said carefully.

"Neither do I. But I have to take the chance that

it's Damiano's game and pay the fifty thousand dollars he's demanding. I think you should, too. I don't know what Damiano overheard you say, but that police chief is dying to solve Betsy's murder, and if he has something to run with, I'll bet he'll do it."

"You may be right," Rod said, his tone noncommittal. "But what could he possibly have on you that would make you a suspect? Certainly not the fact that your mother dated Rob Powell before he married Betsy?"

"It isn't that," Nina said, her voice friendly. "My mother is threatening to say I confessed to her that I murdered Betsy unless I pay the fifty thousand dollars to Josh."

Rod didn't think he could be any more surprised than he already had been, but now his voice was incredulous. "She's *got* to be bluffing."

"Oh, but she isn't," Nina said. "Now if Robert Powell hears that tape on which she's saying how much she hated Betsy, any chance she has with him—which I believe is nonexistent, by the way—will be over. But if this is only Josh Damiano's game, who knows? That's why she wants me to pay the fifty thousand dollars he's demanding—or else. But you see, I know Alison has much more to worry about than my mother being sure I broke up her big romance. I was very nice when the police were questioning all of us twenty years ago." She paused and looked straight into his eyes. "I didn't tell anyone that Betsy was absolutely *cruel* to Alison that night. She was gushing on and on about how proud Selma Fields was that her daughter, Vivian, had won the scholarship. She made sure to mention that Selma was throwing a fabulous party for Vivian, and then the whole family was sailing on their yacht to the Riviera. Alison was fighting back tears. When Betsy floated away, Alison said to me, 'I am going to *kill* that witch.'

"Now isn't that information worth your paying Josh Damiano the fifty thousand dollars he's demanding from Alison *and* the fifty thousand he wants from me? I want to leave here with something.

"Rod, believe me, I hate to do this, but I have no choice. I need every nickel of that three hundred thousand dollars to buy my mother her own apartment and get her out of my life. If we live together much longer, I can promise you, I will kill *her*. I know just how Alison was feeling at the Gala."

She got up. "Before I leave you, I want to say how much I admire both of you. She married you to get an education, but she stuck by you when that fabulous career you should have had disappeared. My theory is that your hold on her is she confessed the crime to you. Isn't that true, Rod?"

Rod reached for his crutches and got to his feet. His face white with anger, he said, "It's obvious you and your mother are cut from the same cloth. Alison is very smart, you know. Maybe she can dig up a few memories herself about how you were hounded for years by your mother because she kept ranting about losing Rob Powell to Betsy. Maybe you snapped and killed Betsy to make Robert Powell a widower. But there's only one problem. In a million years, Alison wouldn't murder anybody."

Nina smiled. "When do I get my answer?" she asked.

"I don't know," Rod said flatly. "Now if you don't mind, will you please let me pass? My wife is coming out of the house, and I want to go to join her."

"I think I'll just settle down on one of these lounge chairs," Nina said cheerfully as she stepped aside to let him pass.

64

Jane went straight from the interview to the kitchen. She had already prepared vichyssoise, a Waldorf salad, and cold sliced ham for lunch.

Robert Powell entered the kitchen a few minutes later. "Jane, I've been thinking. It's quite warm out. Let's eat in the dining room. How many do we have for lunch today?"

Jane could see that his mood was much brighter than it had been in the morning. He was wearing a light blue sport shirt and khaki slacks. His full head of white hair complemented his handsome face. His straight carriage belied his chronological age.

He doesn't look anything like his age, Jane thought. He's always looked like an English lord.

Lord and Lady Powell.

What had he asked her? Of course, how many would be at lunch today.

"The four graduates," Jane hesitated. "That's the

way I still think of them. Ms. Moran, Mrs. Craig, Mr. Rod Kimball, Mr. Alex Buckley, and yourself, sir."

"The lucky nine," Rob Powell said cheerfully. "Or a motley crew. Which is it, Jane?"

Without waiting for an answer, he opened the patio door and went outside.

What's gotten into him? Jane asked herself. This morning it seemed like all he wanted was to get them out of the house. Perhaps knowing that they'll be on their way tomorrow is making him feel good. I don't know what the others said in their interviews, but I know I came off fine.

Filled with self-satisfaction, she began to set the table in the dining room.

Josh appeared in the doorway. "I'll finish that," he said angrily. "You get the food out."

Jane looked at him, surprised. "What's the matter with you?" she asked.

"The matter with me is that I'm not a houseboy," Josh snapped.

Jane had just begun placing the silverware on the table. Startled, she straightened up. Her cheeks flushed, her lips tight, she spat out the words, "For the kind of salary you get, you have some nerve to talk like that about helping out in the house for a few days. Be careful. Be very careful. If Mr. Powell had heard you, you'd have been out the door in a minute. If I report this conversation to him, the same thing would happen."

"Well, listen to the lady of the house," Josh snapped defiantly. "Whatever became of all the jewelry George Curtis gave Betsy? Don't pretend you don't know what I'm talking about. When Mr. Rob was on business trips, I used to drive Betsy to her trysts with George Curtis, and she'd be lit up like a Christmas tree when I took her to meet him. I know she kept it hidden in her room somewhere, but I never heard any mention of it being found. If there's one thing I'm sure of, Mr. Rob Powell had no idea that affair was going on."

"You don't know what you're sure of," Jane whispered fiercely. "So why don't we both agree to keep our mouths shut? Tomorrow at this time they'll all be on their way."

"One last thought, Jane. If Betsy *had* left Powell for George Curtis, she'd have taken you with her, for two good reasons. First, because you waited on her hand and foot. Second, because once she moved out of here and asked Powell for a divorce, he'd have hired private detectives to find out how long that affair had been going on and discovered that you covered for Betsy when he called her from overseas every time he was away on a business trip."

"And what do you think he'd have done to *you* if he knew you were driving her back and forth to her little love nest in his Bentley?" Jane asked, her voice almost a whisper.

They glared at each other from across the table, then Jane said in a pleasant voice, "We'd better get moving. They were told that lunch would be served at one-thirty."

65

After Alison fled from the den, Alex and Laurie did not speak until Jerry, Grace, and the camera crew were gone.

Then Alex said quietly, "Two of our graduates have now given a worldwide audience a convincing reason why one of them might have killed Betsy Powell."

"They absolutely did," Laurie said. "And who knows what Regina and Nina will have to say this afternoon? I would be surprised if all four of them don't bitterly regret getting involved in this program, even for the money."

"I'm sure they already do," Alex agreed.

"Alex, why do you think Powell insisted we all stay here tonight—and that we don't interview him until tomorrow morning?"

"Building up the pressure on all of them, hoping one of them will crack? You and I will be the chief witnesses, if that happens," Alex replied briskly. "My guess is that he's bluffing." He looked at his watch. "I'd better call my office. We're due inside in fifteen minutes."

"And I'm going to try my dad."

Alex sat back in the chair, pretending to look for something in his briefcase.

He wanted to be here for Laurie if Leo Farley did not—or *could* not—answer the phone.

66

Leo's cheery "Hello" took the edge off Laurie's panic.

"I hear you were out on the town last night, Dad," she said.

"Yes, I had a hot date at Mount Sinai. How's your show going?"

"Why didn't you call me when you went to the hospital?"

"So that you didn't come rushing over here. I've had these episodes before. Jim Morris told me to calm down by watching game shows. Right now I'm watching an *I Love Lucy* rerun."

"Then I wouldn't dream of keeping you from it. I'll be down by seven thirty at the latest." Laurie hesitated, then asked, "Dad, do you *really* feel all right now?"

"I feel fine. Stop worrying."

"You make that very hard," Laurie said wryly. "All right, go back to *I Love Lucy*. I'll see you later."

With one hand she dropped the cell phone in her pocket. With the other, she impatiently fumbled for a tissue to brush away the tears that had begun to form in her eyes.

Alex reached into his pocket and handed her his freshly pressed handkerchief. As she accepted it he said, "Laurie, it doesn't hurt to let go a little occasionally."

"I can't," she whispered. "The day I let go, I'll lose my grip for good. I keep hearing that threat ringing in my ears. The only way I have kept my sanity at all is by hoping Blue Eyes keeps his promise that I'm next. Maybe when he kills me, he'll be caught. If he gets away, maybe Dad and Timmy can change their identities and disappear; who knows? But suppose Timmy and I are outside together? Or if I die, suppose Dad isn't here to protect Timmy?"

There was no answer Alex could offer her. Her tears stopped immediately, and he watched as Laurie pulled out her compact and dabbed her eyes. When she looked up at him her voice revealed no sign of stress. "You'd better make that call, Alex," she said. "'Mr. Rob' expects us at the table in exactly fifteen minutes."

67

Chief Penn, the graduates, Rod, Alex, Muriel, and Laurie had gathered at the dining room table when Robert Powell made his appearance.

"How quiet you all are," he remarked. "I can understand why. You are under a great strain." He paused as he looked from one to the other. "And so am I."

Jane was about to enter the dining room.

"Jane, would you please excuse us and close the door? I have a few things to share with my guests."

"Of course, sir."

Powell addressed them: "Are any of you thinking that this beautiful day is exactly the same as the day of the Gala? I remember Betsy sitting at this table with me that morning. We were congratulating each other on our good luck at having such perfect weather. Could any of us have imagined that the next morning

Betsy would be dead, murdered by an intruder?" He paused. "Or perhaps *not* by an intruder?"

He waited, and when there was no response, he went on briskly, "Now, let's be sure I have the details straight. This afternoon, Regina and then Nina will be interviewed. At about four-thirty the graduates will be dressed in replicas of the gowns they wore that night and photographed against the background of films of the Gala. My good friend George Curtis will be standing with you, Alex, sharing his impressions of that evening."

He looked at Laurie. "Am I correct so far?"

"Yes, you are," she said.

Powell smiled. "In the morning I will have my interview with you, Alex—with the graduates present. I hope and expect you will all find it quite interesting. *One* of you especially." He gave a tight smile.

"As to later this evening, everyone at this table, with the exception of Chief Penn, will be staying overnight. After the last scene is finished, the graduates will be driven in individual cars to their hotels. You will pack and check out. Your luggage will be placed in your car. You will have dinner on your own wherever you wish to dine—as my guest, of course—but please return here by eleven o'clock. We will have a nightcap together at that time, then retire. I want everyone to be alert for what I have to say tomorrow. Is that understood?"

This time, as if compelled to respond, heads nodded.

"At brunch tomorrow I will present you the checks

you have been promised. After that, one of you may want to use it to retain Mr. Buckley's services." He smiled a cold, mirthless smile. "Just joking, of course," he added.

He turned to Nina. "Nina, you need not share your car with your dear mother. Muriel and I are going to dine together this evening. It is time to turn the page on the past."

Muriel smiled adoringly at Powell, then shot a triumphant look at Nina.

"Enough of business. Let us now enjoy our luncheon. Ah, here comes Jane. I know she has prepared vichyssoise. You have not lived until you have sampled Jane's vichyssoise. It is indeed nectar for the gods."

It was served in total silence.

68

After leaving the dining room, Regina walked across the yard to the makeup van. The heat outside was a sharp contrast to the coolness of the house, but she welcomed it. After hearing Robert Powell's elaborate plans for the rest of the day and tomorrow morning, she was sure of only one thing: he had her father's suicide note. What more proof would anyone need that she had been Betsy's killer?

For twenty-seven years, since she was fifteen years old, even under oath she had sworn there was no such note in his pocket or around his body.

Who could have had a stronger motive to kill Betsy? she asked herself. And there was no question that Robert Powell was determined to have closure on Betsy's death. That was the whole purpose of his financing the program.

She walked past the pool. Crystal clear, reflecting the sun, brightly patterned lounge chairs scattered around it, it had the look of a stage setting. In the correspondence, they had all been invited to bring swimming apparel.

No one had.

Beyond it, the pool house, a miniature of the mansion, stood unused by anyone but the gardener, who incessantly entered and exited as he fussed over the grounds.

At the production van, Regina hesitated, then pulled open the door.

Meg was waiting, jars of cosmetics lined up neatly on the shelf in front of her.

Courtney was settled in the other chair, reading in front of a shelf of brushes, sprays, and a hair dryer.

This morning Courtney had told Regina that women would kill to have her thick, curly hair. "And I'll bet you'll say that it's a nuisance because it grows too fast."

That's exactly what I *did* say, Regina thought.

She avoided looking at the wall on her left, where the pictures of herself and the other graduates at the Gala had been blown up.

She knew what they looked like. Claire, without a trace of makeup, her hair in a ponytail, her dress high-necked and with sleeves to her elbows. Alison, whose talented mother had made her gown, as she made all her clothes—Alison's father was a produce manager in a grocery store. Nina, her dress daringly low cut, her red hair blazing, her makeup skillfully applied. Even then she looked so confident, Regina thought.

And I had on the most elegant dress of all. Mother went to work at Bergdorf after we lost everything. Even though that dress was reduced a lot, we still couldn't afford it. But she insisted I have it. *"Your father would have bought it for you,"* she told me.

Regina realized she had not spoken to Meg or to Courtney. "Hello, you two," she said. "Don't think I'm crazy. Just gearing up for my interview."

"Claire and Alison were nervous, too," Meg said cheerfully. "Why wouldn't you be? This program is going to be broadcast all over the world."

Regina sank into the chair at Meg's station.

"Thanks for reminding me of that," she said as Meg clipped a plastic sheet around her neck.

This morning, for the picture in the den depicting the four of them after the body had been found and the police had arrived, Meg had applied very little makeup, and Courtney had left their hair a touch disheveled, as it had been the morning after Betsy's death.

Now they were all wearing clothes of their own choice. "Dress as you feel comfortable," Laurie had counseled them.

Regina had chosen a dark blue linen jacket, white shell, and slacks. Her only jewelry was the string of pearls her father had given her on her fifteenth birthday.

Now she watched as with deft strokes, Meg began to apply foundation, blush, eye shadow, mascara, and lip rouge.

Courtney came over, and with a few quick movements of her brush, swept Regina's hair into a half bang and pulled it behind her ears.

"You look great," she said.

"You sure do," Meg agreed.

As Meg was unclasping the sheet from Regina's neck, Jerry opened the door of the van. "All set, Regina?" he asked.

"I guess so."

As they walked back to the house Jerry said comfortingly, "I know you're nervous, Regina. Don't be. Can you believe that Helen Hayes got stage fright every night till the moment she stepped onstage?"

"It's funny," Regina told him. "You know that I have a real estate office. Just this morning I was thinking that the day I got the letter about this program I was so unnerved I did a lousy presentation of a house I should have sold. The owner was a seventy-six-year-old woman who wanted to move into an assisted-living facility. I sold the house for her two months later, and for thirty thousand dollars less than I should have gotten for it. When I get the money for doing this program, I'm going to return my commission to her."

"Then you're one in a million," Jerry said dryly as he slid open the door from the patio to the kitchen.

Regina remembered that earlier in the morning, this patio entrance had been blocked off.

"No one on the patio now, and no sign of Jane," Jerry commented. "I guess she must take some downtime after all."

Where are the others? Regina asked herself as they

walked down the hallway to the den. Are they afraid to be together?

We don't trust each other, she thought. We each had a reason to kill Betsy, but mine is the strongest.

Laurie Moran and Alex Buckley were waiting for her in the den. Laurie's assistant Grace stood to the side. A crew member was still adjusting lights. The cameraman was in his place.

Without being invited, Regina sat at the table opposite Alex. She began to clasp and unclasp her hands. Stop it, she warned herself. She heard Laurie's greeting and returned it.

Alex Buckley was welcoming her, but she was sure his attitude was hostile. When would he produce her father's suicide note? she asked herself.

"Take one," the director was saying, and began to count. "Ten, nine, eight, seven, six, five, four, three, two, one." There was the clap of the slate board, and Alex began.

"We are now speaking to the third of the four honorees at the Graduation Gala, Regina Callari.

"Regina, thank you for agreeing to be with us on this program. You grew up in this town, didn't you?"

"Yes, I did."

"And yet, as I understand it, you haven't been back since shortly after the Gala and the death of Betsy Bonner Powell?"

Try to sound calm, Regina warned herself.

"As I'm sure the others have told you, all four of us were treated as murder suspects. Would you have hung around after that?"

"You moved to Florida shortly after. Your mother followed you there?"

"Yes, she did."

"Wasn't she very young when she died?"

"She was just turning fifty."

"What was she like?"

"She was one of those women who did a lot of good, but hated the limelight."

"What was her relationship with your father?"

"They were one soul."

"What was his business?"

"He bought failing companies, turned them around, and then sold them for huge profits. He was very successful."

"Let's go back to that later. I want to talk about the night of the Gala, starting with when you were all in the den together."

Laurie listened and observed as Regina told the same story as the other girls. They had filled their wineglasses again and again. They had discussed the evening, laughing at some of the dresses of the older women. Exactly as the other girls had, she described the finding of Betsy's body.

"We were young. You must know that we all had our own issues with the Powells," Regina was saying. "By then I know I was relaxed and enjoying being with the others. We refilled our wineglasses, going in and out for smokes. Even Claire was joking about her stepfather being so finicky about smoking. 'Please,' she said, 'don't light up until you are at the end of the patio. He's got the nose of a bloodhound.'

"We were talking about our plans. Nina was going to Hollywood. She always played the lead in the plays in high school and college, and, of course, her mother was an actress. She even joked about the fact that her mother was still riding her because she called Claire and her mother over when they were in the same restaurant, and that's how Betsy met Rob Powell."

"How did Claire respond to that?" Alex asked quickly.

"She said, 'You are lucky, Nina,'" Regina answered.

"What do you think she meant?" Alex asked quickly.

"I have my suspicions," Regina answered honestly. "But I just don't know."

"Let's go back a little," Alex said. "I've seen pictures of your home. It was very beautiful."

"Yes, it was," Regina said. "And more than that, it was a warm and comfortable home."

"But then, of course, everything changed when your father invested in Robert Powell's hedge fund."

Regina realized where he was going. Be careful, she warned herself, he's building a motive for you to have killed Betsy.

"It must have been hard not to resent the fact that virtually all of your dad's money was lost in that investment."

"My mother was sad but not bitter. She told me my father had something of a go-for-the-gold mentality, and he put too many eggs in one basket several times. On the other hand, he had never been reckless."

"But you still maintained a close friendship with Claire?"

"Yes, I did, until we all left Salem Ridge. I guess by unspoken agreement we didn't want to stay in touch after Betsy's death."

"How did you feel coming to this mansion after your father's death?"

"I was very seldom here. I don't think Robert Powell liked having Claire's friends around. We were more likely to get together at the rest of our homes."

"Then why would he have the Gala for all of you?"

"My guess is it was Betsy's idea. Some of her friends were having graduation parties for their daughters. She wanted to outshine them."

"What were you thinking the night of the Gala?"

"Missing my father. Thinking how perfect that beautiful night would have been if he were still here. My mother was a guest as well—I could see in her eyes that her thoughts mirrored my own."

"Regina, at age fifteen you discovered your father's body," Alex continued.

"Yes, I did," Regina said quietly.

"Would it have been easier for you if he left a note? If he had apologized for his suicide and the financial disaster? If he told you one last time he loved you? Do you think that would have helped you and your mother?"

The vivid memory of feeling so happy, riding her bicycle up the long driveway, the salt air filling her senses, pushing the button to open the garage door, the sight of her handsome forty-five-year-old father swaying from the noose, one hand around it as if perhaps he changed his mind too late, shattered Regina's fragile composure.

"Would a note have made any difference?" she asked, choking out the words. "My father was dead."

"Did you blame Robert Powell because your father lost everything in his hedge fund?"

Her last shred of composure crumbled. "I blame both of them. Betsy was up to her neck in deceiving my father, just as much as Powell was."

"How do you know that, Regina? Wasn't it because your father *did* in fact leave a note?"

Alex waited, then went on firmly. "He did leave a note, didn't he?"

Regina heard herself trying to whisper a faint "No . . . no . . . no," as he stared at her, his eyes sympathetic but demanding.

69

Bruno's excitement rose to a fever pitch after he heard Laurie's call to her father. Gleefully, he reflected on how everything was falling into place.

Leo Farley would be in the hospital until tomorrow morning.

Leo and Laurie would take the call from Timmy in the hospital room.

Two hours later, I pick up Timmy, Bruno thought. Leo had already told the director of the camp that he was in the hospital. I'll be in a cop's uniform.

I can pull it off.

I can probably even get away with it.

But if not, it's worth it. The "Blue Eyes" murder case had been in the newspapers for years; still was. If they only knew that I spent five years rotting in prison after I shot Laurie's husband. And all for a lousy parole violation. But in a way, it was *worth* it. Leo Farley and his daughter have spent these five years wondering and worrying about when I'll strike again. Tomorrow their waiting will be over.

Bruno dropped the phone into his pocket and went outside in time to see the police chief's car pulling up behind the studio vans. He was here for lunch.

Bruno walked to the putting green, as far from the chief's line of vision as humanly possible. Here, the chief could not get a clear look at his face.

There was one thing Bruno knew—most cops have long-term memories of faces, even when people age or alter their facial hair.

Or are dumb enough to put themselves on Facebook.

Bruno laughed out loud at that thought.

An hour later he was carefully examining the flower beds alongside the pool when the police car drove away.

That meant the chief wouldn't be back until tomorrow.

Just in time for the Big Show, Bruno thought gleefully.

70

Nina and Muriel did not speak after lunch. Muriel had obviously asked Robert Powell to have a car ready for her for the afternoon, because it had parked at the front door and was waiting for her.

Nina knew what that meant. The expensive new outfits her mother bought on her credit card were about to be put aside in favor of new ones—ones that would also be purchased on Nina's credit card.

Nina went up to her room to try to collect her thoughts until it was time for her own interview.

Like all the others it was a large bedroom, with a sitting area that offered a couch, an easy chair, a cocktail table, and a television.

Nina sat on the couch, taking in the cream-colored draperies behind the bed, the way their edgings picked up those on the panels at the window, and the way the rug and pillow shams coordinated and harmonized. An interior designer's dream, Nina thought.

She remembered that about a year before her death, Betsy had commissioned a complete redecorating job. Claire had told the girls about it.

Claire had said, *"I've been told to bring you over to see it. My mother is giving the grand tour to everyone."*

The "grand tour" came up after she died, Nina remembered. In fact, a college friend majoring in pre-law had warned me it would be a factor in the defense if anyone was accused of Betsy's murder: many, many people knew the layout of the house exactly—and that Betsy and Robert had separate bedrooms.

What is going to happen? Nina asked herself. I'm sure Robert is bluffing. He's making a fool of my mother, and she will turn on me again. Would she honestly be vindictive enough to claim I confessed to her that I killed Betsy?

No, even *she* couldn't do that, Nina decided.

Or could she?

Nina's cell phone rang. She picked it up, and her eyes widened as she saw the number. Quickly she answered, "Hello, Grant."

His voice was warm as he spoke her name.

Nina listened as he told her she wasn't to make any plans with anyone else for Saturday night. He wanted her to go to a dinner party with him at Steven Spielberg's home.

To go with Grant to a dinner party at Steven Spielberg's home! This was the crème de la crème of Hollywood society.

Suppose her mother accused Nina of confessing to Betsy's murder? Or, almost as bad, returned to California with her and picked up where they had left off: living with her, screaming at her all the time, the condo always a mess, wineglasses all over the place, the smell of cigarette smoke heavy in the air.

"Can't wait to see you Saturday night," Grant said.

Don't sound like Muriel, simpering and fawning, Nina warned herself. "I'm looking forward to it so much, too, Grant," she said warmly, but without undue excitement in her tone.

After she disconnected, Nina sat, no longer even aware of her surroundings.

No matter which way she does it, my mother is going to ruin the rest of my life, she thought.

The phone rang again. It was Grace. "Nina, would you mind going over to makeup?" she asked. "They'll be ready for your interview in about half an hour."

71

Laurie and Alex sat in the den and compared notes after Regina's interview.

"Was I too rough on Regina?" Alex asked.

"No, I don't think so," Laurie said slowly. "But when you were finished, I don't think anyone would doubt that there was a suicide note. But why would a fifteen-year-old have taken it?"

"You have your own theory, I know," Alex said. "Don't think I haven't noticed that whenever you ask me my theory, you already have one of your own."

"Guilty as charged." Laurie smiled. "My theory is that there was something in that note that Regina didn't want her mother to read—and that it involved Betsy. Maybe the fact that her father was having an affair with her. That's what I see. Remember how Regina described her parents as being 'one soul'?"

"And that opens up the question—perhaps Betsy influenced her father's reckless business decision to put everything he had into Powell's hedge fund," Alex suggested. "Doesn't that give Regina a strong motive to take a God-given opportunity to punish Betsy?" he added.

"If I were in her shoes and had lost my parents and everything I had because of Betsy Powell," Laurie told him, "I could kill. I know I could."

"You *think* you could," Alex corrected. "Now, tell me what you thought of Robert Powell's speech at lunch. I'm telling you right now that I think he's bluffing, but if one of the people at that table *did* murder Betsy Powell, he or she may believe his threat. He's playing a dangerous game."

72

Nina looked in the mirror as Meg clipped the vinyl sheet around her neck.

"Now, Meg," she cautioned, "this morning you were told to make us look like rag dolls."

"I was told to make you resemble the way you looked the morning Betsy's body was discovered," Meg said matter-of-factly. "Even then you looked better than anyone else."

"I looked passable, but for this interview I want you to make me look a little like her." Nina held up a picture of Grant with his late wife, Kathryn.

Meg studied it carefully. "You resemble her," she observed.

"I *want* to resemble her," Nina said flatly.

She had googled everything she could find on the subject of Grant Richmond. For a major producer, he led a quiet behind-the-scenes life. He had married at twenty-six. His wife had been twenty-one.

They had been married for thirty years before she died two years ago of heart failure from a lifelong condition.

No children, and not a whiff of scandal about them.

So Grant had been a one-woman man, and he had been alone for two years. By now he was probably lonely.

He was pushing sixty.

Nina held up her camera and looked at a second picture. "Who does this look like?" she demanded.

Meg studied it carefully. "This is the same lady, Nina. Is she a relative?"

Nina nodded in satisfaction. It's not just that I'm a good dancer, she thought. I resemble his wife.

"Look, Meg," she said. "She's not a relative, but I want to look like her when you do the makeup."

"Then I can't put that heavy liner and shadow on you."

"That's fine with me."

A half hour later Meg said, "That's it."

Nina looked in the mirror. "I could be her sister," she said. "Perfect."

"My turn, Nina, it's getting late," Courtney said briskly.

"I know." Nina moved into Courtney's chair. Holding the picture, she said, "She had short hair. I don't want to cut mine."

"Don't," Courtney said. "I'll put it up in a twist; same effect."

Five minutes later, Jerry knocked on the door of

the van. When he came inside, he was startled by the change in Nina's appearance.

"Ready, Nina?" he asked.

"Yes, I am." She gave herself a final look in the mirror before she got up. "These two are miracle workers," she said. "Don't you agree, Jerry?"

"Yes, I do," he said honestly. "By that I mean for giving you a different look, not a better one," he added hastily.

Nina laughed. "Good you added those last few words."

As they left the van, Jerry compared the graduates. He liked Nina best. The others seemed to be trapped in their own shells. For women who had been close friends until they were twenty-one, they seemed to have very little to say to each other. When they were on the patio in between shoots, they all grabbed for a book or their smartphones from their purses.

Nina did, too, except when Muriel insisted on talking. She always paid attention when Muriel gushed about what a wonderful man Robert Powell was, and how Betsy had been her dearest friend.

It's as if Muriel is always hoping that Powell can hear her, Jerry thought. She's overplaying her role. I've been around enough film sets to know that.

He and Nina were walking past the pool. "I wouldn't mind taking a swim on a day like this," he commented. "How about you?"

"I'd like to be taking a swim in the pool at my condo. I do that every day, or evening if I work late," Nina said.

What am I going to say? she was asking herself. What kind of questions are they going to ask me? What's going to happen tomorrow when Robert Powell shows us the door? Would my own mother use that moment to swear that I confessed to killing Betsy to her and claim the reward?

You bet she would!

I won't let it happen.

Jerry did not attempt to keep up the conversation. Unlike Regina, Nina did not seem nervous, but he was sure she was preparing herself for the interview.

But then she suddenly said, "There's Creepy Crawly again." She pointed to Bruno, who was at the far end of the grounds behind the house. "What's he doing? Chasing bugs on the plants?"

Jerry laughed. "Mr. Powell is a perfectionist. He wants every shot of the grounds to display them in their normal pristine condition. Yesterday when we were taking pictures of the four of you in different locations back here, he looked shocked when the equipment made tracks in the grass. Then, as you saw, Creepy Crawly, as you call him, came running to the rescue."

"Oh, God, do I remember that he was a perfectionist!" Nina exclaimed. That last night when we were all going back and forth from the den to the patio and Regina put out her last cigarette, she deliberately missed the ashtray on the table and ground it out on the tabletop. I don't think anyone else saw her.

Should I tell *that* story when I'm interviewed?

Again the patio and kitchen were empty.

Grant will be watching when this is on television, Nina told herself as she and Jerry walked down the hallway to the den. I certainly have the least reason to have killed Betsy. No sane person would think that I did it. The fact that my mother blames me for introducing them would never be a strong enough motive for murder.

She stood for a moment at the door of the den. Well, this is it, she thought. Alex and Laurie were waiting for her. I wonder what the others were feeling when they walked in here? Nina asked herself. Could they possibly have been as terrified as I am now?

Come on, I'm an actress. I can carry this off. She gave a brief smile and, with an air of confidence, took the seat opposite Alex.

"Nina Craig was the final graduate being celebrated on the tragic night of the Graduation Gala," Alex began. "Nina, thank you for being with us today."

Her mouth too dry to speak, Nina nodded.

His voice friendly, his smile warm, Alex asked, "What does it feel like to be here again in Salem Ridge, reunited with your old friends after twenty years?"

Be honest whenever you can, Nina warned herself. "It's awkward, even strange. We all know why we're here."

"And why is that, Nina?"

"To try to prove that none of us murdered Betsy Powell," she said. "And that she was killed by a stranger who came in. On the other hand, we all know that you're hoping that one of us will blurt out a confession or give herself away. I certainly think that's what Robert Powell is hoping. And, of course, in a way I can't blame him."

"How does that make you feel, Nina?"

"Angry. Defensive. But I think we all have been feeling like that for the last twenty years, so it's nothing new. I've certainly learned the hard way that you can get used to anything."

Listening and observing, Laurie found it hard to conceal her surprise. Nina Craig was not responding to Alex's questions the way she had expected at all. Somehow, she had expected a more belligerent response from her. After all, Nina had the least reason of all of them to have suffocated Betsy, but her attitude now was one of regret, even when she confessed to anger. And she *looks* different, too, Laurie thought. Softer. What's the reason she had her hair styled in an upsweep? With all the research we've done on her, I've never seen one picture without the flowing locks. She's playing a game, but what is it?

Nina was taking Alex through her childhood.

"Alex, as you obviously know, my mother, Muriel Craig, is an actress. I was kind of born in a trunk. We moved all over in those days."

"What about school?"

"Somehow, between the East and West Coasts, I graduated from grammar school."

"What about your father? I know your parents were divorced when you were very young."

He couldn't stand her, either, Nina thought. But

he got away fast. "They married young and divorced when I was three."

"Did you see much of him after that?"

"No, but he did contribute to my college education." A little, she thought, a very little—what Mother could squeeze out of him in court.

"Actually, you saw very little of him from the time of the divorce, isn't that true, Nina?"

"He tried his hand at acting, didn't make it, then moved to Chicago, remarried, and had four more children. There wasn't much room in that for me."

Where is he going with this? Nina asked herself frantically.

"Then you never had a father in your growing-up years?"

"I think that's obvious."

"Why did you and your mother move to Salem Ridge, Nina?"

"My mother was dating Robert Powell."

"Wasn't she also offered the leading role in a pilot that became a series and ran for six years, and has been on reruns ever since?"

"Yes, that's true. But Powell told her that he didn't want to be married to anyone who would be working all the time."

"Even when her relationship with Powell ended, the two of you stayed in Salem Ridge. That seems curious to me."

"I don't know why. She had rented a condo. There was a very nice old couple next door, the Johnsons. When she broke up with Robert Powell, my mother was offered a flurry of jobs. I had started high school. She paid the Johnsons to look after me when she was working."

Don't dwell on how lonesome it was after the Johnsons poked their heads in to say good night and I was left by myself for the night, Nina thought. And then when Mother got home from a job, she'd start ranting about how hard she was working, and how it was all my fault, over and over again. I'd miss her when she was away, then when she came home I'd wish she was away on a job anywhere else in the world.

"Your mother kept the condo until you went to college, didn't she?"

"Yes. By then all the jobs were on the West Coast. She had bought a condo out there."

"So you spent your semester breaks and vacations with her?"

"Whenever possible. But I was getting summer-stock jobs and grabbed them whenever they were offered."

"Nina, let's talk about the Gala."

Laurie listened as, in different ways, Alex asked the same questions he had asked the other girls. Her answers were virtually the same as those of the other graduates. She, too, insisted that an intruder had to have been the culprit.

"Let's go back," Alex suggested. "Were you surprised when Claire called and told you that her mother and Robert Powell wanted to have a Graduation Gala for the four of you?"

"Yes, but it was a good chance to see the girls again."

"Your mother was invited to attend as well?"

"Yes, but she didn't."

"Why not?"

"She couldn't take the time off. She had an audition coming up."

"Nina, wasn't it because Betsy scrawled on the invitation that she and Robert couldn't wait to see her, and how blessed she was that you had called her over to the table that wonderful day she and Robert met?"

"How do you know that? Who told you that?"

"Actually, your mother did," Alex said amiably. "Shortly before lunch today."

She's building up to saying that I confessed to her that I murdered Betsy, Nina thought. No matter whether anyone believes her or not, that will be the end of any chance I have with Grant.

What was Alex Buckley asking her? How would she describe her feelings about Betsy Powell?

Why not tell the truth? Why not?

"I loathed her," she said. "Especially after I read that note. She was mean. Make that cruel. There wasn't a decent bone in her body, and when I looked down on her dead face, I had to force myself not to spit on it."

73

George Curtis arrived at the Powell mansion at three-thirty. He had been asked to wear the same kind of evening attire he had worn at the Gala. He had a virtual replica of it in his closet. Because it was so warm, he carried his white dinner jacket, shirt, and bow tie on a plastic-covered hanger.

Before going to the club to play bridge with her friends, Isabelle had given him a cautionary note. "Just remember, you think you kept your little romance pretty quiet, but if I was suspicious, don't you think anyone else was? Maybe even Rob Powell? Just be careful and don't fall into a trap. You had the strongest motive of anyone to have Betsy dead." Then, with a kiss and a wave of her hand, she stepped into her convertible.

"Isabelle, I swear to you—" he had begun.

"I know you do," she said. "But remember, you

don't have to convince *me*, and I don't care if you did it anyway. Just don't let yourself get caught."

The temperature had dropped a little, but it was still very hot. George parked his car in the front driveway, picked up the clothes hanger, and walked around to the back of the house. A flurry of activity greeted him. The production crew had their cameras aimed at designated spots on the grounds. He guessed that was where the graduates would be standing while he talked in the foreground with Alex Buckley. He had been told that the background would be a rolling shot of scenes from the Gala.

Laurie Moran approached as soon as she spotted him. "Thank you so much for agreeing to do this, Mr. Curtis. We'll try not to keep you too long. Why don't you wait inside with the others? It's too hot out here."

"That's not a bad idea," he agreed. He crossed the patio with reluctant steps and went into the house. The four graduates were in the main dining room, dressed in the gowns that he recognized were replicas of the ones they had worn that night. Even with the skillfully applied makeup they were wearing, the tension in their faces was unmistakable.

He did not have long to wait. Laurie's assistant Grace came in to take the graduates outside. When she came back for him, he saw that they were all in place, standing like statues against what he knew would be the background of films of the Gala. He wondered what they were thinking. He wondered if every one of them didn't feel as he had that night. I was terrified that Betsy had the power to ruin my marriage just as the children Isabelle and I had prayed for were becoming a reality, he thought. Alison had to have been bitter. She had lost out on her scholarship because of the donation Rob had made to her college. Occasionally I would pick up something in the grocery store where her father worked, and he would always brag about how hard Alison was studying . . .

There's no one in town who didn't hear Muriel tell the story of how Betsy stole Rob from her, and the fact that it was all because of Nina. And from what I hear, Claire had desperately wanted to board at Vassar, but neither Betsy nor Rob would hear of it. "*A waste of money when she has such a beautiful home,*" as Betsy put it. And Regina's father committed suicide because of his investment in Rob's hedge fund.

Who among those girls, amid all the extravagant display, could have avoided feeling bitterness that night? And from the next day on, for twenty years, they had lived under a cloud of suspicion.

George Curtis felt a deep sense of shame. I *did* come back here the night of the Gala, he remembered. It was about 4 A.M. I stood here on this spot. I knew where Betsy's bedroom was. I was crazed with fear that Isabelle would divorce me if Betsy ever told her about us. But then I could see the reflection of someone moving in Betsy's room. There was a light in the hallway, and when the door opened I was almost sure I could tell who it was.

I still think I know who it was. I *know* who it was.

When Betsy's body was discovered I wanted to tell, but how could I explain why I was here at that time? I couldn't. But if I had admitted to what I saw, everyone else who has been under suspicion wouldn't have been going through this hell for twenty years. He felt the guilt wash over him.

Alex Buckley was walking to him. "Ready to go down memory lane, Mr. Curtis?" he asked cheerfully.

74

"How do you think that went?" Laurie asked with concern as she stepped into Alex's car.

Alex was starting the engine and putting up the top of his convertible. "I think we could use some air-conditioning. To answer your question, I think it went great."

"I think it did, too. But it's twenty of seven. I'm so afraid that if we hit traffic we won't be at the hospital when Timmy calls, and Dad will miss talking to him."

"I checked the traffic report a few minutes ago on my iPhone. It's okay. I promise I'll get you to the hospital by seven-thirty."

"One more left," Laurie sighed as Alex drove out of the grounds of the Powell estate. "And now the usual question. What's your take on George Curtis?"

"He's a class act," Alex said promptly. "He's the kind of guy people look up to. Well, why not? He's been on the cover of *Forbes* magazine."

"And it doesn't hurt that he is downright handsome," Laurie said. "Think about it. Curtis is a billionaire, charming, good-looking. Compare him with Robert Powell, at least as far as money goes."

"There is no comparison, Laurie. Powell may be worth half a billion, but Curtis is worth billions."

"Now, think of that frame in the Gala films where George Curtis and Betsy look pretty serious, almost as though they're arguing."

"Are you using that in the background, Laurie?"

"No. That wouldn't be fair. But I do know this: the George Curtises of this world don't get involved with this kind of program unless they have something to hide. Think about that."

"Laurie, you continue to amaze me. I *did* think about it. And once again, I agree with you," Alex told her.

Laurie pulled out her phone. "I'll just alert Dad that we're on our way."

Leo answered on the first ring. "I'm still alive," he said. "I'm now watching *All in the Family*. Another golden oldie. Where are you?"

"On our way down. Traffic is good so far."

"Didn't you say Alex Buckley was driving you here, then back to the Powell place?"

"That's right."

"Don't let him cool his heels in the car. Bring him up. I'd like to meet him."

Laurie looked at Alex. "Would you be interested in meeting my dad?"

"Of course I would."

"Alex accepts with delight, Dad. See you."

75

Bruno was putting on his police uniform when he
listened to the call. Countdown! he said to himself.
After all these years, I get my revenge. There shall be
wailing and gnashing of teeth, he thought. Oh, Leo,
how sad you are going to be. Your daughter. Your
grandson. And all the while they've been searching through hospital records to see if the doctor had
made a mistake on a patient. You were the one who
made the mistake, Leo. When you were a tough
young cop. Too tough. You could have given me a
break when you arrested me but you wouldn't. You
wrecked my life. You cost me thirty years in prison
and then another five for good measure.

Bruno stood in front of the full-length mirror
on the closet door of his shabby apartment. He had
been renting it month to month because, as he had
explained to the landlord, he wanted to be sure that
his job with Perfect Estates worked out. The landlord,

happy to avoid necessary repairs for the present, was delighted with his temporary tenant.

He wouldn't care that I left suddenly, especially since I paid him to the end of the month, and I'm not going to claim the month's security.

As if anyone could damage this dump, Bruno thought.

76

As Laurie and Alex were driving out, the production crew was closing down for the day.

The graduates had changed from their gowns, and all of them as one turned down the offer to keep them. "Laurie really wants you to have them," Jerry explained. "And I can tell you, they were very expensive."

Nina spoke for all of them. "That's just what we need, another reminder of that night."

Their cars were waiting to drive them to their hotels.

When Rod and Alison arrived at their room, they happily closed the door behind them. Then Rod reached for her. "Alie, it's all right."

"It's not, Rod. It's not all right. You know what's on that tape. You know what Josh can do with that." She turned from him and angrily reached into the closet, grabbing clothes from their hangers and throwing them on the bed.

Rod sank onto the couch and unconsciously began to massage his aching knees. "We are going to have a scotch now," he said emphatically. "Then we are going to order a fabulous dinner, either here or out— your choice. We'll order the most expensive items on the menu, courtesy of Robert Powell."

"I couldn't eat a thing!" Alison protested.

"Order it anyhow."

"Rod, you make me laugh when I have no reason to."

"Alison, that's what I'm here for," Rod said cheerfully. He was not about to tell her that he absolutely shared her concern about Josh's tapes—not because of the money, but because of what it would do to Alie if, once again because of Betsy Powell, her chance to go to medical school without taking on a heavy financial burden, was snatched from her.

77

Regina carefully packed the few new clothes she had brought in preparation for the program. *I may be trading these for an orange jumpsuit,* she thought bitterly. *Score one hundred for Robert Powell. He ruined my life when I was fifteen years old, and now he has his big chance to ruin the rest of it. I wouldn't be surprised if he put Josh up to going through my bag.*

But in the note Dad accuses him and Betsy of deliberately setting him up for a scam. Why would Robert want that to come out? Josh must be doing this on his own. I've got to pay him off, she thought. *How ironic—I have publicly made myself more likely to be accused of being Betsy's murderer than if I'd stayed home selling real estate.*

Efficiently, she packed her overnight bag and a large suitcase. *Now where?* she asked herself. *I don't feel like calling for room service. I've got a car downstairs, courtesy of Mr. Powell. Should I?*

Yes, she decided, why not? She would have him drive her past her old house, then take her to the restaurant where she and her parents used to go regularly for dinner.

Auld lang syne, she thought.

78

One more night in the house she hated! Why did I do this to myself?

It was a question Claire had been asking herself since the plane landed. Had it been stupid to make herself up to resemble her mother that first morning? Had she done it to stick it to "Daddy Rob"? Maybe. He'd had the nerve to open the door of her bedroom right after her interview this morning to ask her that very question. Why didn't I ever press charges against him in all these years? she asked herself. Why don't I do it now?

She knew the answer. Because it gave me a perfect reason to kill my mother, and because, with his battery of lawyers, Daddy Rob would have held me up as a demented liar, and my mother would have loved backing him up. That's why I became a counselor, she thought. I wanted to help other girls in my situation. But not many of them told me that *their* mothers accepted the fact that their stepfather came sneaking into their room at night. I know that until I go into therapy myself, I'll never move forward with my life, Claire conceded. He's held me hostage all these years.

There was one way she could get to him. Tonight and tomorrow morning she would again wear makeup and style her hair to accentuate her remarkable resemblance to his dear Betsy. As if that makes a bit of difference in the grand scheme of things, Claire thought bitterly as she picked up the phone to order room service. I wonder if Nina will faint again when she sees me.

And why was she, of all people, the one to faint in the first place?

79

Nina packed, then had room service send up dinner. As she listlessly took a bite of cordon bleu, her phone rang. To her astonishment, it was Grant.

"Couldn't help wondering how the interview went," he said. "Alex Buckley is notorious for shaking up witnesses."

"Well, he did an Oscar-worthy performance on me," Nina said. "Wait until you see it."

"Hey, you sound pretty down."

"I guess I am," Nina admitted.

"Try not to be, but I understand. I was a witness in a fraud case twenty years ago. It wasn't pleasant."

Pleasant! That's a good word, Nina thought as she listened to Grant tell her he was looking forward to seeing her and wished her a good flight.

Nina took a large swallow of vodka from the

tumbler beside her dinner plate. Maybe if I promise my mother to give her all the money left after paying Josh, she'll be satisfied, she thought. Especially if she knows that an A-list producer like Grant is dating me!

80

In Mount Sinai Hospital, Leo was looking at his watch with growing impatience. It was twenty to eight, and Laurie still wasn't there. But just as he was sure she would have to take Timmy's call in the car, Laurie appeared in the doorway. The tall, impressive-looking guy behind her was instantly recognizable as the famous Alex Buckley.

Laurie rushed to hug him. "Dad, I'm so sorry. They should take the East River Drive and bury it at sea. There was a fender bender at 125th Street. You would have thought it was a terror attack for the traffic jam it caused."

"At ease," Leo said, "or you'll be the next one in here with heart fibrillations." He looked up at Alex. "Wouldn't you agree with that, counselor?"

"I certainly agree that your daughter is under a lot of stress," Alex said carefully as he pulled up a chair at

Leo Farley's bedside. "But she's doing a great job with this program, I can promise you that."

"Now, before you ask me again, Laurie, yes, I feel fine, and yes, I get out tomorrow morning," Leo Farley declared. "What time do you wrap up this witch hunt you're on?"

"Hey, Dad, that's not exactly what I would call having respect for my work," Laurie protested.

"I have every respect for your work," Leo said. "But if I had gotten away with murder for twenty years and now I was under a spotlight where every word I said in front of a national viewing audience could be picked over by all the amateur sleuths in the country, I might be driven to do whatever it took to cover my tracks."

Alex saw that both Leo and Laurie kept glancing at their watches. It was five to eight.

"Timmy's late calling. I'd better call the office at the camp again and check to see if anything is wrong," Leo said.

"Dad, you've been calling the office at the camp?" Laurie asked.

"You bet I have. That way I can keep them on their toes and make sure that there's no lapse in security there. What do you think, Alex?"

"In your situation, if I were the parent or grandparent, I would do exactly the same thing," Alex agreed.

The ringing of Laurie's phone brought a collective sigh of relief. Before it rang again, she and Leo were saying, "Hi, Timmy."

"Hi, Mom," a happy young voice answered. "I was

worried that you wouldn't get home in time to have Grandpa with you when I called."

"Well, we're both here," Laurie said.

Alex listened as Timmy described his activities of the day. He was on the "A" swim team. He liked the three other guys in his tent. Camp was fun. It was only at the end of the conversation that his tone became wistful. "I miss you guys. Are you really, really coming up on visiting day?"

"We are really, *really* coming up on visiting day," Laurie promised.

"You bet we are," Leo said emphatically. "Have I ever broken a promise to you, big guy?"

"No, Grandpa."

"Do you think I'm going to start now?" Leo demanded with mock severity in his voice.

The wistful note was gone.

"No, Grandpa," Timmy said happily.

When they said their final good-bye, Laurie looked at Alex. "That's my little guy," she said proudly.

"He sounds like a great kid," Alex said honestly.

"And now I want you two to go get something to eat and start back to Robert Powell's place," Leo said firmly. "You'll be late enough as it is. Laurie, I hope you're going to take a couple of days off after you wrap up this program."

"That's the last thing I'll be doing, Dad. In fact, that's almost funny. Postproduction can be the toughest part of it. But I agree with you—emotionally, this one has been tough. I have to tell you, I hope I'm never under suspicion of having committed a murder."

Alex knew which way Laurie and her father's thoughts were turning. "I'll defend you, ten percent discount," he promised. They both laughed, and when Alex said good-bye to Leo he heard himself saying, "I defended some people in cases about which I'd love to have your opinion. Would you want to have dinner sometime?"

"Sure I would," Leo agreed.

"Can I come?" Laurie laughed.

"There's no question about that," Alex said, his tone now serious.

With a final good-bye to Leo, they went downstairs and left the hospital.

"I love Manhattan," Laurie sighed. "It's home sweet home."

"So do I," Alex agreed. "Look, we don't have to be back to that mausoleum until eleven, and it's only eight thirty now. Why don't we have a relaxed dinner?"

"We were talking about grabbing a hamburger."

"Forget it. Marea on Central Park South is one of the best restaurants in New York. It's always full, but by this time the theatre crowd has gone. Okay with you?"

"Perfect," Laurie said. Relaxed now that Leo looked good and Timmy sounded happy, she knew she would enjoy the evening dining with Alex.

AT THAT VERY MOMENT, BRUNO WAS CROSSING the Tappan Zee Bridge on the way to Timmy's camp.

81

Twenty-four miles away in an equally expensive restaurant in Westchester County, Robert Powell and Muriel Craig were sipping champagne. "To our reunion," he whispered.

"Rob, dear, I've missed you. Oh, how I've missed you." Muriel reached across the table for his hand. "Why didn't you ever call me in all these years?"

"I was afraid to call you. When we broke up I was very unfair to you. I know you had given up the chance to be in that series, and it became so successful. I owed you so much, I didn't know where to begin."

"I called and wrote to you," Muriel reminded him.

"That only made me feel more guilty," Robert Powell confessed. "And I haven't told you yet how absolutely lovely you look tonight."

Muriel knew that was not flattery. She had prevailed on Meg and Courtney to do her makeup and style her hair. She had found a beautiful dinner suit in an exclusive boutique in Bedford. The fact that she had already bought a beautiful dinner suit with matching accessories on Rodeo Drive in Hollywood did not trouble her. She was carrying Nina's credit card.

Robert was saying, "I think we'd better order."

Throughout the dinner, he skillfully intermingled compliments with subtle questions. "I was so flattered to hear that you blamed Nina for calling Claire and Betsy to the table that day, Muriel."

"I could have killed her," Muriel admitted, her voice thick and a little loud. "I was so in love with you."

"And I often thought of you over the years and wondered how stupidly carried away I was, and how much I came to regret it." He paused. "And then, when Betsy was mercifully off my hands, I wish I could have known who to thank."

Muriel looked hesitant, then glanced around the dining room to be sure that the occupants at the surrounding tables were absorbed in their own conversations. Satisfied, she bent forward and leaned across the table as far as she could, getting a smear of butter on the lapel of her new suit.

"Robbie, do you mean you were *glad* when Betsy was smothered?"

"Promise not to tell anyone that," he whispered.

"Of course not. It's our secret. But you know how close my daughter, Nina, and I have always been?"

"Of course I do."

"Well, she was so upset with what Betsy wrote on my invitation, you know, how she wanted me to see how happy you two were and how glad she was that Nina had introduced you . . ."

"I learned about it later, and I was shocked."

"I was hurt, but Nina was furious at her. She knew how much I loved you. Rob, I think Nina was the one who killed Betsy. She did it for me so that I would have another chance with you."

"Are you sure, or are you guessing, Muriel?" Robert Powell's eyes were suddenly alert, his tone of voice sharp.

Muriel Craig looked at him, vaguely aware of the change in his manner. "Of course I'm sure, Robbie. She called me. You remember, I was in Hollywood and she was crying over the phone. She said, 'Mommy, I'm scared. They're asking so many questions.

"'Mommy, I did it for you.'"

82

Jane checked the bedrooms for the last time before they all got back. She had opened the bar in the den and laid out a platter of hors d'oeuvres just as she had done the night Betsy was murdered. She thought, Oh, to be rid of all of them at last!

After several days of all this activity, she was unused to the blessed silence in the house. Mr. Rob had taken that impossible Muriel Craig out to dinner. No question, she looked beautiful, but there was no doubt she already had a few under her belt.

And there was a faint smell of smoke in her bathroom.

Mr. Rob scorned anyone who drank too much or smoked.

Mr. Rob was toying with Muriel. Jane knew the signs. It was similar to the way Betsy had toyed with

Regina's father, until she got him to sink every nickel he had into the hedge fund.

Oh, they were quite the pair of experts at cheating people, she thought with admiration. Plus, Betsy was a two-faced fraud. She had skillfully hidden her little dalliances from Mr. Rob.

That was why Betsy had slipped me little gifts to keep my mouth shut, Jane thought.

But she was worried now. She had missed the fact that Josh had been playing his own little game, black-mailing people he taped in the car.

If Mr. Rob knew she had covered for Betsy, she would be fired at once. He must never know. But who would tell him? Not Josh. He'd lose *his* job, too.

I still have the jewelry that George Curtis gave Betsy, Jane thought as she turned down the beds for the visitors and lowered the shades in their rooms, a job she hadn't done in twenty years—except, of course, for Mr. Rob. Sometimes she put a chocolate on his pillow, just as they did in hotels.

Mr. Curtis had been here this afternoon. Boy, he must have been squirming, she thought, talking to Alex Buckley about the Gala.

After the Gala, Jane had fixed the platter of hors d'oeuvres for the girls and brought them to the den. I was in and out for the first half hour or so and listened to all of them until they really let go on Betsy. Then they started to look at me and I said good night.

If push came to shove, I could make a case against any one of them, she told herself.

She laid her head on Mr. Rob's pillow, just for an instant. Then she pulled herself up and with rapid fingers plumped it again.

Tomorrow night at this time she and Mr. Rob would be alone again.

83

"It's time to get back," Alex said reluctantly. For the last ninety minutes, in between thoroughly enjoying chatting with Laurie over an excellent dinner, he had found himself telling her stories of his own background—how his mother and then his father had died when he was in college, how at age twenty-one he had become his seventeen-year-old brother's guardian.

"He became my 'little guy,'" he said, and then, appalled at his own words, said, "Laurie, I'm sorry. There's no comparison with your situation."

"No, there isn't," Laurie said matter-of-factly. "But I hate it when people weigh and measure every word they say to me. It's a continuing factor of my life. But your brother grew up and is a successful lawyer, and someday Blue Eyes will be captured and this awful burden will be gone. My one comfort is that Blue Eyes swore he'd get me first." She sipped a taste of champagne. "I can drink to that!" she said.

"Put down that glass," Alex said forcefully. "Let's drink to Blue Eyes being captured and rotting in prison for the rest of his life." He did not add, Or being shot between the eyes in cold blood, as he murdered your husband, Dr. Greg Moran.

Reluctantly, Alex signaled for the check.

Fifteen minutes later they were driving toward Westchester on the Henry Hudson Parkway.

Alex could see that Laurie was struggling to stay awake. "Look, why don't you close your eyes?" he suggested. "You told me you didn't sleep last night because you were worried about your dad, and I doubt you'll sleep much tonight, either."

"You're absolutely right," Laurie sighed. She closed her eyes and in less than a minute Alex heard the sound of her soft, even breathing.

He glanced over at her from time to time. From the outside lights of the parkway he could see her profile, and then was pleased when, in her sleep, her head turned toward him.

He thought about how worried Leo Farley was about her being under the same roof as these people, one of whom was surely a murderer—but which one?

And there was something familiar about that gardener. What was it? He had snapped his picture yesterday when he was out on the patio and sent it to his investigator. He had also called Perfect Estates. He had told the person answering the phone that, for security reasons, he was just verifying the names of everyone on the property.

Robert Powell's speech at lunch was clearly an

attempt to frighten one of them into making a move, Alex thought, and whoever that person is may take a last, desperate chance to stop him.

Thirty minutes later he tapped Laurie's arm. "Okay, 'Sleeping Beauty,'" he said briskly. "Time to wake up. We're here for the night."

84

Bruno was in the office at the camp. The counselor on night duty had been summoned from his cabin.

Toby Barber was twenty-six years old, a good sleeper, an early-to-bed type. Rubbing his eyes, he came into the office to confront Bruno, authoritative in his police uniform, a concerned look on his face. "I'm sorry to disturb you, Mr. Barber," he told Toby, "but it's very, very important. Commissioner Farley has had a major heart attack. He may not make it. He wants to see his grandson now."

Bruno was a good actor. He stared straight into the young counselor's eyes.

"We've been warned to take particular care of Timmy," Toby said, trying to come fully awake, "but I do know that his grandfather called the head counselor today and told him he was in the hospital with a heart condition. I'll call my boss right away on his cell to get his permission. He's visiting friends at a birth-day party."

"Commissioner Farley is dying," Bruno said, his voice laced with fury. "He wants to see his grandson."

"I understand, I understand," Toby said nervously. "Just one phone call."

There was no answer on the phone.

"He probably doesn't hear it," Toby said worriedly. "I'll try again in a few minutes."

"I am not waiting a few minutes," Bruno thun-dered. "The commissioner is a dying man who wants to see his grandson."

Thoroughly intimidated, Barber said, "I'll get Timmy. Just let me help him change."

"Don't change him. Put on his bathrobe and slip-pers!" Bruno ordered. "He has plenty of clothes at home."

"Yes, of course. You're right. I'll get him."

Ten minutes later Bruno was holding the hand of a sleepy Timmy and putting him in his car.

His mind was racing with a combination of tri-umph and anticipation.

85

Robert Powell arrived home to receive the first of his overnight guests.

Muriel rushed upstairs to change her jacket. Horrified when she looked in the mirror, she freshened her makeup and brushed her hair. She walked downstairs trying not to show that she was unsteady on her feet. When she came into the den, she saw that Nina was the next to return. She saw the expression of contempt in her daughter's eyes. Wait till you see, she thought as she went over to Rob to kiss his cheek. He put his arm around her tenderly.

Claire, Regina, Alison, and Rod arrived within a few minutes of each other. Laurie and Alex were last, but within ten minutes all had gathered and were in the den.

Jane stood at the bar to pass out wine and cordials.

Robert Powell held up his glass. "I cannot thank you all enough for being with me, and I apologize that you have had to endure this ordeal for twenty years. As you know, I, too, have been under a terrible cloud of suspicion. But I am happy to say that tomorrow morning, during my interview, I will announce to the world that I now know who killed my beloved Betsy—and I will name that person. So let us have this final toast to the relief that is to come, and say good night to each other."

There was absolute silence in the room. The platter of hors d'oeuvres, so carefully prepared by Jane, was ignored.

Everyone put their glasses down without speaking and began to leave the room.

Josh was hovering in the hallway, ready to assist Jane with collecting the glasses and turning off the lights.

Laurie and Alex waited until the others were upstairs to say good night to Robert Powell.

"That was a pretty strong statement, Mr. Powell," Alex said flatly. "And very provocative. Do you really think it was necessary?"

"I think it was absolutely necessary," Robert Powell said. "I have spent many years going from one to the other of those four young women, trying to imagine who went into my wife's bedroom and stole the breath from her body. I know Betsy had her faults, but she was exactly right for me, and I have missed her for twenty years. Why do you think I never remarried? Because she is irreplaceable."

Where does that leave Muriel Craig? Laurie wondered.

"And now I wish you a very good night," Powell said briskly.

Alex walked Laurie to the door of her room. "Keep your door locked," he said. "If Powell is right, someone is right now trying to decide what to do. Crazy as it sounds, someone might blame you for setting up this program."

"Or blame you for driving every one of them to admit she hated Betsy, Alex."

"I'm not worried," Alex said quietly. "Go to bed and lock your door."

86

Regina sat on the edge of the bed. I know he means me, she thought. Josh must have given him the suicide note. I wonder if I'll still get the money. I can use it for my defense. For twenty years I've wanted an end to this. Well, I have it now.

In robotlike fashion she changed into pajamas, went into the bathroom, splashed water on her face, turned off the light, and went to bed. Then, sleepless, she stared into the dark.

87

Alison and Rod lay side by side, their hands clutched under the light covers.

"I did do it," Alison said. "I know I was in Betsy's room, and I was in the closet watching."

"Watching what?" Rod asked quickly.

"Someone holding the pillow over Betsy's face. But Rod, it wasn't someone, it was me."

"Don't say that!"

"I know it's true, Rod. I know it's true."

"You don't know it's true. Stop saying that."

"Rod, I'm going to go to prison."

"No, you're not. And for one reason: I couldn't live without you."

Alison stared into the darkness and came to realize the truth that anger had hidden from her. She said, "Rod, I know that you have always felt that I married you so that you could send me to medical school. I may have believed that myself. But you weren't the only one who fell in love the first day of kindergarten. I did, too. It's a terrible thing, but I know I have wasted twenty years hating Betsy Powell."

She laughed mirthlessly. "If only I had had the satisfaction of knowing what I was doing when I killed her."

88

Claire sat on the couch in her bedroom, making no attempt to sleep.

So he actually did love my mother, she thought. From the time he started coming into my room less than a month after we moved in here, I allowed it for her sake. I could see that she was so happy, and I wanted to keep her that way. I was sure that if I told her, she'd move out of here, and then where would we be?

Back in a tiny apartment. She dated men along the way, looking for what Robert Powell could give her. We were so close when I was little. I felt I owed it to her. It was my big secret, making that sacrifice for my mother. Counting every night he didn't come near me as a blessing. Then I overheard them talking. He was telling her about the night before, and she was pleased I was so responsive.

Damn her, damn her, damn her.

I smothered her in my mind from the time I was thirteen. If I was the one who did it that final night and somebody saw me and is saying so now, so be it, so be it.

89

Nina did not attempt to go to bed. Instead she sat, legs crossed, replaying in her mind the events of the day. Was it possible that her mother had carried out her threat? She's a good actress, Nina thought, and who wouldn't believe her?

I didn't know that Robert Powell was so bulldozed by Betsy that he didn't see her for what she was. Or maybe he *did* see her for what she was and found it thrilling.

If Rob has been playing up to my mother these couple of days, she's obviously been fool enough to fall for it. If she's said I confessed to killing Betsy, it's impossible for me. And when Rob shows her the door tomorrow, she can go straight to the police chief to claim the reward. What, if anything, can I do about it?

90

As the last light went out in the house, Bruno got out of the car. He had given Timmy a sleeping pill and now had him slung over his shoulder. Carefully he climbed over the fence, moving slowly to be sure not to disturb him. He carried him into the pool house and opened the door of the utility room. He laid him on the pile of blankets he had prepared for him and loosely tied his hands and feet.

Timmy stirred and murmured a protest when Bruno tied a relaxed gag around his mouth, then fell back into a deep sleep.

Bruno knew he had to be picked up tomorrow morning by the landscaper's truck. There would be no explanation for him not being there. But the kid should be okay until I get back, he thought. Even if he wakes up, he can't get out and he can't pull the gag off. His hands are tied behind him.

Now that the end was near, he knew that he was

not only deadly calm, but would *stay* deadly calm. He looked down at Timmy's sleeping face. There was enough light from the full moon that he could see it clearly. "You would've looked just like your daddy someday," he said, "and your mommy is right in that house and doesn't know you're here. Wait till she finds out you're missing."

He knew he should leave but could not resist reaching into his pocket and taking out a tiny case. He opened it and took out shiny bright blue lenses and put them in his eyes. He had worn them that day because they would stand out just in case anyone got close enough to describe him. He remembered how he had heard Timmy's wail five years ago: *"Blue Eyes shot my daddy."*

Yes, I did, he thought. Yes, I did.

He took out the lenses, saving them for tomorrow.

91

Leo Farley could not sleep. The cop in him was sending him a warning. He tried to brush it off.

Laurie is okay, he reminded himself. I'm glad Alex Buckley is in that house. It's obvious that he likes Laurie, but more important, he knows she's facing a potentially explosive situation tonight with that bunch in the same house.

Timmy sounds great, and I'll see him Sunday. Then why in hell am I so sure that something is seriously wrong? Maybe it's just all these heart monitors on me. They'd drive anyone crazy.

The nurse had left a sleeping pill on his night table. "It's not strong, Commissioner," she had told him, "but it will take the edge off and let you get some sleep."

Leo reached for it, then threw it back on the table. I don't want to wake up half-groggy, he thought angrily.

And anyhow, I know it won't help me go to sleep.

92

At three o'clock in the morning, Jane got quietly out of bed, opened the door of her room, and padded along until she reached the room where Muriel Craig was sleeping.

Her noisy snoring was sufficient proof that she was under the influence of excess liquid refreshment. Jane tiptoed over to the bed, bent over, and raised the pillow she was holding. Then, with a sudden quick movement, she jammed it over Muriel's face and clasped it down.

The snoring stopped with an abrupt gagging sound. The strong hands of her attacker held the pillow like a vise. Muriel began to gasp for breath.

Her hands flew up and she tried to push the pillow away. "Don't bother," someone whispered.

Any remnant of the fog in her brain disappeared.

I don't want to die, Muriel thought. I don't want to die.

Her long fingernails dug deep into the back of her assailant's hands, and for a moment their grip loosened. Muriel pushed away the pillow and screamed. But then the pillow came back even more forcefully over her face. "You didn't think I'd let you have him," Jane hissed, her voice ragged and her tone vicious as she again clasped the pillow tightly over Muriel's face. "Maybe they know I killed Betsy, but you won't get a chance at him. *He's mine. He's mine.*"

Throughout the second floor, everyone heard the scream and felt utter disbelief.

Alex arrived first, wrestling with Jane and throwing her to the floor. As he turned on the light, he saw that Muriel's face was blue. She was not breathing. He pulled her out of the bed, laid her on the floor, and began CPR.

As Robert Powell ran down the hall, Rod and the four graduates came rushing from the other direction. Wild-eyed Jane looked from one to the other of them and began to flee, still clutching the pillow.

"You?" Powell shouted and began to follow her. "It was *you?*"

Stumbling and gasping, Jane ran down the stairs and through the kitchen. Shoving the patio door aside, she ran into the darkness, not knowing where to go. She was beside the pool when Robert Powell grabbed her.

"It was you," he said. "All this time it was *you*? For twenty years I have seen you every day and never suspected for one minute that you killed my Betsy."

"I love you, Rob," she moaned. "I love you, I love you, I love you."

"You can't swim, can you? You're afraid of water, aren't you?" With a sudden motion, he shoved her into the pool, then buried her frantic pleas for help by shouting: "Jane, Jane, don't be afraid, we'll help you, Jane, we'll help you. Where are you?"

When he was sure that she was sinking, he continued running past the pool house and down the driveway until, exhausted, he sank onto the ground. That was where he was found when a squad car came roaring around the driveway. A policeman knelt beside him. "It's all right, Mr. Powell, it's all right. Do you know which way she went?"

"No." Robert Powell's breathing was labored, his complexion ghastly white. Just then the outdoor lights burst on, and every corner of the grounds became visible. "Maybe the pool house," he breathed. "Maybe she's hiding in there."

Sirens screaming, other squad cars began racing down the driveway. Ed Penn was in one of them.

"Look in the pool house," the policeman with Powell shouted.

One of the officers raced to the door of the pool house and was pushing it open when another cop shouted, "She's down here."

He was standing by the pool looking down. Jane, faceup, was lying at the bottom. Her eyes were open and her fists were closed as if she were still grasping the pillow. The officer dove into the pool and struggled to bring her to the surface. The other officers helped him drag her out of the pool and they positioned her on the ground. They pumped her chest and applied CPR. After several minutes they stopped their futile attempt to revive her.

INSIDE, ALEX HAD MANAGED TO GET MURIEL'S heart beating. The graduates and Rod were standing motionless in the room. As Muriel fought her way back to consciousness, she moaned, "Rob, Rob."

Nina's hysterical laughter could be heard through the house.

93

Bruno stood on the sidewalk for a full fifteen minutes before Dave Cappo pulled up in the grounds van promptly at 8 A.M. Dave was bursting with excitement as they headed for the Powell estate.

"Did you hear everything that's going on?" he asked.

"What's that?" Bruno asked, saying to himself, I don't care.

"Somebody tried to kill somebody at the Powell place last night."

"What?"

"It was the housekeeper. She killed Powell's wife twenty years ago," Dave said breathlessly. "She tried to do it again to someone else last night, but she got caught in the act. She tried to get away and fell in the pool—turns out she couldn't swim."

Did they find Timmy? Bruno thought in terror.

"What do you think of that?" Dave was asking. "I

mean, for twenty years those four graduates have been under suspicion, and it turns out none of them did it."

"What's happening up there now?" Bruno asked. If they found Timmy, I can have Dave take me home right now. I can say I don't feel well. I can be out of this town in minutes. Timmy doesn't know who picked him up. But they'll come looking for me fast . . .

"Oh, just the usual stuff," Dave said. "The medical examiner took away the body. From what I hear, the housekeeper was standing there holding the pillow over the face of the mother of one of the graduates. Her name is Muriel Craig. She's an actress."

Bruno knew he had to respond. "Oh, I've heard of her." They haven't searched the pool house, he thought. They wouldn't have any reason to start searching now. I'm going to see it through.

Usually Dave dropped him off in the driveway. "I don't know if they'll let you in, but we can try. Then you can tell us everything that's going on now."

The car was stopped by a policeman. "I'll have to check inside," he said. He phoned and received the answer.

"Mr. Powell says to let him in. He can start working on the putting green that's outside the area the police have roped off."

Trying to look casual, Bruno got out of the car and walked slowly to the pool house. He passed the pool. The body was gone. He went in, closed the door, and rushed to the utility room. Timmy was awake. He was squirming on the mound of blankets. Tears were running down his cheeks. Bruno knelt beside him. "Don't cry, Timmy," he said. "Mommy's coming soon. I'm going to give you some cereal and let you go to the bathroom. Then Mommy will take you to see Grandpa. Is that okay?"

Timmy nodded.

"Now you have to promise me that you won't try to call out when I let you eat. Is that a promise?"

Timmy nodded his head again.

There was a small bathroom off the utility room for the use of any of the grounds help. Bruno carried Timmy into it and stood with him over the toilet. "Let it go," he said. It'll be your last time, he thought.

He placed Timmy back on the blankets, went into the kitchen, and brought out Cheerios, milk, and orange juice.

"I'm going to pull down the gag," he said. "I'll let you eat, but make it fast."

His eyes terrified, Timmy obeyed.

When he was finished, Bruno retied the gag, again being sure that it was not too tight. He pushed Timmy down on the blankets. "If you try to make any noise, no one will hear you," he warned. "If you're very, very quiet, I promise Mommy will come to pick you up."

Bruno reached for a rake, carried it out of the utility room, closed the door, and locked it.

He went outside and began to poke at the grass around the putting green with the rake.

94

Before the police responded to the 911 call, Josh had rushed to Jane's apartment, where he searched for and found the hidden jewelry George Curtis had given Betsy. Now it was securely in his pockets with no one the wiser. He had been surprised that Jane was the one who had killed Betsy, even though he had always suspected she was crazy about Mr. Rob.

At nine o'clock everyone who had stayed overnight came down for breakfast. They barely spoke to each other. The realization that they were now free of any suspicion that one of them had taken Betsy's life was just beginning to sink in.

Muriel had refused to go to the hospital and stayed in bed until the medical examiner had left with Jane's body. Her throat swollen, her voice husky, she had already begun to realize that now Robert was really alone, and he would know that she had lied to him about Nina's confession. But on the other hand, she thought, maybe he will understand that I lied because I love him so much. To that end, she finally got up, showered, carefully made up her face, and brushed her hair. When she was finished, she dressed in a light sweater, slacks, and sandals. She hoped the rapidly spreading bruises on her throat would show Rob how much she had endured for him.

Chief Ed Penn and other detectives had spent the hours after the incident individually questioning everyone in the house. All of their accounts were consistent. From all initial appearances, Jane had acted alone in trying to kill Muriel. From all initial appearances, Jane had accidentally fallen into the pool as she fled from the house.

Under these circumstances, he reluctantly agreed to the fervent request by Laurie and Alex to allow them to finish the program. "The investigation is not over," he told them firmly. "Everyone will have to come in to give formal statements. But as long as no one tries to go into the roped-off areas, I'll let you continue."

In the den, Laurie and Alex were waiting to hold the final interview with Robert Powell.

The others had been invited in to watch. By then they were all packed and dressed, desperate to be away. Still hardly able to believe that the nightmare was over, they filed into the den and sat behind the cameras, waiting for Robert Powell.

95

Mark Garret, the camp director at Mountainside, stared incredulously at Toby Barber. "You mean you let Timmy Moran leave with a stranger last night?" he asked.

"His grandfather is dying. A policeman came for him," Toby said defensively.

"Why didn't you call me?"

"I did, sir. You didn't answer your phone."

With a sinking heart, Garret realized that Toby was right. He had taken off his jacket, and in the noise of the party could not have heard his cell phone ring.

I spoke to Leo Farley yesterday, he tried to reassure himself. *He told me he was in the hospital.*

But he also warned me that the person who killed Timmy's father had threatened him and his mother. Suppose he was the one who picked up Timmy?

Desperately afraid, Garret picked up his phone. Leo Farley's number was on his desk, ready to reach at any time in case a threat to Timmy materialized. He could only hope and pray that Leo Farley had indeed been in an emergency situation.

Farley answered on the first ring.

"Hello there, Mark," he said. "How are you doing?"

Garret hesitated, then asked, "How are you feeling, Commissioner?"

"Oh, I'm okay now. In fact, I'm getting discharged this morning. I spoke to Timmy last night. He's having a great time with you at the camp."

There was nothing Mark Garret could do except blurt out, "Then you didn't send a cop for him last night?"

It took seconds before Leo could absorb what he was hearing. His nightmare was happening. It could only be Blue Eyes who had taken Timmy.

"You mean despite all my warnings you let my grandson go away with a stranger? What did he look like?"

Garret asked Toby to describe the policeman.

In despair, Leo heard a description matching the one that elderly Margy Bless had given to the police five years ago of Greg's murderer: below average height, kind of bulky-looking . . .

Leo asked, "Did he have blue eyes?"

"I asked Toby. He didn't notice. He was very tired."

"You fool!" he shouted as he broke the connection.

He ripped off the wires that were monitoring his heart. In his mind he could hear the words Blue Eyes had shouted to Timmy: *"Tell your mother that she's next. Then it's your turn."*

Frantically he dialed Ed Penn's phone. If he kept to his threat, Blue Eyes would kill Laurie first. He had to be heading for her now—and pray God, with Timmy still alive!

96

Robert Powell, haggard and worn but impeccably dressed in a shirt and tie and summer-weight jacket, quietly listened to the greeting from Alex. The graduates were stationed behind him.

"Mr. Powell, this is hardly the way I expected this program to end. Did you ever know or suspect that Jane Novak had murdered your wife?"

"Absolutely not," Robert Powell said wearily. "I have always suspected that it was one of the graduates. I was not sure which one, and I wanted the answer. I wanted closure. I *needed* closure. I am not a well man; my days are numbered. I have just learned that in addition to my other medical problems, I have a fast-moving form of pancreatic cancer. Before too long, I will be joining my beloved Betsy in heaven or in hell."

For an instant, there was silence.

"I am planning to leave five million dollars to each

of the graduates. I know that, in different ways, Betsy and I have damaged each and every one of them."

He turned to look at them, expecting expressions of gratitude.

Instead he stared at identical expressions of contempt and disgust.

97

"It's time," Bruno said. "We're going to have you call Mommy." He had put the shiny blue contact lenses back in his eyes.

Timmy looked up into the blue eyes that had haunted him for more than five years of his young life. "You shot my daddy," he said.

"That's right, Timmy, and let me tell you why. I didn't want to be a criminal. I wanted to break away from the mob. I was only nineteen. I could have had a different life. But your hotshot grandfather caught me driving drunk. I begged him to let me go and told him that I was reporting to the army the next day. But he arrested me. Then the army wouldn't take me, and I got back with the mob. I broke into a house, and the old lady in it had a heart attack when she saw me. She died. I got thirty years."

Bruno's face became contorted with anger. "I could have done anything. I can build computers. I can break into any computer or phone. I had figured out how to get even with Leo Farley. I was going to kill the people he loved—his son-in-law, his daughter, and you. I got your father, but they sent me back to prison on a stupid parole violation for another five years. Now you know, Timmy, and it's time to call Mommy."

LAURIE AND ALEX WATCHED AS THE GRADUATES walked out of the room, leaving Robert Powell sitting alone. Silently Laurie nodded to the crew to pack up. There was nothing more to be said.

Alex felt the vibration of his phone ringing in his pocket. It was his office; the investigator he had assigned to find out about the landscaper.

"Alex." His voice was urgent. "The landscaper you asked us to check out. He is not Bruno Hoffa. He's Rusty Tillman, who served thirty years in prison. He got out five and a half years ago, a week before the doctor was shot. He went back to prison on a parole violation, and got out five months ago. We ran his picture—"

Alex dropped the phone. Unbelieving, he stared at Laurie. She had been about to step out onto the patio. He heard her phone ring as he frantically shouted, "Wait, Laurie!"

She was already out on the patio, her phone to her ear.

"Timmy, you're not allowed to call me during the day," she said. "What's wrong, honey?" And then she looked up.

The pool house door was opening and Timmy, in his pajamas and robe, was coming out, hand in hand with the gardener. He was holding a rifle pointed at Timmy's head.

With a shriek Laurie began to race across the lawn.

Chief Ed Penn was roaring toward the Powell estate. "Don't turn on the sirens," he warned his driver. "We don't want to alert him. Tell all units to report to the Powell estate."

The policeman in the squad car behind the estate had received the urgent message, had cut through the woods and was climbing the fence. Although a highly skilled marksman, Officer Ron Teski had never fired his weapon in the line of duty. As he sprinted toward the backyard, he realized this might be the day he had trained for. Blue Eyes dropped Timmy's hand and, laughing, let him run to Laurie, who was running toward them from eighty feet away.

The squad car carrying Ed Penn came racing around the circular driveway. Penn, his gun in hand, frantically took aim at Blue Eyes. The shot missed its mark.

By now Laurie had reached Timmy and was bending over to pick him up. Wanting to finish the task the way he had envisioned, Blue Eyes took aim at Laurie's head. As he was about to fire, Officer Teski's first shot cut into his shoulder. Spinning, Blue Eyes raised the rifle and tried to point it in Laurie's direction. His finger was on the trigger as he felt an explosion rip through his chest.

Blue Eyes' body fell to the ground accompanied by

the sound of breaking glass. The bullet he had fired crashed through the window of the den where Robert Powell was still sitting. With a puzzled expression, Powell raised his hand to what remained of his forehead and then fell from the chair.

Seconds later, in a foreshadowing of what was to come, Alex Buckley was wrapping Laurie and Timmy in his arms.

Epilogue

Six months later, there was another reunion of the graduates—this time on a much happier note.

It was Alex who suggested they get together at his apartment on New Year's Eve. The developments in their lives had been extraordinary, and he said it was time to share them.

They sat together and compared notes over cocktails while Ramon prepared dinner.

Claire had gone to a therapist, able at last to talk about what Robert Powell had done to her. "It wasn't my fault," she was now able to say with conviction. She had started to use makeup again and was quietly content to no longer conceal her resemblance to her mother. Now she sat, a very pretty woman, laughing with her old friends and telling them about her new social life.

Regina's first action when she received the money

from the Gala Reunion had been to return the commission Bridget Whiting had paid her. The real estate business had picked up, and a bigger home with an office attached was within her grasp. It gave her enormous pleasure to know that her ex-husband and his rock-star wife were in the midst of a bitter divorce. Zach spent almost all of his free time with her.

Nina was engaged to Grant Richmond. She had willingly turned over her share of the Powell and production company money to her mother, with the proviso that they never have any contact again. Muriel, typically, was telling everyone how much Robert had loved her, and that they had planned to be married before the dreadful accident that took his life.

Alison was attending medical school in Cleveland, commuting from home. She joked that it was hard to keep up with her fellow twentysomething students. She shared the joyous news that she was three months pregnant. Rod had stunned her by saying he was going to be her fellow student. For years, it turned out, he had wanted to become a pharmacist himself.

The four graduates were all saying that Robert Powell was shot before completing his final attempt to make up for what he had done. They were asking each other whether, if he had lived, they would have taken his money. They admitted to each other that they would have accepted it after all they had been through.

George Curtis had been invited to the party, too. Listening, he realized he had gotten off easy. Robert Powell had never suspected his relationship with Betsy. Isabelle had forgiven him. He could have saved twenty years of anguish, but had been too much of a coward to do so.

At the dinner table George smiled as he thought about the announcement he was about to make. Robert Powell had promised to give the graduates five million dollars but had died before he could change his will. George was going to give each of them the five million that would have come from Powell. George knew in his heart that he was trying to make up for the damage his twenty years of silence had inflicted on them.

Three of the graduates had gone to Chief Penn with the recorded threats from Josh, who was now out on bail, awaiting trial. A search warrant had revealed the jewelry Jane had stolen in his apartment. Since Jane had taken it from Betsy, it was now part of Betsy's estate. When Josh's trial and his appeals were over, it would be released for Claire to dispose of as she wished.

Alex, listening to the four graduates, marvelled at their resilience, and then he looked at Laurie. For the first time in the nearly six years since Greg's death, she and Leo had left Timmy with a neighbor who was a babysitter. He saw how their faces now were transformed by the easy laughter they shared with the others. It had been incredible for them to learn that a seemingly routine DUI arrest Leo had made as a young patrolman had been viewed by Blue Eyes as the event that had ruined his life—driving him to

Greg's murder and forcing them all to live under the threat of violence for so long.

The *Under Suspicion* series had taken off, as Laurie had predicted.

Alex knew it was too soon to let her know how deeply in love with her he was. She still needed time to heal.

I can wait, he thought, as long as it takes— however long that is.

Turn the page for an excerpt
from Mary Higgins Clark's
exciting #1 *New York Times*
bestselling novel

The
Cinderella
Murder

Now available in print and ebook

1

It was two o'clock in the morning. Right on time, Rosemary Dempsey thought ruefully as she opened her eyes and stirred. Whenever she had a big day ahead she would inevitably wake up in the middle of the night and start worrying that something would go wrong.

It had always been like this, even when she was a child. And now, fifty-five years old, happily married for thirty-two years, with one child, beautiful and gifted nineteen-year-old Susan, Rosemary could not be anything but a constant worrier, a living Cassandra. *Something is going to go wrong.*

Thanks again, Mom, Rosemary thought. Thanks for all the times you held your breath, so sure that the birthday upside-down cake I loved to make for Daddy would flop. The only one that did was the first one when I was eight years old. All the others were perfect. I was so proud of myself. But then, on his birthday when I was eighteen, you told me you always made a backup cake for him. In the single act of defiance that I can remember, I was so shocked and angry I tossed the one I had made in the garbage can.

You started laughing and then tried to apologize. "It's just that you're talented in other ways, Rosie, but let's face it, in the kitchen you're klutzy."

And of course you found other ways to tell me where I was klutzy, Rosemary thought. "Rosie, when you make the bed, be sure that the spread is even on both sides. It only takes an extra minute to do it right." "Rosie, be careful. When you read a magazine, don't just toss it back on the table. Line it up with the others."

And now, even though I know I can throw a party or make a cake, I am always sure that something will go wrong, Rosemary thought.

But there was a reason today to be apprehensive. It was Jack's sixtieth birthday, and this evening sixty of their friends would be there to celebrate it. Cocktails and a buffet supper, served on the patio by their infallible caterer. The weather forecast was perfect, sunshine and seventy degrees.

It was May 7 in Silicon Valley and that meant that the flowers were in full bloom. Their dream house, the third since they'd moved to San Mateo thirty-two years ago, was built in the style of a Tuscan villa. Every time she turned into the driveway, she fell in love with it again.

Everything will be fine, she assured herself impatiently. And as usual I'll make the birthday chocolate upside-down cake for Jack and it will be perfect and our friends will have a good time and I will be told how I'm a marvel. "Your parties are always so perfect, Rosie . . . The supper was delicious . . . the house exquisite . . . ," and on and on. And I will be a nervous wreck inside, she thought, an absolute nervous wreck.

Careful not to awaken him, she wriggled her slender body over in the bed until her shoulder was touching Jack's. His even breathing told her that he was enjoying his usual untroubled sleep. And he deserved it. He worked so hard. As she often did when she was trying to overcome one of her worry attacks, Rosemary began to remind herself of all the good things in her life, starting with the day she met Jack on the campus of Marquette University. She had been an undergraduate. He had been a law student. It was the proverbial love at first sight. They had been married after she graduated from college. Jack was fascinated by developing technology, and his conversation became filled with talk of robots, telecommunications, microprocessors, and something called internetworking. Within a year they had moved to Northern California.

I always wanted us to live our lives in Milwaukee, Rosemary thought. I still could move back in a heartbeat. Unlike most human beings, I love cold winters. But moving here certainly has worked out for us. Jack is head of the legal department of Valley Tech, one of the top research companies in the country. And Susan was born here. After more than a decade without the family we hoped and prayed for, we were holding her in our arms.

Rosemary sighed. To her dismay, Susan, their only child, was a Californian to her fingertips. She'd scoff at the idea of relocating anywhere. Rosemary tried to wrest her mind away from the troublesome thought that last year Susan had chosen to go to UCLA, a great college but a full five-hour drive away. She had been accepted closer to home at Stanford University. Instead she had rushed to enroll at UCLA, probably because her no-good boyfriend, Keith Ratner, was already a student there. Dear God, Rosemary thought, don't let her end up eloping with him.

The last time she looked at the clock, it was three thirty, and her last impression before falling asleep was once again an overwhelming fear that today something was going to go desperately wrong.

2

She woke up at eight o'clock, an hour later than usual. Dismayed, she rushed out of bed, tossed on a robe, and hurried downstairs.

Jack was still in the kitchen, a toasted bagel in one hand, a cup of coffee in the other. He wore a sport shirt and khakis.

"Happy sixtieth birthday, love," she greeted him. "I didn't hear you get up."

He smiled, swallowed the last bit of the bagel, and put down the cup. "Don't I get a kiss for my birthday?"

"Sixty of them," Rosemary promised as she felt his arms go around her.

Jack was almost a foot taller than Rosemary. When she wore heels, it didn't seem so much, but when she was in her bedroom slippers, he towered over her.

He always made her smile. Jack was a handsome man. His full head of hair, now more gray than blond; his body, lean and muscular; his face, sunburned enough to emphasize the deep blue of his eyes.

Susan was much more like him in both looks and temperament. She was tall and willowy, with long blond hair, deep blue eyes, and classic features. Her brain was like his. Technically gifted, she was the best student in the lab at school and equally gifted in her drama classes.

Next to them, Rosemary always felt as though she faded into the background. That too had been her mother's appraisal. "Rosie, you really should have highlights in your hair. It's such a muddy brown."

Now, even though she did use streaks, Rosemary always thought of her hair as "muddy brown."

Jack collected his long kiss and then released her. "Don't kill me," he said, "but I was hoping to sneak in eighteen holes at the club before the party."

"I guessed that. Good for you!" Rosemary said.

"You don't mind if I abandon you? I know there's no chance of you joining."

They both laughed. He knew all too well that she would be fussing around over details all day.

Rosemary reached for the coffeepot. "Join me for another cup."

"Sure." He glanced out the window. "I'm glad the weather is so good. I hate it when Susan drives through rainstorms to get here, but the weather prediction is good for the weekend."

"And I don't like that she's going to be going back early tomorrow morning," Rosemary said.

"I know. But she's a good driver and young enough that the round trip won't be a problem. Though remind me to talk to her about trading in that car of hers. It's two years old, and already we've had too many visits to the garage." Jack took a final few sips of the coffee. "Okay, I'm on my way. I should be home around four." With a quick kiss on Rosemary's forehead, he was out the door.

AT THREE O'CLOCK, BEAMING WITH SELF-satisfaction, Rosemary stepped back from the kitchen table. Jack's birthday cake was perfect, not a crumb astray when she flipped it over and lifted the pan. The chocolate icing, her own recipe, was relatively smooth, with the words HAPPY 60TH BIRTHDAY, JACK, written carefully, word for word.

Everything is ready, she thought. Now, why can't I relax?

3

Forty-five minutes later, just as Rosemary was expecting Jack to walk in the door, the phone rang. It was Susan.

"Mom, I had to work up the courage to tell you. I can't get home tonight."

"Oh, Susan, Dad will be so disappointed!"

Susan's voice, young and eager, almost breathless, said, "I didn't call before because I didn't know for sure. Mom, *Frank Parker is going to meet me tonight*, about maybe being cast in his new movie." Her voice calmed a little. "Mom, remember when I was in *Home Before Dark*, just before Christmas?"

"How could I forget?" Rosemary and Jack had flown to Los Angeles to watch the campus play from the third row. "You were wonderful."

Susan laughed. "But you're my mother. Why

wouldn't you say that? Anyhow, remember the casting agent, Edwin Lange, who said he'd sign me?"

"Yes, and you never heard from him again."

"But I did. He said Frank Parker saw my audition tape. Edwin taped the performance and showed it to Frank Parker. He said that Parker was blown away and is considering me for the lead in a movie he's casting. It's a movie set on a campus and he wants to find college students to be in it. He wants me to meet him. Mom, can you believe it? I don't want to jinx myself, but I feel so lucky. It's like it's too good to be true. Can you believe that I might get a role, maybe even the lead role?"

"Calm down before you have a heart attack," Rosemary cautioned, "and then you won't get any role." Rosemary smiled and pictured her daughter, energy exuding from every bone in her body, twisting her fingers through her long blond hair, those wonderful blue eyes shining.

The semester's almost over, she thought. If she did get a part in this movie, it would be a great experience. "Dad will certainly understand, Susan, but be sure to call him back."

"I'll try, but, Mom, I'm meeting Edwin in five minutes to go over the tape with him and rehearse, because he says Frank Parker will want me to read for him. I don't know how late it will be. You'll be having the party, and you'll never hear the phone. Why don't I call Dad in the morning?"

"That might not be a bad idea. The party is from six to ten, but most people linger on."

"Give him a birthday kiss for me."

"I will. Knock that director off his feet."

"I'll try."

"Love you, sweetheart."

"Love you, Mom."

Rosemary had never become used to the sudden silence that followed when a cell phone disconnected.

WHEN THE PHONE RANG THE NEXT MORNING, Jack popped up from reading the newspaper. "There's our girl, bright and early by a college student's standards for a Sunday."

But the caller wasn't Susan. It was the Los Angeles Police Department. They had difficult news. A young woman had been found just before dawn in Laurel Canyon Park. She appeared to have been strangled. They didn't want to alarm them unnecessarily, but their daughter's driver's license had been retrieved from a purse found fifteen yards from the body. A mobile phone was clutched in her hand and the last number dialed was theirs.